Denning was Impudent, Insufferable, Infuriating— and Irresistible!

Young and beautiful heiress Emily Carnavon could have had her pick of England's most fashionable beaux and high-born noblemen.

Instead she chose a man who had been barred from the best circles and welcomed by the worst elements in all the realm.

What was more, instead of being humbly grateful for Emily's affection, this shocking scoundrel actually implied that she was not good enough for him—and left her biting back her tears of rage and loss.

A proper young lady would have forgotten the cad then and there. But Emily could not afford to be a proper young lady—not when she was a young woman so desperately, defiantly and determinedly in love. . . .

D0943209

Look for the others in this
great Regency Romance series:

MY LORD RAKEHELL

BOW STREET GENTLEMAN

Bow Street Brangle

Margaret SeBastian

POPULAR LIBRARY • NEW YORK

Published by Popular Library, CBS Publications,
CBS Consumer Publishing, a Division of CBS Inc.

August, 1977

Copyright © 1977 by Arthur M. Gladstone

ISBN: 0-445-04040-8

Chapter I

"Police are a plague and Peel is twin to perfidy!—and I'll not stand quietly by while he spreads his contagion into the midst of Milliken's!" roared General Beresford as he brought his fist crashing down upon the highly polished mahogany table top. Chin thrust out, scowling fiercely, he sat down, even his act of resuming his seat one of defiance. Seated, he looked about fiercely, a challenge to all burning in his eyes.

Lord Ashburton, president of the membership committee for the Milliken Club, sighed and pushed his chair back, but he did not rise. With easy grace he brought his hand up to his chin and regarded the general for a moment. If the general were to gain his point, the nomination would be defeated and a great deal of trouble and controversy stirred up. He let a moment pass before he spoke.

"My dear Alonzo," he began in a soft voice, "we have before us Lord Carnavon's nomination of one Edward Denning for membership in our club. Now, we are a group of gentlemen joined together over the years, a select company which quality it is the duty of this committee to protect and preserve. I do not see any reason that you should calumniate the Honorable Robert Peel, a much respected member of the government and of our own little society, much less cry out upon a topic of political significance that can have no bearing on the policies of Milliken's, which is a purely social body. We are convened to adjudge Mr. Denning's qualifications and suitability as a friend and companion. His politics are most certainly not in question here. Therefore, Sir Alonzo, I regret to inform you that your remarks are not only in questionable taste, they are entirely out of order."

"Of course, my lord, I do beg your pardon and that of all of you gentlemen for my outburst," said General Beresford in an apologetic tone, "but I beg you will understand and consider that the content of my remarks, if not their mode of expression, is most pertinent to the matter in hand; namely, the qualifications of this upstart, Denning. I tell you now that nothing on earth will prevent me from placing a black ball in the box and I do not care who knows that it is mine; not Peel, not Carnavon, and certainly least of all Denning!

"My lord," he went on, "when you refer to Milliken's as a small society of select company, you do the club and the membership a disservice because you disguise—nay, you *erase* our true significance. There is my old commander, His Grace of Wellington; there is Peel, the Home Secretary; there is Carnavon; there is yourself; all these are men of great power and tremendous influence."

Lord Ashburton smiled. "You are too modest, General, when you exclude yourself. You have more than made your mark in the military—but you were making a point?"

"A simple one. This club is comprised of gentlemen of wealth and attainments, and one thing we all of us have in common is breeding. Now, I have heard of this Denning. His name is ever on the lips of every felon and evildoer in London, if not in the kingdom. Oh yes, he has notorious feats to his credit, but what is he truly? Who is he? He is a common, vulgar *runner*, and his breeding is so suspect that no one can say what it is. More than all this, about him there must ever be the distant effluvium

6

of the police. And as to that last"—he paused and looked about the table slowly—"I equate that with treason!"

The various members of the committee shifted uneasily in their seats. The general raised his hands to forestall interruption.

"You do not like the word, gentlemen? Then you must know how I, a man of the military, must despise it—but I do not think we need to discuss it further. There is enough against this Denning—of course you all are aware that that is not his true name—I say, there is enough against the man to make all further discussion a mockery. What of his heritage, his breeding, his blood? The fact that he is referred to as the Bow Street Gentleman must speak volumes in that regard and not, I say, to his credit. We know absolutely nothing of his antecedents—"

Sir Giles Boville cleared his throat.

The general looked in his direction and paused.

Sir Giles cleared his throat again and his voice was heard to mumble heavily: "Name of Denning perfectly proper. Legitimate, quite. Adopted son of the Honorable Alexander Denning, Chief Magistrate, Bow Street."

"Hah!" sneered the general. "A bachelor's son! Need I point out to you gentlemen the significance of that pedigree?"

"Nv'th'less, legitimate. Chancery. All 'n order!"

Lord Ashburton intervened. "Sir Alonzo, that imputation is most uncalled for. There is nothing to say that he is Denning's. In any case, it is my opinion that Denning's adoption of the fellow when he is all of five-and-twenty, at least, is a most remarkable circumstance and can only vouch for the character of the young man."

"Fiddlesticks, my lord! Denning would vouch for the devil himself if he but carried a truncheon with a crown upon it or was bedecked with a scarlet waistcoat. In short, gentlemen, *any* Bow Street runner must indeed be a pet of Denning's."

"Well really, Alonzo, that is most uncalled for!" interjected Lord Ashburton. "I ask you: What of his being

7

nominated by my Lord Carnavon? Now there is a testimonial you cannot find exceptional."

"Can I not? Bethink you, gentlemen! My Lord Carnavon's sponsorship is suspect because it is to the greatest degree self-serving. This bachelor's son is betrothed to wed Carnavon's daugher—and we all know what *she* is!"

The gentlemen about the table exploded into harsh and angry rejoinders. In fact, such expletives as they thought to contribute to the conversation had rarely ever been heard in the ultrarespectable precincts of Milliken's, and the austere walls seemed to tremble with indignation. "Cad!" and "Boor!" and "Blackguard!" and even "Bloody Puritan!" echoed through the chamber.

Lord Ashburton smashed his gavel down so sharply that the haft snapped and the wooden head rebounded off the table.

The gentlemanly uproar subsided into fitful murmurings.

"Gentlemen, such deportment is unheard of and unforgiveable!" he exclaimed. He turned to General Beresford. "And you, sir, have, I hope, spoken out of ignorance. Lady Emily is a dear, sweet young lady whose unfortunate birth has been legitimized by our sovereign, the head of our church. It was a gracious and most rare distinction. You, sir, as a soldier in the service of His Majesty, must be the last person to refute or even question the act of your supreme commander—not to say anything of introducing into this discussion that which should be forgotten, especially as it casts a stain upon the fair name of her ladyship."

"Gentlemen, gentlemen, it was not my intention to cast aspersions upon anyone, but I am a military man and am inclined to be blunt. I have nothing of a personal nature against her ladyship—or against young Denning, for that matter. For one thing, neither the one nor the other is in my acquaintance. But that is all beside the point. We all of us have acquaintances, even friends, who we would never think to put up for membership in Milliken's. And that is exactly the case that is before us now. I am only

8

trying to lay before you an inescapable conclusion. People like this Denning will do nothing for Milliken's. You confer the rights and privileges we hold in common amongst us upon this parvenu, and it will be made to appear that we are giving our blessing to a system which in a free country must of necessity be odious and repulsive, and which no country, free or otherwise, ever has or ever can carry into beneficial execution; namely, a uniform metropolitan police force! We have got one advocate amongst us already, Peel; to elect another—and of such questionable origins—must give to all the world the impression that Milliken's stands foursquare behind a domestic military force, of and for the government in power, and one that is to be staffed by all manner of bastards!"

This time there was no uproar in the chamber as the general ceased his peroration and sat down. There was no sound at all as member looked at member, each raising a questioning eyebrow.

Lord Ashburton, a frown distorting his usually placid countenance, looked about the table. "Does any gentleman wish to offer a further comment?"

There was no response.

"Then I move that we vote upon the nomination of Mr. Edward Denning to membership in the Milliken Club, my Lord Carnavon, sponsor."

The motion was duly seconded.

His lordship palmed the two balls next to his hand, the one white, the other black, and pressed one of them through the hole in a little wooden box sitting in front of him. His action was a practiced one and executed so that no one could observe which ball he had voted. He slid the box to the gentleman seated to his right who performed the same little ceremony, and so it went to each in his turn.

When the box with its seven agate balls rattling within came back to him, Lord Ashburton slid back its lid and glanced inside. He flipped the box over and the balls

9

rolled about every which way on the table top. They were all of them black!

There was a shocked silence in the room. Never before in the history of the Milliken Club had a nominee been unanimously turned down.

Lord Ashburton looked about the table at each committeeman and with a sigh asked: "Well, now, who is so brave as to inform Carnavon how it went?"

General Sir Alonzo Llewellyn Beresford stepped out onto the street. His mood was one of satisfaction that he had singlehandedly preserved Milliken's from encroachment and taint. Yet the indignation and the anger that the business had engendered within him still smoldered. The meeting had been a short one, fortunately, so he still had the time for a brisk march back to his residence in Mayfair. It was exactly the thing he needed to cool himself off and, at the same time, it would serve as a tonic to bolster his appetite. He had a particular fondness for tea and was wont to make a sumptuous repast of it. His housekeeper, aware of her master's penchant for the early evening meal, went to particular pains to see that cook did it justice.

The general regarded the sky for a moment and nodded. He was sure that there would be sufficient light for his stroll. Dusk was still a little time off.

Shouldering his stout walking stick as though it were a saber, as was his usual manner with it, he set off in a most military manner. He had a tendency to parade rather than to stroll, and he carried his saber—beg your pardon, his cane—the way he was used to do it as a junior officer in the cavalry. Observing him march, one could almost imagine the steed he seemed to be astride.

To avoid the congestion along St. James Street, after he had passed White's bow window with its little group of superannuated bucks forever on the watch for a pretty face or a shapely feminine figure (he saluted them with his cane as he stalked by), he turned into a by-lane and proceeded onto Queen's Walk, where he turned north and continued his stroll alongside Green Park.

He was something over a furlong from the crossing at Piccadilly when it happened.

The sun was just beginning to drop behind the trees in the park and the shadows were beginning to stretch out along the walk as from behind him he caught the sound of running footsteps, not loud but stealthy. More than one person was coming up on him and all on tiptoe.

The walk was deserted; the sounds gave him a distinctly uneasy feeling. He whirled about and his suspicions were confirmed on the instant. Three rough fellows were coming at him. The one in the lead had unsheathed a wicked, broad-bladed knife. The second, just behind, appeared to be unarmed. The third and last, excessively large and excessively clumsy, was wielding a cosh—the short, easily concealed little sack filled with lead and sand for administering blows with stunning effect.

The general's fighting blood came to the fore and, believing offense to be the best defense, he strode forward to meet his adversaries, his stick at the ready. His move caught them by surprise and, in the instant's pause, his cane came slashing down upon the knife-wielder's wrist with telling effect. The man screamed with pain as the knife clattered down upon the pavement. Clutching at his damaged limb, the thief ran off into the gathering darkness, cursing loudly.

The general prepared to receive the next onslaught only to discover all was confusion in the ranks of his enemies. It seemed the second fellow had stumbled and fallen into the path of the third, bringing the latter down upon him in one great tangle.

For all he was past his fiftieth year and retired, General Beresford had never let his skills in the martial arts languish. He was on the pair in an instant, slashing with his stick.

His very first stroke hit its mark, but not squarely. It caught the burly footpad on the shoulder. Nevertheless it was more than the fellow wanted and he leaped to his

11

feet, howling with pain, and scurried off into the darkness to join his mate.

Before the third man could do the same, a backhanded slash of the cane bounced off his head and laid him out. He was not knocked unconscious, but he was badly dazed. General Beresford gave him no chance to recover. He pinned him where he lay, the ferrule of his cane thrust firmly against the fellow's chest.

The general stood there, studying the man's face. He was surprised that it should look at all familiar to him, but he was sure he had seen the fellow before. He shook his head. No, that was hardly likely. It was just because it was a finely featured face, for all it was unwashed and the countenance of a petty villain.

A look of sense was beginning to come back to the downed man's eyes. The general got quite a turn as he suddenly found himself being regarded with a rather devilishly charming smile. Why, the fellow was actually chuckling.

Said the general sternly: "You've not a thing to laugh at, my fine friend!"

The man said: "General Sir Alonzo Llewellyn Beresford, I presume. My pleasure, sir."

The general gasped and almost withdrew his weapon, for the fellow's diction was pure Etonian.

"How do you know my name?" he demanded.

"It is my business, sir. If you will allow me to rise, I shall deem it an honor to make myself known to you."

"Not on your life, you scoundrel! It's the lock-up for you and you shall just remain where you are until I can summon assistance."

"I assure you, sir, it will be along presently, and in a state of mild exhaustion, I imagine."

"What? More confederates! I warn you, sir, I'll crack your skull like a walnut if they do but come close."

"Then you will allow me to give him warning I am sure. My head is still ringing from your blow. I have no taste for another portion."

12

"You had better; and no tricks, mind you, or you will be the first to suffer."

Without budging from his supine position, the man shouted: "Shamus! Stand fast! Show yourself!"

"Are ye hurt bad, Neddie lad?" boomed out a voice from the darkness.

"No, just a bit foggy. I shall be all right, but the general is upon the alert and will lay my head open if you make any suspicious move. Light up so that he can see you, and make your identity plain!"

"Aye!" the voice boomed out. There was a striking noise and a lantern's light glowed, flickered, and began to shed its rays. It was lifted up and revealed the features of a craggy-jawed, snub-nosed, gray-haired fellow. Considering the height at which the lantern was held, the holder surely must have been a giant.

"General, sir, I be Shamus O'Shaughnessy, Bow Street runner, and I'd be obliged if ye'd let me chum arise wi' no further hurt to him."

"Not on your life, you scum! I know what you runners are! A pack of thieves and cutthroats! I have already disabled two of you and captured a third. I'll see you all get the King's Justice!"

The man on the ground chuckled. "General, there is a pistol in my belt. Take it as our pledge we mean you no harm."

"Eh? Does your confederate possess a similar weapon?" the general asked as he tried desperately for a reasonable estimate of the situation.

"Yes, sir. I am sure you must realize that if he were out for your blood, he could have easily fired at you instead of taking the trouble to parley."

General Beresford withdrew his walking stick from the fallen man's chest and declared: "I appear to have been outflanked, and by a superior force."

The fellow came to his feet in an easy, graceful movement which bespoke a well-conditioned chap in his prime. He was not at all put out over the general's assault upon him, but responded good-naturedly: "That

13

did not seem to faze you at the outset, sir. My compliments upon a most brilliant little campaign. But be assured the reserves were ready at hand, and you never were in the least danger."

"Just who the devil are you, anyway?" demanded Sir Alonzo.

"Edward Denning of Bow Street, sir. My credentials." He slipped out a leathern card case and proffered it to the old soldier.

Ignoring the case, the general exclaimed: "Why then, you must be the Bow Street Gentleman! I have heard of you!"

"The very same, sir."

"Yes, I have heard tell of you! But what the devil have you to do with me? Why should you have joined in an unprovoked attack upon my person? Why, in God's name, are we standing about even discussing the business?" the general demanded, with growing irascibility.

"Well, sir, I can give you *some* answers as will satisfy you that it was most necessary, but there appears to be more to the business than I have a knowledge of at the moment. If there is some place where we can talk confidentially, you may be able to supply me with certain information that will help to augment the little I have at present."

"You say it is necessary? Well—er—I suppose so. There is my club, Milliken's, just over on St. James Street. We can have a room to ourselves."

Denning burst into laughter. "I hardly think the membership will be pleased to see you enter their hallowed halls in the company of a pair of ragamuffins such as O'Shaughnessy and I appear. I know from first hand how stuffy they can be about something like that."

"Yes, of course! What could I have been thinking of!" he exclaimed in confusion. "Of course that will never—hey? You did say 'at first hand'? Y-you have been inside Milliken's?"

"Does the name John Hanford strike a familiar note, sir?"

"Hanford? Hanford! I have it! Peel and Carnavon vouched for him and—*You!*"

"Yes, sir," said Denning with a smile.

"The devil you say! Why, I could have sworn your references were unimpeachable! It is no wonder that I thought you looked familiar to me. Oh, but I say, Hanford was every inch the gentleman while you . . . Damn, I feel a fool to have been so taken in!"

"Thank you, General Beresford. I take that as a high compliment."

"I assure you I never intended one. Tell me, Denning, it is some sort of game you are playing, passing yourself off as a gentleman? I think you should be brought up on charges of trespass, gaining a membership in Milliken's under false pretenses."

"I assure you, sir, I was under orders in His Majesty's interests. I cannot say more than that, you will understand."

"Why, you are nothing but a damnation spy!"

"You'll not be telling me, sir, that *you* have never had recourse to using spies against your enemies in the field."

"Well, of course not—but damn it all, man, that is no style for a gentleman!"

"But then, General, even as you have made it plain, I am no gentleman."

"Ah, yes, I quite forgot. The trouble with you, Denning, is that it is so blasted difficult to keep it in mind that you are not! Well, it would appear that Milliken's is no place for us. Perhaps there is some tavern where we might—"

"No, sir, that I must refuse. Until I am sure of what is going forward against you, I may not be seen in your company. If our birds were to get their wind up, they'd fly off and we should have all of our work to do over again."

"What's that? I do not comprehend you."

"Look you, sir, we are going to have to let it out that I was placed under arrest, but that I managed to give the

15

slip to Johnny Law. Remember that they saw me down and you standing over me. They have got to expect, therefore, that I was taken into custody. We have to go to this trouble to keep me free to remain a conspirator with them. Now all this would be for naught if they ever got wind of the fact that I am not the dustman I pretend to be. If I were to be seen in your company, it must give everything away."

"I still do not see what all this is in aid of," protested the general.

"Sir, it is most necessary that you do. Perhaps it is presumptuous of me but, as it is dark, I could go with you to your house for a short discussion of the case and there we would be free from observation and eavesdrop."

The general frowned. "Well, I suppose so. I cannot say that the stench of you is particularly attractive. Young man, you have a way with you of telling me just enough to whet my curiosity but hardly enough to satisfy it. Very well, it is a short walk past Piccadilly. You can make all this business plain to me in my library."

A large lamp was burning low in the library. General Beresford turned it up and directed the two runners to be seated. He turned from his tending of the light and, catching sight of Denning's face, he gasped. "Good heavens, man, you are all over blood! I must have served you better than I knew, and you have been bleeding all this time!"

Denning's hand went up to his face involuntarily and he felt the stickiness there. "Damn it all! And I have a dinner engagement with the Trenchards this evening! I cannot let my lady see me like this!"

The general gave a tug on the bellrope and when his man promptly answered, he instructed him to fetch water in a basin and clean rags. In a little while both he and O'Shaughnessy were busily at work examining the wound and cleaning away the dried blood. They were all relieved to find that it was only a minor cut, just above the hairline where the grazing nature of the blow had spent a good deal of its force in the young man's thick mane. Of course, the spot was quite tender to the touch but, aside from the copious flow of blood which was now stanched, no greater effects were to be expected.

"The general be quite a hand wi' basin and bandages!" O'Shaughnessy declared in compliment.

"I dare say I have had occasion to gain that knowledge at some cost," retorted the general, a satisfied smile upon his face as he gazed at his handiwork. "There! I think you'll do now."

His man came and cleared away the basin and materials and the general resumed his seat. "Now then, suppose you tell me what it is all about. I gather that you were not a part of the attack upon me."

Denning was putting tentative fingers to his wound. He said: "Thank you, sir, for your kind attention to my head. Now I must acquaint you with all the circumstances—and without the least delay or I shall be late for my dinner. I dare say, when we have done here, I shall have to move with all the speed of greased lightning if I am not to be over-late."

Said the general: "Far be it from me to keep a man from his lady. Although I am deadly anxious to know what it was that led up to the episode on Queen's Walk, I can understand how you are pressed and would invite you to call upon me here the first thing in the morning, say about ten? I could wish, however, you rid yourself of that horrid aroma before you came."

The young man smiled. "Indeed I surely will, and I thank you for your forbearance. Before I go, please promise me you will guard yourself tonight, making sure your house is secure."

"Great heavens! Do you think they are coming back after me? Surely they are just a pair of footpads—No, that cannot be, for you were with them. Blast all! Now I regret my forbearance!" he declared sulkily.

"If you'd rather I stay and explain . . ."

"No, no. I'll take your advice, you may be sure, but do

you go on and see your lady. Oh, by the way, Denning, this is a devil of a time to tell you, but I am sure you will understand. There is nothing personal intended in it. You might inform my Lord Carnavon that his nomination of you has been blackballed."

Ned Denning had just arisen from his chair and was on the point of departing with O'Shaughnessy. He turned to the general and his face was white. His tone, however, was quite calm as he asked: "If you know the reason for their disapproving of me, I would be obliged to you if you would inform me of it, Sir Alonzo."

"Of course, my boy, of course. I am a member of the committee and I can assure you that it was no under-handed thing. Nothing disgraceful to you or ourselves. You see, it was merely a matter of background. You will admit you've got none. After all, the crowd at Milliken's is a bit of a select group, an elite as it were. We all of us are men of distinction with impeccable breeding. It is obvious you could never fit yourself in with such as we. I am quite surprised Carnavon did not realize it. And then, of course, there are your associates. You do go about all day in the company of the lowest of the low. Well, I am sure you can appreciate how that just is not in the style of the Milliken Club. Do not take it to heart. I am sure there are any number of clubs that will throw open their doors to the son-in-law of Carnavon. He is a very powerful and influential man with all of *them*, I dare say. His banking interests, you know—Ah, but of course you do know! Well, good night, Denning. I shall be looking forward to seeing you tomorrow morning."

"Yes, general. Thank you, sir, and good night to you." He was all courtesy, even donned a smile; but O'Shaughnessy knew that his young and remarkable boon companion had been hurt to the quick.

When they had gone, the general commented to himself: "Amazing fellow, that Denning. Decent sort of chap, really. A shame he is not a gentleman."

Chapter II

"Look, you two," said my Lord Carnavon as he pushed his chair back from the dinner table, "I sense there is something in the wind between you and, whether it is to be love and kisses or another of your interminable brangles, I for one want no part in it. So, having finished my dinner, I shall partake of my brandy and my cigar in the library. When you have done with whatever it is that is brewing up, come to me and we can have a chat."

He chuckled as he got to his feet and lit his cigar. Then, the cigar in his mouth, a glass in one hand and the brandy decanter in the other, he sauntered out of the dining room.

Lady Emily, a concerned expression on her face, regarded her love with anxious eyes.

"Ned dearest, you have said so little all evening long, I cannot blame papa for withdrawing. Is there something wrong between us? Oh, I hope there is not. With our wedding so close upon us, I fear we should never have time to settle it. I should hate it so much to have to wed a groom with whom I am having a quarrel," she ended with a chuckle.

Ned regarded her with great love in his eyes, but there was about his expression an air of hopeless longing such that it quite broke Lady Emily's heart to see. She

19

frowned in puzzlement. It was just the sort of look she might have expected if Ned were suddenly about to leave her.

"Ned, my love! Whatever is wrong?" she cried, and the slight note of panic in her voice was unmistakable.

Ned could not bear to remain seated with the expanse of the table between them. He got up, came around and found a seat close beside her. In an instant she was in his arms, hugging him tightly as he clung to her and kissed her with a deep ardor. A farewell kiss? Yes, he had quite made up his mind.

Gently he disengaged himself from her arms, and stood up.

He said: "Emily, if I did not love you so dearly, I should not have had to say this. I could have let the world go hang and have taken my happiness without thought or care; but I do love you—more than my life; and I'll not see you unhappy through any fault of mine."

She looked at him, an uncertain smile on her lips. Affecting a light manner, she said: "Really, Ned, must you forever be melodramatic—especially at a time like this?" She reached up her arms invitingly towards him.

He stepped back in a gesture of denial. "No, Emily, I am quite serious. I cannot think when I have ever been more so. I have had news today which tells me that I am not the man for you. I can never make you happy."

A frown of annoyance came to mar the clear smoothness of Lady Emily's brow. "Ned, this is utter nonsense! You have already made me happy because you love me. I am happy this minute because you are near me—but I assure you, if you are to continue in this fashion for *another* minute, I shall be quite *un*happy with you!" Her eyes were flashing sparks as she ended.

"Look at me, Emily! What do you see?"

"Why, Edward Denning, the man I love!"

"Hah!" he sneered. "And who, pray tell, is Edward Denning? Edward is a name I never answered to until I was past eighteen years of age—and Denning? Aye, it is a respected name and, for as long as I have used it, I hope I have not disgraced it. But it is not *my* name—it is a hand-me-down! Mr. Denning gave it me with just such instruction. He hoped that by lending me his name it would act upon Lolly, the mudlark, to make of him a trustworthy man—and that was his sole purpose."

"You lie and you know it, Ned! He was determined to afford you the chance to turn your talents to better things than pilfering. He would have had you assist the law instead of breaking it! And he was right to have so wished it!

"Perhaps in the beginning it was in the nature of a loan, but he never had cause to regret it, and he had made you his heir long before he took the trouble of adopting you for his son. The name Denning is yours and rightfully so, even more so than that mine is Trenchard, for you have earned for yourself your right to your name. It was only my father's love for me and the feeling that life had sadly wronged my dead mother that explains his great efforts to have *me* legitimatized. No, Ned, you can wear the name Denning with all pride. And Uncle Alec has every right to equal pride in that his adopted son should be the most brilliant runner of Bow Street and the obvious choice to succeed him as Chief Magistrate when he is ready to step down.

"Now, I beg you, Ned, no more of this nonsense. Lolly, the master thief, is no more—only Ned Denning remains." She chuckled at a thought. "I will admit I should like to have known Lolly. Oh, he must have been an impudent rascal, from what Shamus has told me, hardly the stuffy melodramatic ass I love now with all my heart and soul."

"My lady—oh, Emily, you are making this so damned difficult!" cried Ned as though he were in pain. "I wish you would not look at me so!" He turned his back to her. "Emily, you are mistaken. Lolly is not gone nor will he ever depart from me. I was a fool to think that he could. In fact, I know now that it is Lolly who is the real me and Ned Denning the feeble masquerade. Even though the world has not been apprised of the facts, yet are they not all fools. They sense that I am not real. They know only too well that I am not of the gentry—"

"Who dares to say so?" demanded Lady Emily, rising from her chair in anger. "They have only to look at you! You have the manner, you have the grace, you have the courtesy—"

"But I do not have the lineage! Who is to say what strange origins I spring from? No, Emily, it will not wash! I shall never be accepted; and I cannot in all conscience, though it breaks my heart to say it, I cannot in all conscience ask you to descend to the limbo of society which I inhabit."

"Limbo of society! Edward Denning, if I did not love you so well I should throttle you! You are to be son-in-law to Carnavon! That should be enough to *force* society to accept you on *any* terms!"

"Well, society does not agree with you! I was informed but a few hours ago that the membership committee of Milliken's found my qualifications not up to their style. I have not the associates, I have not the calling, I have not the *breeding* to meet their standards. No, Emily, I am not Edward Denning, truly—I am merely Lolly, all decked out in the trappings of a Bow Street Runner!"

"They did not dare!"

"They most certainly did!"

"My father will be furious with them! I shall inform him at once! He'll change their minds for them quickly enough!"

"And to what end? I have not the least doubt that my Lord Carnavon can force them to swallow me whole, but I should never, ever be truly accepted. No, Emily! You may tell your father to withdraw his nomination of me and thereby avoid for himself further embarrassment. And you may tell him further that I relinquish all claim to the hand of his daughter. Lolly is not fit to kiss the hem of her skirt!"

"Ned! No!" screamed Emily as she rushed to him and clutched him in her arms, tears in her eyes. "No, Ned, no! I'll not have it!" she repeated over and over again.

Tiny muscles in his jaw were working as he gently took her by the shoulders and stared into her eyes.

"My lady, we all of us suspect that my birth may well have been without exception. My speech, my manner seem so to indicate it, but to suspect is not to know, and only knowledge counts for anything in this world. I am resolved that one day I shall come to that knowledge and, good or bad, I shall know who I am. But one thing I am not and that is a giddy fool. I realize it may take me the rest of my life to discover it and I cannot ask you to wait. You are young and have a full life that is just beginning, as the acknowledged daughter and heiress of Carnavon. If by some miracle I should manage to accomplish the task I have set for myself and in some little time, then I shall be back to join in the ranks of your suitors. Then shall I have a name to offer you—my own true name—unless it turns out to be one that is little better than Lolly."

Even as he spoke, Lady Emily was studying him out of eyes that had ceased their weeping. Though her cheeks were still moist, her eyes were glittering.

She nodded. "Yes, I begin to see what it is. You cannot stand the thought of being married to me and having to face down society. Oh, I know what is said of me and despite the King's patent. I am still Carnavon's bastard, and that you cannot stomach. Oh yes, it is all too clear! This renunciation of yours is just a pose! You do not love me half so well as you claim! You would prove yourself my superior so that you might then condescend to me. Well know you, Edward Denning or Lolly, whichever: Bastard child or no, I am a *Trenchard!* And no one condescends to a Trenchard! Not for money! Not for love! If you persist in this craziness of yours, I shall wish never to see you again!"

Ned, very pale of face, stepped back and bowed.

"My Lady," he said. He turned on his heel and strode out of the chamber.

"Ned!" she cried. "Do not do this thing!"

As the door closed behind him, she fell into a chair and stared unbelievingly after him.

Some few moments later, when Lord Carnavon came in to see what was keeping the happy pair, he was shocked to discover only his daughter. And she was weeping bitterly.

Ned Denning appeared promptly at ten o'clock the next morning at General Beresford's residence and was ushered into that gentleman's presence. The general was seated in his drawing room and arose to greet the man from Bow Street.

"Well, skewer me and roast me!" exclaimed the general, smiling broadly. "It is truly remarkable, Denning, how you can transform yourself! Damme, you are Jack Hanford once again! I say, have a seat."

"Thank you, sir. I—"

"Tell me, Denning, you look a bit peaked. I say, I am awfully sorry if it was my blow—"

"No, no, General, my head is quite all right this morning. I don't suppose I slept too well, I am sure."

"Good. Good. I should be saddened indeed if I had—"

"Of course you did not, sir. You may rest easy on that score. It is not the first time something of the sort has happened to me. But I would to business if you do not mind."

"Of course. I pray you will proceed."

Denning then proceeded to relate how he in the interests of another case had gone to a flash house . . .

"A flash house?" asked the general. "I have heard the term before but am not at all sure of it."

"Sir, a flash house is a thieves' tavern, a place of the lowest repute which caters to delinquents of every sort of criminality. You see, sir, a thief will never sit amongst honest men, it is not in his province to do it, nor would he trust himself with such people. And so these vulgar dives are where he hangs out. Now, we do not shut these places up for the very good reason that not only do they serve us as listening posts to lead us to wanted coves,

24

but, as often as not, we can find our man in one or another of them."

"Do you say that these knaves will just sit about and wait for a runner to nab him?"

"Well, it is not quite like that, sir. We runners receive as a regular salary but one pound five a week, and naught else for expenses while in the city. It is enough to put a little meat into a man but never heart, so it has become the custom for runners to look the other way unless there is some reward connected with a particular felony. It is not a good system, but a man has got to live. What is the result? We generally let the charleys and the petty constables concern themselves with matters of little promise in the way of a return and take to ourselves the cases the solutions to which will gain some hefty reward to the runner. The result is that, for the most part, we runners tend to concentrate upon finding and restoring to its owner stolen valuable property. It pays far better than apprehending murderers. Only in cases where the person slain is of note, so that the government or the family posts a handsome reward for the head of the perpetrator, are the runners at all interested."

"Well, yes, yes, that is nothing new, and I think I see what *you* are driving at; but you have not answered my question."

"Well, the thieves are fly to this system, too. And as long as they believe that nothing they have done warrants the posting of a reward, they are content to take their ease in these flash houses—and, truly, they are quite secure there."

"I see. No more than one might have expected from Cits. Now, if the army were running things, it would be a bit different, I can tell you."

"I am sure it would, sir, but to get back to—"

"Just one moment, Denning. I could not mistake your drift and I, too, am 'fly.' I suppose after I hear your tale, you will expect me to post a reward *pour encourager les autres* as the Frenchies would say."

"Certainly, I should not have the slightest objection,"

25

replied Ned with a smile, "but that is a matter which is entirely up to you. Mr. Denning, the magistrate at Bow Street, frowns upon the practice and the runners are on notice not to encourage it. But he admits he can do little to halt it and prays fervently, along with myself, that Mr. Peel will gain sufficient backing to get his reform bill passed. That will most assuredly put an end to it and allow us to pursue any and all criminals, reward or no."

"Hah!" snorted the general. "That is rubbish! I can just see Peel and his great police army charging down a street after a pickpocket or perhaps a sniveling area sneak. Nonsense! And, if it should come to pass, he'd learn that it was so soon enough!"

"I beg your pardon, General, for having to contradict you, but you are suffering under a misconception. That is not the way it will work at all."

"Do you say he does not propose a multitude of thief-takers in uniform? What is that but an army?"

"If one leaves it at that, of course. But an army is a body of men deployed in great masses. That is not at all in Mr. Peel's proposals. No, sir, it is more that each one of the new constables would be assigned a beat to patrol, something like a sentry, but not the same. He would not be there to challenge everyone passing by. His very presence, visible to all, must be deterrent to a thief and, should a crime be committed on his beat, the citizens can turn to him for immediate aid. The entire city would be subject to constant patrol by these men. No, they will not wipe out crime, but I think you can appreciate that such an attack as was made upon *you* could never have been carried out with such boldness had there been a constable patrolling along Queen's Walk."

The general pressed his lips together in thought. "Aye, there *is* something in what you say, Denning. But what of a situation such as you claim I am in peril. Surely, if I were to call in this new-style sentry of yours to attend me and pursue the facts in the case, his post must go unmanned while he does so. Why, sir, in the army he could be shot for leaving his post!"

"Sir, it is my fondest wish that Bow Street will be relieved of its patrolling duties and be assigned exclusively to the investigation of such matters. We, of any body, have the experience and the training for it. As it is, we do so now, but only in addition to other duties—the watches and pursuits that can be as easily handled by officers less expert than we. Just think of it, we can be called out to the farthest reaches of the realm—nay, the empire—and we are but eight men! Do you wonder that hard as we work, crime is rampant upon our streets and, with each passing day, it grows in numbers and violence? I tell you, sir, something has got to be done and Peel's proposals are the best answer I know. A decent policeman laboring for a decent wage, and the country at large would be a deal safer for us all!"

"Hear! Hear!" cried the general, laughing and clapping his hands. "I say, Denning, Peel could do worse than have you stand up in the House and debate his bill. Well, I must admit I had not thought of it like that and, as I like to believe I am a fair man, I shall have to do some further thinking about what you have just told me. That, at least! I dare say," he continued, "you have had to work with some interesting cases in your young career. Come to think of it, it was you who solved the kidnapping of Lady Emily Trenchard and brought the fiends to justice. Of course that goes to explain how you got yourself into his lordship's good graces and the lady pledged to you, does it not?"

"It was the occasion for my first becoming acquainted with my lady, yes," responded Ned coolly.

"Yes," said the general. "You do not look like a fellow to let the grass grow under your feet."

"Sir, I resent the imputation! And, for your information, the engagement has been broken off!"

The general looked wise. "I should have thought it never ought to have been plighted in the first place. I dare say Lord Carnavon has come to his senses and given you the boot. Really, Denning, you do carry things a bit too far. You should have known better than to have set your hopes upon a prize so far above you."

Ned leaped to his feet and glared at the general.

"General Beresford, you are being most insulting to me! If it were not my duty to keep you from harm, I should call you out!" declared Ned heatedly.

"Son, I like you, but I call a spade a spade and you had best get used to it."

"Then understand this, sir. It was I who broke it off and, if that thought gladdens your heart, I did so because of the news you gave to me last night. If I am not good enough for Milliken's, I am certainly not good enough for my lady!" Ned had gotten to his feet and was glaring down at the older man.

The general was shocked. He looked up at the young man and frowned.

"For such a reason? For pity's sake, don't you love the girl?" shouted the general, getting red in the face.

"Too much to drag her down to my level so that people such as you, sir, can make a mock of her!" shot back Ned, just as hotly.

"You, sir, are a damned fool! But blast me if I ever though a membership in Milliken's would cost—Denning, old boy, I do beg your pardon! How the devil was I to know that so much depended upon your election? You see, lad, I was holding forth against you only on principle, don't you know. Principles have got to be maintained. But then you have to consider I did not know *you*, son. Oh, damme, there are always exceptions, aren't there? There have got to be exceptions! Can't follow one's principles every minute! A man would be a damn fool to try. I say, Denning, stay put, why don't you. Don't do anything rash. I'll have Ashburton reconvene the board and we'll have you within the portals of the Milliken Club inside of a wink."

Ned shook his head and smiled bitterly. "Truly, General, I thank you for your willingness to reconsider, but it would be to no avail. Until I can discover my origins, I am honor bound to avoid my Lady Emily. If and when I can come to her with just claims to a respectable station in life in my own right, I shall once again plead my suit with her. But, until then, I remain Edward Denning of Bow Street, nothing more. Now I would put all of this aside and continue with our first order of business, namely: acquainting you with the facts leading up to the assault upon you and what they may portend."

"Sit down, Denning!" snapped the general irritably.

Ned reseated himself and would have begun to speak, but the general raised a hand to admonish him to keep silent, and he held his peace and waited.

Finally General Beresford, frowning heavily, said: "Denning, I am convinced that I have wounded you sorely. You cannot help but consider me hateful in every respect—and I cannot say you have no right. Yet you sit before me and calmly prepare to go into the details of some possible peril to me as though you were concerned for me. I'm sure, given the chance, you'd much prefer to have at me with rapier or pistol. How am I to trust in you?"

"My dear General, you may well believe that I have little love for you and your ilk, sir, but I have even less for the blackguards who assaulted you and if, as I believe, there is someone hiding behind some false facade whilst hired underlings attempt to do his bloody work for him, then you may believe that for him I bear a positive hatred. It is my duty to apprehend him and what I feel for you has not the least bearing on it. Sir, even if you will not cooperate with Bow Street in this matter after I have aired my suspicions, you may still rest assured that, until we can resolve the circumstances that underlay last evening's business and can demonstrate to our own satisfaction, if not to yours as well, that no peril threatens you, we shall not rest."

The general's eyes narrowed and he studied the younger man carefully. "Very well, Denning, I shall hear you out, but do not think you have heard the last word as to Milliken's. For all I have objected to your election, you *shall* be a member. Perhaps you are not a gentleman

29

by blood but blast my hide if you would not have earned your commission on the battlefield and *that*, my dear sir, is gentleman enough for me! Bow Street Gentleman they call you, do they? I had thought it a mockery, but I am here to state it is an appellation of honor and it befits you well, sir. Why, if Peel had the sense he was born with, he'd find himself fifty such as you and to the devil with all the rest of those police sentries and armies of his!"

"You flatter me, sir!"

"I do not think so. I have heard tales of you—who has not?—and I never gave them much credit. I took you for a blowhard like old Townshend. There's an example of a runner who talks a great game about himself, but it is different with you. It is other people who speak of you and in terms of the greatest admiration. Now that *is* a difference! Aye, I do not think I flatter you one bit and am prepared to listen to what you have to say to me in all seriousness."

"Thank you, general. That is most encouraging. Perhaps we shall get along after all is said and done."

"I am sure we shall, sir. Now, do you proceed to detail for me what you have learned."

Ned related how at the Brown Bear, a flash house located across the street from the Bow Street Police Office, he had happened to overhear a strange bit of conversation. Two disreputable characters, who were not familiar to him, were huddled over their mugs of grog mumbling together when he caught the name "General Beresford." Having heard of the general as being a celebrated hero of Wellington's campaigns, the mere mention of his name in such a vulgar haunt was sufficient to pique his interest.

He had resorted to the Brown Bear, which was actually a tavern whose premises comprised the ground floor of the disreputable dossing ken, the Russian Hotel, to see if he could learn the whereabouts of a wanted malefactor and, as was his wont, had come into the place in disguise. He had elected the guise of a seedy dustman trying to cadge the price of a cup o' grog.

It was, therefore, the easiest thing for him to approach the two men and let them know that he was a good fellow to work a lay and that he was ready for anything they would care to lead him to. After exchanging knowing glances, the two men told him they had in mind to go on the prigging lay. They had their ogles on an old swell whom they intended to snabble for the rhino he carried. One of them drew his knife and flourished it at this juncture to demonstrate his skill. The cove, spokesman for the two, then went on to say they could always use another gutsy bloke and if he'd come in with them, they'd let him take anything that he was lucky enough to find on the body—or the body itself if he'd a mind to peddle it to the resurrectioners—except for brass. They'd keep that.

Naturally Ned was immediately greatly excited at such a profitable prospect and asked with all enthusiasm who they were going to make easy. They replied that it was none of his business and that if he wanted in, he'd have to do what he was told and no questions. He was all acquiescence and gratitude, agreeing to do whatever they asked of him. They ordered him to meet with them that afternoon in front of the Milliken Club and not to draw any attention to himself. Ned then suggested a pint of grog all about to seal the pact. There were toasts to Bow Street's confusion, and he left them to seek out O'Shaughnessy.

He arranged for the big man to dog the trio and be prepared to act in reserve if the need should arise. Then Ned went to inform the Chief Magistrate what had occurred and what he planned to do about it all. Mr. Denning approved the plan and immediately began a discussion with his adopted son anent the underlying purport of the crime, both of them agreeing that here was something unusual. To contemplate murder when, for a mere disabling blow upon the head, all would be made accessible to them, called for deep contemplation. Mr. Denning relied upon Ned to arrange it so that the assault would miscarry without endangering the intended victim, whom they were sure was General Beresford—at least that was the only hint they had to go on. By doing so, there was a good chance that Bow Street might then find itself in a position to determine if there truly was something more of assassination here than robbery.

So, with the magistrate's blessing and a warning to be careful of his own safety, Ned repaired to James Street that afternoon and joined up with his unsavory companions.

The two thieves could not have been more pleased when their quarry chose to go by way of the fairly deserted Queen's Walk, and they initiated their nefarious activities with the greatest expectations. Ned's heart sank when he realized how well for them it *had* begun, and he immediately brought the larger man with the cosh down with his act of stumbling and falling into him. He was about to draw his pistol and slay the knife-wielder when, to his great relief and satisfaction, he witnessed the general quickly disarm and disable his assailant.

"So you see, sir, as far as I am concerned, the crack on the head you dealt me was a small price to pay to see how well everything had gone off," he ended with a smile.

"Of course, if I had but known, I should never have—"

"Please, General, it is quite all right. In fact, it was just the touch that was needed to give an authenticity to the exercise. If they should have stopped to observe what was happening, they could never have doubted that I had been nabbed. So my disguise is preserved, and I may continue to deal directly with them again as circumstances may require."

General Alonzo shook his head, "It sounds stuff to me, and I think we should all have been better served if the rascals were taken up and hung out of hand. I do not see anything in what you have told me to say that this was not a waylaying in the ordinary way. Assassination bespeaks politics and I am no politico—unless it is Peel who has taken umbrage at my vociferous opposition to his police reform," he declared laughingly.

Ned smiled. "Then just let us call it attempted murder. And, as it is obviously premeditated, there has got to be some dark purpose behind it. Our experience tells us that such a foul deed is rarely resorted to for such small gain."

"Oh, pshaw! Since they would hang for the theft of a shilling just as surely as for a slaying, I do not see that it can make a whit of difference to them how they treat their victims."

"Yes, General, that is a very good point you make, and it is one Mr. Peel is giving his attention to, you may rest assured. But, sir, we are not debating a proposition before the House of Commons. This is no parliamentary proceeding we are concerned with here. We are dealing with a man's life—your life, sir! Can you not appreciate that you must give us the benefit of any doubt, and humor us with your cooperation?"

The general replied with a shrewd look in his face: "And suppose I were to say to you, Denning, that I shall cooperate with you but that I shall not put up a farthing of reward money, what then?"

Ned's face fell. "In that case, sir, I can only promise you the services of two runners, O'Shaughnessy and myself, and the support of Mr. Denning, the Chief Magistrate. The other runners will never be tempted to assist us, and our own effectiveness in the matter will, therefore, be much diminished."

"I see. How would *you* share in the reward if it were payable?"

"It would be allotted amongst those runners who participated with us. Mr. Denning's personal resources are open to me in my work, as of course you will understand, and I see to it that O'Shaughnessy never feels the need to sell his services to the highest bidder. If it could be done, Mr. Denning would see to it that all of us runners were paid properly instead of having to subsist on reward monies. That, too, sir, is a matter of some importance

33

that Mr. Peel deals with in his proposals."

The general laughed. "You never let up on a fellow, do you, Denning?"

Ned chuckled. "I apologize, sir, if I have tried your patience."

"Well, I admit you might have, but that your points are so cogent. Now, I should say my life is worth at least five hundred pounds. Do you think that will be sufficient to entice the necessary assistance?"

"That is more than generous, sir!" exclaimed Ned, in great surprise.

"Not at all! I could as easily have made it a thousand, since I am sure I shall not have to pay a penny of it."

"I hope you are right, General Beresford."

Chapter III

Lord Carnavon put down his newspaper with a rattle and rose to greet his daughter as she came into the morning room.

"Have you had your breakfast, my lady?" he asked, studying her face carefully. She appeared wan and rather disconsolate.

She nodded.

He embraced her, placing a fatherly kiss upon her brow.

"Come, sit with me. I would speak with you."

He held a chair for her alongside his own and then sat himself down.

"After a night's rest, tell me, my dear: do you still condemn Ned's renunciation in so harsh a light?"

"No, papa, it was only that I was so upset with him that I charged him with condescension. Oh, why must he be such an adorably stuffy prig!"

"Well, I am relieved to hear you say so. As you well know, my dear, it took me some getting used to, that I should have a nameless runner for son-in-law, and but for old Denning's adopting him to make him something easier for me to swallow, I do not know that you and I should not still have been at tenterhooks over him. But that is all water under the bridge now, and I *have* gotten used to the idea. In fact, having got to know that lad, I'm damn proud of him and consider he will be quite an asset to us Trenchards. Then to have it all come to naught in one lover's quarrel—well now, my dear, that would be a bit much!"

"But, my lord, whatever am I to do? Must I sit alone through the years, praying against all hope that he will find himself?"

"No, of course not, my love. He is a bit of a fathead in certain things, but never fear. Give me a little time, have a little patience. I shall have no trouble with the membership committee, except for that hard-grained, hard-mouthed Beresford. Never did like the fellow, but I'll find a way to win him over, you may rely upon it. Beyond Milliken's, I'll see Ned elected into so many clubs, I dare say I shall be at the greatest expense paying his fees. And I know the boy. Gentleman in fact or fiction, he'll fit into any of 'em without a ripple. Of course there will always be a Beresford about, but his ilk are easily ignored. Why, damme, if it comes to that, I'll buy Ned a knighthood—or better yet, a regiment! Yes, that's the ticket, a colonelcy, by Jove! It must certainly take General Beresford down a peg and the lad need not give up a thing. His executive officers would be only too delighted to manage the regiment in his absence—"

"No, my lord, I beg you will do no such thing. Ned is my problem and I will handle it."

"Ah, now that is the daughter of our house speaking! Of course, my sweet! But if I can be of the least service to you, you have only to say so. I'll not interfere unless you wish it. Are you feeling any better?"

She conferred a bright smile upon him. "Yes, papa, much. He has made me miserable, and so I shall do the same for him, until from sheer exhaustion he must flee back into my arms where he belongs."

"It sounds a Spartan romance to my ears," his lordship remarked with a chuckle, "but vastly entertaining. I think I shall enjoy every facet of your little plot."

"Oh, papa!" cried Lady Emily, blushing, as she came

36

to him in some confusion to hide her flaming cheeks against his chest.

He patted her comfortingly upon the shoulder and remarked: "Of course we shall let the notice of your betrothal stand. That, in itself, must cause him some embarrassment, I should think. *He* can hardly disavow it."

Lady Emily let out a gurgle of delight.

He sighed. "Well, my dear, I must leave you now. Peel and I have much to discuss if we are to get his police bill through Parliament. We are working upon a plan that will get the essence of the idea approved and thereby prevent the opposition from defeating it by chewing on what is, for them, the more unappetizing consequences. Still it will call for great skill and careful planning if we are to succeed. Truly, my little love, I never thought I would be put to so much trouble just to see my daughter married. If only your choice had fallen upon a fellow somewhat less pigheaded, somewhat less upstanding and, perhaps, something more of a wastrel, I am sure we should have had not an iota of the fuss this love of yours is raising. Imagine a father having to raise an entire Metropolitan Police Force just to keep the bridegroom happy! Oh, I say! Now that is a wedding gift befitting a Trenchard!"

Both father and daughter laughed merrily at the thought, and my lord left his little dove, quite pleased to see that she had got her good spirits back.

"Ah, ye dirty scum, ye! Leavin' a cove to be battered to death!" shouted Ned as he gave the bigger of the two thieves a shove and began to dance about him, his fists raised in an awkward caricature of a prize-ring stance. Suddenly he stopped his prancing, tore off his cap, and bent his head to exhibit a swath of filthy bandages clapped about his ear and temple.

"That's what ye left me for, ye lumpin' rogue! Leave me in the lurch, will ye? I'll lump you proper, I will! Carn, put up your mauleys an' I'll bash yer boko till the claret runs, ye bloody, white-livered funker!"

The big man sneered and slammed his ale mug down upon the table as he ponderously rose to his feet. Ned began to dance about like a bantam cock, his fists striking out in all directions, but keeping some three or four feet back from him.

The other thief grabbed his chum's arm and yanked him back, nodded at his seat and the hulking thief, with a growling sneer, sat down.

"Aw, Raike, let me polish 'im proper," he complained. "I'll shut 'is noise fer 'im!"

"No, Benson, I'll handle this." Raike grinned mirthlessly at Ned and beckoned him to approach. "All right, Filcher, me beauty, come along now an' jine us. Have a pot o' brew! Say, we all o' us is chums, lad! That's a rare fellow!" he exclaimed, all heartiness, as Ned very indignantly took the offered seat.

"Ho, John Belcher! A pot o' brew fer me pal, Filcher, here!"

The tavern keeper came over with a foaming mug of ale and slapped it down upon the table. Raike handed him some coins and Belcher ambled back behind the bar.

"Naw then, mate, how come you are about, free as a bird? I could've sworn O'Shaughnessy came out o' the shadders and nabbed ye—"

"Well, burn your bum! Ef ye seen as much, why'd you let 'im? I had me the devil's own time of it givin' the big beak the slip. Ye could've lent us a hand!" cried Ned, hot with indignation.

"O'Shaughnessy? What, have ye gone queer in yer cock-loft? I lost me pig-sticker, and Benson's never a match fer 'im! And what's more, the ol' gent was making that stick o' his sing, I tell you!"

"You don't have ter!" grinned Ned, making a show of rubbing his head. "Just ye mentionin' it an' me bone-box aches all over again!"

"Ah, there's a good lad!" exclaimed Raike. "No hard feelin's. 'T was a close one all around, waren' it, Benson?"

"It war, b'gum, it war a close one," rumbled Benson, grinning.

"So ye give the overgrown harman the slip, eh? 'T war a neat bit o' work. O'Shaughnessy's not one ter be gulled easy."

"It'll take more than the likes o' that lubber to keep his bunch o' fives on the likes o' me!" boasted Ned.

"Well, you're a rum-duke to come inter this bozzing ken! Doncher know Bow Street is just over the way?"

"So let it be! There ain't no reward out fer me."

"No, but O'Shaughnessy knows yer now, you perishin' luny! An' ef he should nab yer again, he'll make yer squeak an' all o' us 'll be dancin' a Tyburn hornpipe outside o' Newgate!," Raike pointed out, making a graphic garroting demonstration about his own neck.

"Bah!" sneered Ned. "'T is sure as a gun, I'll see the bilger beak afore he ogles me and I'll make beef quicker 'n he can blink."

"An' supposin' Denning's wi' 'un?" scowled Raike.

"The Bow Street Gent?" asked Ned, suddenly hushed.

"Aye, his nibs, hisself. He's one as 'll see you afore ever you sees him!"

Ned leaned back with a disdainful laugh. "Garn! Ye're bammin' me! The Gent'd never come into this flash-ken. He'd surely dirty up his little finger!" and his laughter became uproarious.

"Hush, ye bloody fool! Doncher know nothink! Why, he can dress hisself ter look like yer own brother! You must 'a' been in quod long years not ter know that!"

Ned's eyes went round with horror. "Yer don't say!" he breathed.

"Aye, I do say! Now let's make beef afore he does turn up. We can't talk here!"

They got up from the table, Ned looking about him, shaken and fearful, huddling close to Benson as they made their way out of the Brown Bear. Outside, on Bow Street, Raike led them across the thoroughfare and they had to dodge nimbly about to avoid the rumbling carts lumbering past. They went through an alleyway and came out on Drury Lane. Following Raike's lead they arrived at a battered-looking lodging house which they entered. They climbed up two flights of stairs and came to a halt on the landing while Raike, producing a large key, opened the door. It was a bare and dingy room they entered, which boasted some odd chairs assembled about a rough-hewn deal table, stained with much use. From a small cupboard, Raike produced some tumblers and a bottle as they all took their seats at the table.

"Now, here's spirits to warm a man's innards! Not like that thin grog John Belcher dishes yer with."

They drank the fiery stuff and then proceeded to get down to business.

Raike said: "Filcher, yer don't look like much but I likes yer style an', furthermore, I have sold the cove wi' the brass who's supportin' this lay on a third mate, and he's agreed to stand holes on 't. How say you?"

"Raike, yer me chum fer life! Count me in!" exclaimed Ned, full of enthusiasm.

"Bono! Let's talk!" A look of distatse suddenly filled his face and he began to sniff the air. He looked at Ned with a scowl and exclaimed: "Blister my bum, but, Filcher, you stink! Fer Christ's sake, we ought to douse you in the Thames! Bad as that is, it smells sweeter 'n' you do!"

Ned fired up at him: "Yer don't have ter point yer boko at me, Raike! I be a dustman an' all us dustmen stinks!"

"Well, give it over, hear! No wonder the gaffer was fly to us! He whiffed *you*! 'T is no disgrace fer a cove to reek a bit, but you are bloody awful! Now you get out of it or ye'll have no part of this lay!"

"All right, Raike. But what about the lay? What's in it fer me? There's more to it than the swag we finds on him or I'm off me chump!"

Raike grinned at him evilly and a guttural chuckle escaped from Benson.

"Now ain't we the knowin' one!" sneered Raike.

Ned made it a compliment by simpering in a pretended embarrassment of modesty. "Aw!" he giggled.

"Well, it so happens ye're right, cully. We aims ter clap a stopper on the gaffer swell and now that yer know, yer *in!*"

"Not fer a watch 'n' chain and a sparkler, I ain't!"

"No, not fer a watch 'n' chain 'n' sparkler yer ain't!" mimicked Raike.

"Then fer what, I axes yer?" demanded Ned.

"Fer thirty-five quid, that's fer what!"

Ned began to count on his fingers, frowning. Then he cried: "That's fer naught, that is! I make it not twel' poun' apiece an' that's not near enough to snaffle a cove!"

"An' what, pray tell, does a dustman expec' fer his sarvices, me lord? Ye can have the corpus. 'T is an old one but good fer ten guineas at least."

"Ah!" said Ned. "That's more like it. I'm in!"

They shook hands all around and drank a toast to the success of their enterprise.

"Nah then," said Ned, banging his tumbler down upon the table, "who sports the rhino fer the reckoning?"

"None o' yer business!" snarled Raike. "Ye'll be paid."

Ned looked him up and down. "Not by you I won't! I wants to know who's the party as is standing buff fer the lay."

"None o' yer damn business, I said!" Raike roared angrily. There was a growl from Benson in support.

"Rot me guts ef it ain't!" snarled Ned right back at him. "I got ter know! I ain't about ter do it on tick! How do I knows ef he kin pay ef I don't know who he is? I ain't in this fer friendship, y' unnerstan'."

"Yer kin take me word fer it, cantch'er?"

"La-di-da! An' who in blazes 'r you?"

"I oughter scrag yer fer that!" exclaimed Raike, livid with fury.

Ned put a hand to his throat and rubbed it soothingly. "Nah, nah, keep yer hair on! 'T is only a matter of trust. Fer certain there'll be a reward fer this lay and the lads

41

from Bow Street will be hard at us to see us nabbled proper. So ef we don' trust each other at the start, one way 'r another, the Robin Redbreasts 'll be up wi' us 'n' we'll all o' us go up the ladder."

Raike scowled and involuntarily twisted his neck about to relieve its tenseness. "Shut yer clack-box! 'T is no fit thing ter be mentionin'!" Begrudgingly, he went on: " 'T is Bartholomew. Now are ye satisfied?"

Ned nodded vigorously. "I thanks ye kindly. For there's a gent wi' blunt enough to pay the reckonin'."

Ned, now all enthusiasm, proposed they go right out and snabble the old man.

Raike shut him up and said that they had raised the wind with their attack and would have to lay low for perhaps a fortnight to let the wind die down. They had to make it look like murder for loot, and to move too soon must certainly raise the suspicion that more than just an assault by footpads was involved.

Ned immediately complained that what with his having to give over his vocation as a dustman, he'd have nothing to live on. Raike handed him a fistful of coppers with the warning he had better make it do.

In two weeks' time, it was agreed, they were to meet at Raike's room again, and until then they were to lay low and not be seen together. The conspirators then indulged themselves with another toast to their success, and the meeting was adjourned. . . .

When Ned had finished his report to General Beresford, the latter nodded and promised his fullest cooperation. They shook hands upon it and Ned took his leave.

Chapter IV

Despite a tendency towards choler, General Sir Alonzo Llewellyn Beresford was not shunned by society. He was a gentleman of some charm, and his friends were more than willing to make allowances for his occasional spells of irascibility, attributing them to his lifelong exposure to His Majesty's Service. The general did most of his socializing at the Army Club, where the entertainment, as one might have expected, consisted in the main of old battles being constantly refought, usually with far greater wisdom and dash than originally. His membership in Milliken's was in the nature of an honor to him, he having been one of Wellington's masters of strategy and known to be quite quite close to the Iron Duke. His visits to Milliken's were in the nature of bracers, opportunities to mix with the nation's powerful and to learn at first hand how the country was faring. Although he was on retired status from the service, he was by no means retired from living and enjoyed immensely engaging in violent debate with any of the great figures with whom he rubbed elbows in that exclusive sanctum.

So it was that he had had, on more than one occasion, serious discussion with Lord Carnavon on various matters as one member to another. But, since they did not move in the same circles otherwise, their acquaintance was more a tolerance of each other than anything more intimate. It came as a surprise to the general, then, when he received a note from his lordship inviting him to call.

Now, a man whose plans and proposals for conducting successful campaigns had received not only the approval but the accolade of Wellington could have been nothing less than astute, and the general's mind quickly came to an understanding of what lay behind the invitation. He smiled to himself and prepared to meet with Lord Carnavon. He was looking forward with some anticipation to an interesting period of conversation with the powerful peer.

At the appointed hour, he presented himself at the Trenchard town house and was admitted by a footman, who respectfully extended his lordship's regrets that he was for the moment occupied and that his lordship would be indebted to him if the general could wait upon him. Of course the general was quite willing to do so, and he was led into a comfortable anteroom.

There he discovered that he was not to wait alone. Another visitor was in the room, a gentleman who was seated near the window, spectacles on his forehead, studying a sheaf of papers. Perhaps an attorney, thought General Beresford.

The other party was a few years his senior and neatly clad, but his clothes were neither stylish nor new. Although not threadbare, mind you, they had seen much wear, as the shine about the knees attested.

The general nodded at the gentleman and looked about him to find a comfortable seat. To his surprise the gentleman smiled and arose, extending a welcoming hand even as he put the general under an unabashed scrutiny from a pair of unusually penetrating eyes. The general, in some doubt, accepted the hand and was even more surprised when the gentleman exclaimed: "Ah, General Beresford, this is indeed a pleasure, but I could wish the circumstances that make you known to me were a deal less sordid."

The general smiled uncertainly and said: "I do not recall that we have ever met, sir."

"Of course. I am Alexander Denning of Bow Street. I

44

say, why not make yourself comfortable and we can have a little chat."

The general was suddenly quite embarrassed. Denning's presence could only mean that Lord Carnavon was going out of his way to bring pressure to bear upon him. Instead of his coming to meet with only an irate prospective father-in-law-to-be, he was going to have to face an irate father as well. It was something more than he had bargained for.

Yet, as he gazed into the clear, intelligent eyes of the magistrate, he could not detect one sign of rancor. The man was smiling pleasantly enough as they took their seats, and he began at once to plunge into conversation.

"My dear General, in regard to this matter of—"

"My dear Mr. Denning, before you begin upon me, I would say that I regret the business and have already apologized to your son. I shall see to it that the situation is mended with all due haste—although I should hesitate to term it sordid in any sense."

Now surprise shone forth in Mr. Denning's eyes. His eyebrows shot way up so quickly that his spectacles dropped down upon his nose. He pushed them back up with an unconscious gesture and exclaimed with an uncertain laugh: "My dear General, you do not have a thing to say to it! It is *we* who have our work cut out for us to protect you and at the same time run the malefactors to earth—and apologize to Ned? What in the world do you have to apologize for, to him of all people? Oh, do you think it is because of the crack upon the head you dealt him? I bid you put your fears to rest. It was not to be avoided, and it was quite understandable. It was one of those unpleasantnesses that every runner comes to expect, then thanks his Maker that it was not worse."

"Oh, that nonsense!" exclaimed the general, somewhat relieved. "No, of course I can do nothing about that, and I am quite willing to leave the business in your hands completely. I do not take it so seriously."

Puzzlement grew in Mr. Denning's face. "If not that

nonsense—and I assure you it is not nonsense at all, but a most serious business for you and ourselves—if it is not that, what exactly *do* you have reference to?"

"Why, the defeat of your son's nomination for membership in the Milliken Club! Had you not heard?"

"No, I had not. That puppy never tells me anything! I begin to understand now why *I* have been called here."

The general was quick to proceed to his apology. "Well, sir, there is not the slightest need for vituperation. I shall explain to Lord Carnavon—"

"Oh, bother Lord Carnavon! Make any explanations to him you care to! It is Lady Emily I am come to see and at her express wish. I could not for my life understand why the little dear should have sent me such a desperate plea for my help. I thank you, sir, for having made it clear to me, but I do not thank you for what you have managed to stir up for me. I shall have my hands full with my lady and I'll not thank you for that either."

"I shall do all that is possible to make amends. I have come to respect and even admire that son of yours in a very short while. I did not know the lad when I harangued against him at the club. It was nothing personal, you see. Just a matter of principle."

"Aye, principle and there's the rub! I do not have to be told that now Ned must believe he is not worthy of my lady, and if you know the least thing about my lady, then you know that she will engage in combat to the death with anyone foolhardy enough to cast aspersions on Ned, not excluding Ned himself. Yes, I can see all too clearly what has happened. General, you do not realize it, but you have managed to precipitate us all into a brangle of the first magnitude. Oh, if only he were blood of my blood, not any of this could have happened."

"I hope you will pardon my saying so, Mr. Denning, but the lady sounds a shrew."

"Oh, she is, she is! A shrew, a vixen, a termagent, utterly spoiled and a complete little darling."

The general smiled. "Ah, a rare one, in short."

"Aye, a rare one—and Ned's a fool!"

46

"I should very much like to make her ladyship's acquaintance."

"Oh, you shall, General, you most certainly shall! You do not think that I am about to face my lady without reserves, do you—especially as the culprit behind it all is so ready to hand? When you have done with my lord, I beg you will come to my rescue. I am sure I shall need you desperately."

The general chuckled. "She sounds a delightful creature, and I shall gladly come to your assistance in full panoply."

"Thank you, sir, and I am Alec to my friends."

"And to my friends, I am Alonzo!"

"We are well met, Alonzo!"

"Indeed we are, Alec!" And the two gentlemen arose from their chairs and shook each other by the hand with great warmth.

At that moment Lord Carnavon entered the room, accompanied by the gentleman with whom he had been closeted.

"Well!" exclaimed the Home Secretary, the Honorable Robert Peel. "Upon viewing this scene of incredible amity between opposing champions, I do wonder if I have gained an adherent or lost one!"

Said General Beresford: "It is more than likely that you have gained one, sir! I would bring to your favorable notice, one Denning of Bow Street."

Mr. Peel laughed jovially. "Say no more! Be it father or son, I am bored to distraction with encomiums upon their respective excellences. I dare say one or the other of 'em has had you by the ear. They are both of them hard men to defeat in debate, sir, and if you have been vanquished, I compliment you, sir, and welcome you to the fold. Well, gentlemen, I am pressed and must take my leave. Remember me to my lady, my lord. Oh, yes, after today's sesions, it will be wise if we sit down together again and compare notes. Good day, all!"

There was a shaking of hands and the Honorable Mr. Peel departed.

Then Lord Carnavon did not turn to General Beresford but to Mr. Denning instead, and there was a troubled expression on his face as he inquired of him: "Alec, has my secretary been remiss? I had no idea that you were waiting or that you even were expected today. I will apologize—"

"No, no, my lord. It is not you I have come to see. I have received a summons from Lady Emily and have rushed over to assure her that the heavens have not fallen in."

Lord Carnavon laughed. "You have my sincere condolences, Alec."

"My lord, I pray you will not hold the general too long. I will require his aid if I am to reassure her ladyship that, willy-nilly, Ned shall be convinced not to toy with the affections af a Trenchard—though truly, by this time, one might have thought he had learned that lesson well."

Lord Carnavon smiled but, at the same time, he was frowning. He looked a question at General Beresford.

The general gave him a stiff little bow. "My lord, perhaps it will save time if I apologize to you for my ill-considered outspokenness at Milliken's and assure you that I will mend the matter to your satisfaction at the earliest possible moment."

Lord Carnavon's brow cleared. "In that case I should be delighted if you would join me in a friendly coze, my good sir."

"No, no, my lord!" protested Mr. Denning. "If you are satisfied, then I needs must have the general to serve as my buckler against my lady."

"Very good!" exclaimed his lordship, laughing heartily. "I'll join you in the fray."

"I pray you will not. One Trenchard at a time is the most my stomach can bear so early in the morning."

His lordship laughed again. He wished them both a good campaign and returned to his office still chuckling.

General Beresford remarked: "Alec, I admire that you

are on such easy terms with his lordship. The man's power in the realm is awe-inspiring."

"Lord Carnavon will stand upon his dignity—and I assure you the dignity of a Trenchard is something to behold—but he insists that I treat him with all informality. He claims that as we are both parents of a most oddly assorted pair, before me he can only stand as my equal in our joint misery."

"Misery? He looked anything but miserable as he left us. I have met with him on occasion at our club—a most formidable peer I thought him. Here at home I swear I did not recognize the gentleman, he is so easy."

Mr. Denning laughed. "I can well imagine it. Our joint misery, you will of course understand, is a conceit for our happiness that two such headstrong people as are our heirs have consented together to wage their wars between themselves and, if ever they are committed to the blessed state of matrimonial strife, we shall all of us breathe more freely."

"Ah yes, but Ned Denning has informed me the question of his birth denies him entree here."

"Oh, he has come to that, has he? Well, of course, after your little outrage, it is only to be expected," commented Mr. Denning with a sigh. "Ah, here is my lady's maid come to fetch me. Come, Alonzo, and make your peace with my Lady Emily."

Exactly what he expected to find in Lady Trenchard, General Beresford could not have said, but certainly he was not prepared for what he did discover.

The two gentlemen entered into the drawing room and, instead of anything like a sedate reception, Mr. Denning was immediately overwhelmed by the onslaught of one vivacious brunette young lady with sparkling, dark eyes and cherry-red lips, as she dashed herself into his arms and kissed him on both cheeks. General Beresford could not repress a twinge of jealousy at the warm scene.

"Oh, Uncle Alec, it is so good of you to come!" she

cried. "I am sorry to have kept you waiting, but Adelaide could not get my hair right and I would not be caught in less than perfection by my future august parent!"

With that she subsided in a deep and respectful curtsy except that it lost something as she could not repress a giggle. As she arose from it, she turned her merry eyes upon the general and, smiling, exclaimed: "How very sweet of you! You have brought me some military hero, I'll take my oath!"

The general chuckled. "A hit, a palpable hit, my lady!" he replied as he bowed to her.

As she returned his salutation with another curtsy, Mr. Denning said: "Allow me to present to you, my lady, Sir Alonzo Beresford, His Majesty's General, now retired. You were right on the mark. The general served under Wellington and was one of his principal aides throughout his campaigns. He has managed to see action at Waterloo, Salamanca, and places too numerous to mention. He has had more than one mention in the dispatches, I can assure you."

The general could not help but be pleased at the look of interest that appeared in Lady Emily's eyes. He flushed a little and remarked: "My dear Alec, there is no call for you to lay it on so thick."

"Oh, but do let him, Sir Alonzo! I am sure Uncle Alec does not exaggerate, and I am so thrilled to have met you!" exclaimed my lady. "It is not often I get to meet a gentleman of such gallant achievement."

"My lady, I think *you* are now doing it too brown by far," protested Sir Alonzo. "Surely you do not expect me to believe you when you say you do not often meet with such as I. I cannot doubt that you must meet with His Grace, my commander, fairly frequently, what with your father and the duke both being engaged in politicking."

She shook her head sadly. "No, never in the months since I have come out of Bedford, have I even caught sight of the great man. I do declare, it is the despair of my life. That tyrant of a father of mine promises and promises; but either he is too busy or the duke may not be disturbed. And when I threaten to call upon His Grace by myself, I am threatened with a spanking. Now you really must admit I am much too old for that childish nonsense," she said in a most serious and confidential manner, and then went off into a gale of laughter as she quipped: "So I do not tempt fate!"

For a moment the general was nonplussed to hear with what gross disrespect she referred to her father, but then it struck him that not only was it all lighthearted frivolity, not to be taken seriously for a moment, but that the little minx was exerting herself to put him at his ease as pleasantly as she could. His heart went out to her at once.

He said: "My lady, if you will trust yourself to me, I should deem it a great pleasure to have you make a call with me upon His Grace so that I may present you to him. I should do it not so much as to ingratiate myself with you as to confer a particular delight upon His Grace."

Lady Emily beamed. "You are a true gallant, sir, and if you were but two years younger, I am sure I must lose my heart to you."

The general burst out laughing. "More like two plus twenty, I am sure!"

"Sir Alonzo, I think I shall come to like you very much indeed," she said.

"I pray you will, my lady, but I fear you will *not* after I have told you in what way I have transgressed against your happiness."

The general was astonished to see how quickly the young lady's expression went from cheerfulness to soberness, and her eyes fixed themselves upon his face. She waited for him to speak and suddenly he was no longer at ease.

"My lady—er—damme, I did not think this would be so difficult! My lady, the thing of it is that it was due to my efforts in great part that Mr. Edward Denning was denied membership in the Milliken Club—"

Sparks of anger kindled in Lady Emily's eyes and the general rushed on, praying to avoid a scene.

"—but I committed a grievous error, and do promise to see it rectified at once. My lady, I humbly beg your forgiveness, and state that had I known something more of the character of your fiancé, I should never have acted against his and your interests. I am sure you will excuse me, for my intentions were of the best. A man's breeding is ever of the utmost importance, and we of the membership committee cannot easily drop the bars or we abrogate the very principles upon which Milliken's was founded; and that, my dear lady, is to restrict the membership to the elect of the nation: men of intellect, achievement, affluence, and *breeding*. If we were to overlook any one of these qualities in our members, why, Milliken's would not be Milliken's! But, of course, young Denning is just that exception that proves the rule, and I can no longer doubt that his joining our ranks would *not* necessarily be a discredit to Milliken's, don't you see?"

The general rested his case with a feeling of satisfaction for having clearly justified his position in the first instance and, now, in the second as well. But, as Lady Emily continued to stare coldly at him, he found that his satisfaction did not restore his ease.

There was silence in the room as Lady Emily sat rigidly, a stiff expression on her countenance, and contemplated the general. Finally she spoke. "General Beresford, indeed you are a brave man or you would never have dared to face *me* with such drivel. There is a stain, sir, on my own birth that even His Majesty's patent will never erase. It was only through my father's influence, and because of the affection that his sovereign has for him, that I am being forced down society's throat. Yet, for all of that, I am still Lord Carnavon's bastard child. Who is to say that Edward Denning's origins are as tarnished as are my own, only because they are unknown? As to the other qualities Milliken's holds dear, he has them all, thanks to his stepfather here present, and to his own sweet self—"

"My lady, of course I am in full agreement," the general hastened to assure her, "but, as I said before, I was not aware of his accomplishments and of all his most commendable qualities at the time. I assure you again I will see to it that all is amended. It was but an honest error. There was no personal affront intended. It all can quite easily be gotten over."

"Do you think so? I know Ned and I think not! Oh, it shall be got over all right, but in due time, and I have my work well laid out for me if I am to achieve it in any good time. You have broken his heart, and, in doing so, you have broken mine. Now I have got to convince my melodramatic imbecile of a love that he has no need of the Milliken Clubs and the General Beresfords of this world. As for you, sir, this is my father's house and *I* cannot deny you it, but until Ned Denning sees fit to speak to you again, then and then only will I!"

Mr. Denning spoke up; there was a tight little smile on his face. "Well now, that is not so bad, Alonzo. I thought surely she would have sentenced you to being drawn and quartered at least. My lady, I am pleasantly surprised at your forgiving humor and I compliment you upon your good grace in the matter."

Lady Emily regarded Mr. Denning, her eyes full of suspicion. "Uncle Alec, I do not care for your sarcasm one little bit. I am in deadly earnest, you know."

"I know, my dear, I know; but you see, the thing is that the general here is in a bit of peril, and Ned cannot help but speak with him from day to day, because he has taken on the task of seeing to it that Sir Alonzo comes to no harm."

Lady Emily clapped her hand to her mouth and burst into laughter. "Oh, dear! Now you have ruined everything! And here I was thinking what a perfectly marvelous little scene I had just played!" Then her face filled with concern and she looked directly at Sir Alonzo. "But I dare say that if Ned is on the case it must be something quite serious."

The general was entranced. Never before had he encountered such rapid transition of moods in anyone, and they were not evanescent in the least. Lady Emily had the quality of being very sincere even though it appeared that, as in this instance, one moment she was angry with him and the next she was truly troubled for him.

General Beresford, thankful for the respite, immediately began to deprecate the seriousness of the business, but Mr. Denning would not have it. He put up a hand and shook his head.

"No, Alonzo, I wish you would not treat the matter so lightly. We have come upon further information that confirms our worst suspicions, and we are well met this day, for I would let you know how deeply endangered you are."

The general raised a doubtful eyebrow. "Well, Alec, if you insist. Perhaps we can talk it over at the Army Club. I am sure my lady's patience would be tried past all bearing—"

"No, no, this is a most excellent place—better here even than at my office in Bow Street. One cannot be too confidential in these matters."

"But, my dear Alec, in my lady's presence?" asked the general, giving the magistrate a querying look.

Mr. Denning stared straight at him and said, very deliberately: "Yes. My lady is to be trusted implicitly. She is to be a policeman's wife, and in that capacity she cannot help but be put in possession of the most confidential aspects of her husband's business. And, as she loves her husband, it can never go further than her ears, for it may well place her husband in the greatest jeopardy if she could not keep these matters to herself. Am I correct, my lady?"

"But of course, Uncle Alec."

"And furthermore, my lady is a rare one. I do not think it at all condescending of me to listen with all seriousness to any comment she may care to make upon our progress." He chuckled. "That, I am sure, my respected son will find a most difficult thing to live with."

"Oh really, Uncle Alec! How bad of you to say so, even if it is true," exclaimed Lady Emily with a little gurgle, as her face turned a lovely shade of pink.

General Beresford said: "My lady, I hope you will find it in your heart to forgive me for the anguish I have caused you."

"It pains me to say so, Sir Alonzo, but I fear I must. My horrid father-in-law-to-be has insisted that I do, as you have just heard."

The general smiled and shook his head in wonder. It was not the easiest thing to follow the little lady's moods, but it was a delight to try.

"Thank you, my lady. I am very much relieved."

"Well, now to something which you will find a deal less pleasant. If I may have your attention," requested Mr. Denning. "We have learned the identities of your assailants and something more. If it had not been for that latter, the thieves would now be in irons; but fortunately for them—at least for the time being—it turns out that they are in someone else's employ. Their task, my good Alonzo, is simply to do you in."

"Well, if what you say is true, it must be the simplest thing," said the general. "Arrest this evil genius as well."

"But it is not so simple, for this evil genius is truly such—a man by the name of Bartholomew. And he, I can assure you, is but one further step—one more foul rung of this conspiratorial ladder. We *cannot* take him—yet!"

"What can be his interest? I number no Bartholomew in my acquaintance."

"Obviously he has been hired to arrange your demise for the benefit of a party or parties unknown—and that is exactly what can be expected of Bartholomew. He is a man of no visible means of livelihood, but affects a spurious gentility and a true opulence in his style. The source of his wealth is crime of every description. We have come to suspect—and that is a weak word in this instance—that in every rancid pie baked up for the discomfort of our citizenry, Bartholomew has more than just a finger in it. But he is clever, he is. We have yet to uncover one shred of evidence against him of a nature cogent enough to convince a jury of his criminal implications."

"Bah, that is no way to go about the business! In the army a touch of the cat, a hot day's ride upon the breech of a cannon, and he'd give you enough of confession to hang his own grandmother!"

"So it may be in the army. But this is not the army. This is England, and we have got to prove a case before we can proceed to punishment. Star-chamber proceedings went out of style over one hundred and fifty years ago."

"Well, I am not about to permit such audacity free reign against me. The man pretends to be a gentleman, does he? Very well, I shall support his pretensions—to the point of inviting him out upon the field of honor, and I warrant you he will not leave it breathing!"

Mr. Denning laughed. "Ah, if only all our cases could be resolved so simply! First of all, my dear Alonzo, I must inform you that the duello is a breach of the law, and I should have to take you in charge, before the deed if I heard about it in time, after it most certainly, if you had managed to survive—which last I surely doubt, as Bartholomew would have gone to the greatest pains to see to it that you never lived long enough to make your appearance."

"But then he would be known for a coward and poltroon!" protested Sir Alonzo.

"And you would be dead! The very thing we could wish to avoid, and he to accomplish."

Lady Emily interposed: "My dear General, I shall not permit my respected uncle to toy with you longer, or we shall be at this entertainment forever and a day. Slaying or otherwise impeding this Bartholomew will hardly discourage the man who has engaged his services. He will only seek out other villains to accomplish his evil design."

"Ah, yes, I see. How foolish of me not to have done so. I suppose I am not used to this sort of warfare at all.

Well, Alec, I dare say you have something to propose?"

"Ned has rejoined the assassins and has now gained their confidence. That is how we have come to be so knowledgeable. Our strategy is to lull the enemy into believing that their intentions are completely unknown to us. In this false freedom from suspicion that they are enjoying, it is the most likely thing that they, or Bartholomew, will do something, say something, that will give us the clues we need to the identity of the third party, so that we may close the trap upon all of them. In a word, Alonzo, I am proposing that you act as bait—er—no, a bait may be consumed—let us say a decoy, rather."

"Ah, you begin to interest me greatly. I cannot say I approve of Ned Denning's associating himself with such lowly cutthroats, but I suppose it cannot be helped. Well, of course, I shall not mention a word of this to my colleagues at Milliken's. They would hardly approve."

There was a tolerant smile upon Mr. Denning's lips as he cautioned: "Nor must you mention any part of this business to anyone else either."

Lady Emily chortled. "Oh, Sir Alonzo, you are precious! And completely incorrigible!"

"Now then, Alonzo," the magistrate went on, "one further caution. It is not beyond possibility that you will encounter Ned in this duty. If he is garbed in anything less than the highest fashion, you are not to notice him—"

"Oh, I say! After what I have done to him, I should be a complete cad to cut him!"

"You will be a complete fool and he a dead man if you do not! General, this is war!" exclaimed Mr. Denning, losing patience.

There was a pained expression on General Beresford's countenance as he struggled with the notion. "I—I think I begin to comprehend. But, damme, this is a most ungentlemanly—and unmilitary—approach to the enemy!"

"I should agree with you, sir," said Lady Emily, "if the enemy consisted of gallant gentlemen like yourself. But you forget that dash and glory play no part in this business. Your death, achieved in any way that is foul, will be their victory. Ours will be to see them frustrated in their attempts, and hung by the neck in any way the law of the land dictates we may!"

"Hmmmm," mused General Beresford. "Sort of puts the odds on their side a bit, I should think."

"Aye, it does, but, if you will sit still for it, we shall have our first good crack at bringing Bartholomew down. And all of London will breathe easier to see the fiend destroyed."

"Good God!" exclaimed the general. "Never in my life did I ever conceive that sitting immobile before the enemy would be the best part of strategy. Alec, my hand on it! Of course I shall be with you all of the way!"

Chapter V

In her heart of hearts, Emily never believed that Ned would not come around in a day or two to an understanding of exactly how foolishly he was behaving. After all, this was the nineteenth century! The days of knightly vows and sincere dedication to inane ideals were long gone, recollections of them reposing only in that great receptacle of nonsense, Malory's *Morte d'Arthur*, and in such more recent works as *Santo Sebastiano; or, The Young Protector*, no more saner for its recentness. These she had little patience with, preferring Sir Walter Scott for something more robust and Miss Austen for something more delicate. But, as Mr. Edward Denning had not seen fit to make an appearance that day, or even the next, and as she found Sir Walter and Miss Jane poorer company than what she wished, she finally sent a note to Bow Street.

By dusk, no answer had been returned, and she sent another, this time to the home of Mr. Alexander Denning, with whom Ned had taken up residence after his adoption had gone through. Not that that had been so easy to accomplish, his moving in with his new father. For some weeks after he had been officially declared the adopted son of the Honorable Alexander Denning, Ned had resisted all attempts to convince him that he would not be imposing on his new father. It was not until the magistrate, who had been watching over him ever since the first time he had appeared as a mudlark on charges before him at Bow Street, and one of very tender years, finally lost all patience and ordered the brilliant Bow Street runner out of his paltry lodgings and into his own modest but extremely comfortable house.

"Damme, Ned, I'll not have you shame me before the world! Now you do as I say or, by heaven, I'll disown you!" Since at the time Mr. Denning the elder had been adoptive father to Mr. Denning the younger (then twenty-five years of age) for all of nine days, the removal of the latter to the former's residence was accomplished with all good grace and a great deal of jesting.

There was no answer to Lady Emily's second note either, and she began to worry. If Ned was truly adamant in his avowal, the chances were excellent that they never would become man and wife. After all, Mr. Denning some years back had exerted himself to unravel the mystery of Ned's beginnings and, for all his well-known perspicacity, had had to give it up as hopeless. He had concluded that Ned, from his speech alone, must have come from a good family; but was lost, strayed, or stolen at a very young age to wind up a thief on the banks of the Thames. He suspected foul play, but had not been able to uncover any clue to it for all his studying of past police reports in all quarters of the realm. Even reference to the newspapers produced nothing of any consequence. The fog of years passing seemed to have obliterated every trace of the lad's history.

It stood to reason that if Mr. Denning had failed to solve the mystery, with all his experience and all the resources at his command, what hope could there be for Ned to accomplish it? Yes, the matter was become quite serious. Somehow she had got to disabuse Mr. Edward of his silly notions and bring him back to his love; namely, herself.

The following day she thought and she thought and, as a result, was quite distracted all day long. Her father never noticed because he was quite taken up with visits and visitings. All the politicos were in a turmoil. Peel was preparing to present his detestable legislation in Parliament and, between pressure from him and pressure from my Lord Carnavon, the wheels of the new liberalism were beginning to budge. Although the Home Secretary was not a particularly flamboyant type—and certainly no radical—he was persuasive and had an excellent sense of the temper of his colleagues in the Commons. What was more, he could trade and bargain with the best.

As for Lord Carnavon, his power was derived from finance; his bank spread far and wide its tentacles of gold. The threatened withdrawal of the least of them could gain a vote in support of Peel.

Nevertheless, Mr. Peel was beginning to find too many objections to various details of his plans for a Metropolitan Police Force. And so, to retain the concept at least, bit by bit these details were sloughed away. He was willing to allow it because he felt that so long as the *idea* of the New Police was salvaged, there would be time enough to force back into the establishment the necessary items of organization, pay, and jurisdiction as future developments required that they be spelled out. But it was a monstrously complicated task. He was grateful to have the powerful Trenchard peer in his support.

The long and the short of it was that Lady Emily found herself quite tried and quite bored—and *that* was a new experience for her!

When, before her elevation to legitimacy had been accomplished, she had been residing on her father's estate of Ravenswold in Bedford, she had had all manner of friends amongst the local gentry, good friends who understood the unfortunate circumstances of her birth and did not hold it against her. The fact that she was the acknowledged heir of Carnavon and the mistress of Ravenswold certainly made no small contribution to her standing in the community. And the fact that she was not in any sense a mere by-blow of his lordship, but the child of a true love that death had seen fit to end before the final vows were taken, was common knowledge. His lordship's love for his only child was never a thing he had been ashamed of, and he had kept her at Ravenswold not on his own account, but to spare her the slurs and indignities she would have been made to suffer in the much harsher and heartless society of the capital.

Now she was truly a lady in every sense of the word—and betrothed. As soon as the announcement had been promulgated and she was no longer a matrimonial prospect, it was the most natural thing that her callers began to drop away. She had not cared because she had Ned and he was all she wanted. Well, now it was beginning to appear that she was not to have Ned—for the time being at least—and as her father was all taken up with the matter of police reform, she had not even his company. So it was that she was become bored; it was not a thing she knew how to suffer well.

Having to spend her time considering ways and means of bringing her love to his senses, out of this self-sacrificial obstinacy, was not at all a happy diversion. Especially as there would be not the slightest effort required if she could but get him in her arms and alone. Apparently he was wise to just that probability, and was not about to let her get so close to him as to put undue strain upon his resolution. Reason enough that was that he would not respond to her messages. She was sure that, given time, she would find a way, but for now it was giving her the headache, and she realized that she could not devote every waking minute of her day to the problem without encouraging an onslaught of the megrims. What she needed was a companion. Even as she thought of it, her hand dropped down to the side of her chair and reached for something that was not there. Of course! King Alfred! Oh how she wished he was by her side!

No wonder she felt that she had not a friend in the world! It had been so many weeks since she had said farewell to him at Ravenswold. She wondered how he was getting on in her absence. The thought of the shaggy blackness of His Majesty brought a smile to her lips and gave birth to a resolution in her heart to speak at once to her father. The very first chance she got, she would beg him to bring King Alfred to her. Surely that big brave fellow must help her to fill her time more pleasantly than she had been able to do the last few days.

The first chance came at dinner that night. My Lord Carnavon, suffering from an overdose of politicking and also from a desire to spend even a little time in the charming company of the one he loved before all others, decided to stay in that night, dining and conversing with my lady. Well may he have regretted that decision.

"Papa, I am lonely, desolate, and forlorn!" remarked Emily as the meal came to a close. She sighed deeply.

"I take it, then, that Ned is standing by his vow and has not called?"

"He has not even answered my letters!"

"Bufflehead! What are you going to do about it?"

"I have not made up my mind."

"I have always considered him an excellent catch, for he has qualities that are rare. He has courage, devotion, loyalty, and I dare say he can be a tender, loving—"

"Papa! You are not making me feel any better!"

"Er—yes, but what I mean to say is that he is also pig-headed to a fault. Correct me if I am wrong, but it seems to me you have had trouble with him on the score of his social inferiority from the very beginning. One begins to suspect that he is even more snobbish than we are, forever waving his undefined station in life in our faces."

"Oh, papa, you know it is not that! It is simply that he is very sensible of the fact that neither the circumstances of his birth nor those of my own can bear the light of scrutiny. But yes, he *is* a fool on that score, a lovable fool, for together we can face the world and be happy, if he would but realize it."

"Well, my dear, as I have said time and again, he is

your problem. From what Denning tells me, he is having his hands full with the lad on a similar score. Ned refuses to settle into his filial status as a proper son should and they are constantly at bickering over his place in Denning's household. Alec complains to me that he has enough of Bow Street runners during the day. Now, it seems, he brings one home with him each night. And it has gotten a deal worse since the breakup of your betrothal."

Indignantly Emily retorted: "Our engagement stands! That much, at least, he shall never achieve!"

"Well, I could wish there was some way to bring an end to this idiocy of his!"

"Believe me, I shall find a way—but, in the meantime, I am lonely and would have company."

"I suppose we could give a ball and force his attendance as we did at your coming out."

"No, I have no wish for so much company as that. I have it in mind to bring King Alfred to London. I do miss the dear fellow so."

Her father stared at her incredulously. "What! You would bring that monster here to this house? Never! Why the City of London itself is to small to kennel the beast!"

"Oh, poo! How you do exaggerate! His Majesty is perfectly well behaved and can be so quiet you will never know he is about."

"Hah! Never know he is about, when even his snoring is enough to make the walls tremble! Where, I pray you will tell me, do we have adequate quarters for the monster? I rule out the stables at once! My bloods would never consent to share their fine stalls with a dog who needs at least as much room as any one of them."

"Oh, bother your bloods! Anyway, His Majesty would never condescend to sleep in a stable!"

"Well, I certainly do not propose to erect a great hall of a kennel for him on our limited grounds."

"Nor would I think of putting the dear fellow in a kennel! After all, he is royalty! He would never forgive me!"

"Then exactly where do you propose to keep him, may I ask?"

"With me. Here in the house," she replied serenely.

"Over my dead body you will!" shouted his lordship. "That is all I need—to have that great hound of hell decide to share my bed with me of a night!"

"You need have no worry on that score. There will always be someone about to tend him and keep him happy."

"Ha-happy?!" exclaimed his lordship. "So now is it that I am to hire a platoon of keepers from the zoological gardens to keep us all from harm? No! I say. Absolutely no! If you must have a dog, I shall have my man of business find you a cute little lapdog. You will then have your wish for company fulfilled and be in the height of fashion at the same time."

"Fustian to fashion! King Alfred is more than just a dog and I'll not be satisfied with less. I have raised him from a pup and he is the only thing that is mine, all mine!"

"Emily, you are speaking like a child! Everything I have, you have!"

She smiled. "And everything I have, you have, papa; therefore, I would have you share with me the affections of His Majesty, King Alfred."

"I shall consider them shared without further proof or demonstration! Now, Emily, I think this discussion is ended. Think of the expense! Our bills for board would be doubled! Nay, trebled, I'll wager! And who would see to him when you were away? No, it is out of the question! It is too nonsensical an idea to even waste one's breath over!"

"Oh, that is too silly of you, papa! He costs no more to feed than a horse or two, I am sure—and, anyway, you are paying for his food out at Ravenswold even as we talk."

His lordship raised his eyes to heaven. Emily grinned, for she knew she had him on that point at least.

She went right on demolishing his objections. "As to a keeper, yes, I do agree and I have thought of the perfect solution. You remember Timmie? When he is not engaged with attending upon His Majesty, if you are nice to me I might even lend him to you for a tiger. He is a bright boy and very engaging, and what he does not know about horses and dogs is not worth knowing."

"My lady, your concern for my comfort quite overwhelms me. I do not know how I ever managed all these years to get along so well without the presence of a thirteen-year-old scamp of a boy. Why King Alfred is twice his size!"

"Your sarcasm, papa, is quite lost on me, I assure you. I am not so much larger than Timmie, and King Alfred has never objected to my handling of him. Besides, he loves the boy. I tell you it is the perfect answer."

"Enough, Emily! I have said no, and no it shall be!"

Emily regarded her father with a hurt expression. Her dark eyes began to sparkle with tears. A few rolled down her cheeks.

"Emily! None of that! We are Trenchards and can stand buff for minor disappointments. And you know that when I have made up my mind, there is no one on earth who can make me change it."

Emily sat looking at him, her hands in her lap, her tears not abating.

His lordship went down in defeat. "No one except one miserable brat of a daughter, that is!" he declared, shaking his head at himself.

In a flash she was on his breast, smiling happily through her tears, declaring he was the best father she had ever had.

He chuckled and kissed her warmly. "If I love you more than life itself, I can hardly put my ease above your happiness. Oh well, it will put a bit of life into the place to have a boy and a dog about, I suppose. Aye, and I have an idea that London itself will never be the same for King Alfred's invasion of it."

He paused for a moment and then he remarked thoughtfully: "You know, I do think I kind of miss seeing the old boy at that."

Squatting close by the river was a squalid tavern, the Oak and Rose, known with some affection as the ol' Muck 'n' Mire by its patrons. It was situated just beyond the reach of the tides of the Thames and shared with that mighty stream an affinity for mud, brought into its precincts in copious amounts upon the boots of its custom, watermen all, haunters of the wharves, the embankments, the quays, and the river itself. They were of various diurnal occupations connected with trades deriving from the river and its commerce: fishermen, warehousemen, stevedores, and such; but came the night and, by and large, they all shared one trade—that of mudlarking. In effect it was thievery along the waterfront. It encompassed anything from stripping corpses found floating in the river to breaking into chandlers' storerooms. Their trademark was river mud. One can suppose that to some it was all great fun, hence mudlarking. Then again, it may have been sheer irony, that term; for no respectable felon from inland had any taste for their company, except and unless he had got to quit the country in a hurry. Then it was mudlarks, ho! to secure him safe passage out of the port of London.

The mudlarks were a society to themselves, much as a pack of wolves are. And, too, they tended to be more morose than to other brothers of the cross. They were easily given to violence and fought grimly and bloodily. The losers in their petty strifes and squabbles were generally to be found floating face down upon the breast of Father Thames by the River Police, the following morning.

With one exception, they had no great heritage, their most diligent efforts to achieve renown never obtaining for them more than the cursory attention of landsmen, for the simple reason that they never ventured farther inland than quayside in their exploits. The only exception was one man, a very young man—or at least he had been until O'Shaughnessy (bad cess to him!) had shot him to death attempting to collar him. His name had been Lolly and he had been a true gent. He could hold his own with the nobs as though he were every bit as good as they. When deep in their cups, the mudlarks would always hark back to the times some eight and nine years before when Lolly, at the head of a band of much older thieves, had carried mudlarking right into Goldsmith's Hall itself. Ah, but he had overreached himself that one time, and it had been his last exploit. He had gained the attention of Bow Street with his raids beyond the river, and they had caught up with him in the end. It was a shame to have lost him because he had conferred a rare glory upon the trade. Also, it was a lesson to them all to stick to their lasts, namely the river and its mud, the things they knew best. And so they would sigh for those few golden years when Lolly had almost succeeded in making of mudlarking a respectable lay.

But to Raike and Benson, who had no use for mudlarks and had never heard of Lolly, the ol' Muck 'n' Mire, distasteful as its company was for them, had its use this one time as a hole in which they could plot together safe from any chance observation by Filcher—for it was against Filcher they were plotting.

They were huddled together over a tiny table in a corner of the vast ramshackle chamber and Raike was saying: "Shut yer gob box, ye overstuffed barrel of lard! I ken very well no dimber cully'd be found dead in this crib but we be safe from Filcher here an' he's got no part in this gab."

Benson rumbled something and nodded.

"Now this is what I say," continued Raike. "It makes no difference to Bartholomew how the job gets done so long as it is done. He's willin' to sport the tin fer three blokes but that ain't ter say as three blokes is necessary ter nap the regulars. Now if just us two blokes was to nap 'em, why there'd be a'most six quid more fer you 'n' me!"

Benson nodded ponderously. "Aye, I'll snaggle Filcher a'ter it's done and there'll be no noise from him."

"No, yer bloomin' ijyit! We kin do it bowman wi'out

68

'im. We don't need Filcher at all! That way he got no right to split wi' us—but he can still colleck the corpus ef 'e wants it." Raike went off in a cackle at his jest.

Benson did not see that it was at all humorous, and he frowned. "But you said the corpus be worth ten guineas!" he protested.

"Oh, you stupid lump! Yer not a bit brainier than Filcher! Does yer wants ter go trottin' all over Lunnon wi' a dimber gaffer's corpus on yer back? What'll ye say to a charley as stops yer? The old gent had a wee drop too much and yer his bosom chum seein' him home safe? Look at yer, yer couldn't even pass fer a copper penny in a pot o' gold guineas!"

The metaphor was completely over Benson's head, but he was content to accept it that Raike did not approve his idea.

"Well, is it bowman wich yer?" asked Raike.

Benson nodded.

"Bono! We'll not wait the fortnight out and afore Filcher can know what's o'clock, it'll all be a fetter complee, as the Frenchies would say."

Benson grinned in admiration of Raike's erudition and nodded his wholehearted agreement.

Chapter VI

My Lord Carnavon was nothing if not efficient in all his business, and it is to be believed, therefore, that all who served him shared in that virtue to a high degree. So it was not surprising when, upon the third morning after my lady had requested her boon of my lord, that the Trenchard domicile was shaken to its foundations and left much battered and bruised by the advent of a small boy and a very large dog.

Soames, the Trenchard butler and an eyewitness to the invasion, was on the rack. Each horrid gash in the gleaming, highly polished parquet floor was as though inscribed in blood on his heart. But he stood his ground staunchly and never fled from his post. Admittedly it was by the greatest effort of his will that he managed to maintain his usual well-composed demeanor. Considering his fear and torment on the occasion, he surely can be forgiven the slight tremor in lip and leg that could not be denied.

He had never in his life seen such an horrendous beast. It was not a dog—it was a DOG! In fact it was a very horse of a dog! It could not have been less than seven and a half hands high at the shoulder and its hoofs, or paws, were at least as large as a great man's

71

palm, if not larger. And it was covered all over with a perfectly repellent black shag.

As to its weight and strength, he feared to guess, nor did he have much time to give it much consideration as he and the two Trenchard footmen found themselves thoroughly occupied snatching up endangered ceramic ware and skittering costly chairs and refectory tables out of harm's way.

The room was filled with action of a most demonic sort, and the shrieks and hoarse, deep-throated barks only added to the pandemonium. The well-scrubbed, elfish-eyed farm boy who appeared to be an appurtenance of the beast did absolutely nothing to control it nor, bless her soul, did my lady. For all that they had come to cherish and love their charming mistress, it was a little bit much to see her suddenly become quite the maddest member of the odd trio, all gurgles and laughter as the monster charged at her like a bull, oversetting her again and again and then stopping in the midst of this mad rite of welcome to thoroughly wash her face with a great pink tongue.

Seeing those huge, dripping, ivory sabers so close to her petite, adorable features gave the strongest of the three servitors qualms; but it was amazing, and the greatest relief, to see that never for an instant was there truly the slightest cause for worry. Lady Emily banged away on the great dog's head times innumerable and he only wagged his tail the harder. She hung about his neck and crooned a welcome to him and no one could deny that he understood for he crooned a paean of love into her face in reply.

As the throes and spasms of the meeting subsided to be replaced by mere pantings and chucklings, Soames, infinitely relieved that the walls had suffered no damage, was able to regard the animal in a more tempered light. Yes, he had heard mention of such beasts. They were born and bred somewhere in the New World, he understood. Well, what could one expect of those people over there! They had no taste in anything, considering that they had already carved out for themselves territories, states, and nations the least of which was larger than England herself! Very indecent of them to act so coarsely! It could hardly be surprising that they should breed their dogs upon the same extravagant scale, the braggarts! Surely Mother England had suffered enough at their hands, must they now go about exporting their foul-bred monsters to her shores? So disrespectful of them—although, he thought as he gazed at the animal, now relaxed and quiet, when it is still it appears a rather sedate and majestic beast. Nice expression, too. The eyes are soft and intelligent and—yes, there is a bit of the clown about them. But those teeth! And that awfully great size! Oh well, my Lady Emily was an adorable creature. One could therefore be excused if one were to make allowances for her execrable taste in canines. For all of that thinking, Soames could not help but feel that ominous times lay ahead for the members of the Trenchard household.

Despite King Alfred's tumultuous reception into Lord Carnavon's mansion, all the troubles his lordship had foreseen never came to pass. True, there was an occasional crash as another decorative piece of crockery made disastrous obeisance before the passage of His Awful Majesty; and, too, Soames's pride and joy, the floor in the large reception hall, was damaged to the extent that only carpenters could restore its gleaming beauty; but, other than that, King Alfred proved a surprisingly mild-mannered sovereign who was always willing to unbend and accept a tidbit or two from his lieges in exchange for a royal salute with his large, moist tongue.

In twenty-four hours the household was quite back to normal, with Timmie in awe, from his head to his toes, of Soames and electing to attend the senior servitor whenever his attendance upon the great black dog was not required. Soames was quite taken with the lad and proceeded, under the guise of looking to keep the lad from standing about idly, to initiate him into the rites and mysteries of butlering. It provided my Lord Carnavon with much amusement to see how his callers and guests reacted to the appearance of his butler coming in to serve with his thirteen-year-old appendage close behind, aping his every move with the delightful gawkiness that only a lad of his age could manage.

Soames, long in his master's service, dared to introduce this new feature into the appointments of the mansion for he suspected that my lord would be amused and that, even if he did not approve the idea of a page, he'd not raise any fuss when he let Soames know it would not do. But it never happened; Timmie was accepted into the household with much less fuss than was his canine charge.

There was one person in the Trenchard domicile who in the end was quite relieved to find that King Alfred was more than competent to take over one of her responsibilities. That was Adelaide, Lady Emily's personal maid. Adelaide as abigail had the duty of acting as chaperone to her mistress, and, being city-bred, was not at all up to the idea of a stroll that might go on for an hour or two almost every day. A half hour in the park was as much as she cared for, but that was as nothing to Lady Emily, who was used to walking and riding over the brad meadows of the Trenchards' Bedford estate. With King Alfred's coming, this daily ordeal was spared her. Lord Carnavon, who was very well acquainted with King Alfred's qualifications as chaperone, had no objection to the arrangement, believing that His Majesty could protect his mistress against even a hint of incivility with greater effect than a hundred Adelaides.

Needless to say, the sight of the stylish and petite young lady strolling through the park with the huge dog lumbering alongside of her, completely untethered, was cause for stares and comment. Some of the braver bucks did accost her, but they found it exceedingly difficult to conduct themselves in any improper manner under the mournful but alert gaze of her companion. That she was the daughter of Lord Carnavon and known to be promised to the renowned Edward Denning of Bow Street may have also worked to keep their deportment unexceptionable.

But Lady Emily was still not content. She experienced a need to talk to someone, someone who might be more appreciative of King Alfred's fine qualities and would see beyond his great size and his great teeth. For a reason she could not fathom, and did not try, her choice fell upon General Beresford.

For all that the elderly gentleman had done to set Ned apart from her, there was an appeal about him that drew her to wish to get to know him better. After all, she told herself, Sir Alonzo had been most repentant, and even before he had made his confession of wrong-mindedness she had felt a strong liking for the retired warrior. He was certainly a deal more charming than an old soldier had any right to be, and his ease with her was not the artificial courtesy of military training. He had a more natural, bred-in-the-bone as it were, sort of grace. In any case, she thought it would be great fun to spring King Alfred upon him. She was sure he'd never mind the big fellow at all.

The day that Lady Emily decided to pay a call upon General Sir Alonzo Beresford was a very nice day, nice enough to permit the lowering of the hood on the darling little pony phaeton her father had had made for her. It was drawn by a pair of small but nicely spirited bloods. Needless to say, my lady was marvelously well turned out as she drove about in it.

Today, for the first time, she had His Majesty, King Alfred, beside her, fully occupying the seat with her so that from offside she could not be seen, and it appeared that he was the sole occupant of the tiny equipage. Of course his great shaggy form, by comparison, made the phaeton appear to be even smaller than it was.

From the other side, her ladyship was in view against the black background of King Alfred's head and shoulders and, from this view, he appeared to be even more monstrously large than he was, by comparison with the dainty and charming picture his mistress made.

The sight of the two of them trotting at a brisk pace along the thoroughfares of London was quite enough to bring all traffic to a standstill. Many a gentleman suffered a stiff neck later from too much craning and twisting about to see Beauty and her Beast come to life before his very eyes.

Naturally, Lady Emily was delighted with the stir she was causing, and laughed aloud with the greatest glee as she went along, her dark eyes flashing and the red ribbons of her driving bonnet streaming behind like glorious banners. King Alfred, too, must have been enjoying the drive, for he encouraged her greatly with deep baying barks.

Soames had supplied her with the complete directions for reaching the General's residence and she had not the least trouble in finding it. She dismounted from her little carriage, King Alfred leaping down and coming to stand beside her, eyeing with some suspicion the young lad who came dashing out to take her vehicle in charge. The boy quickly slowed to a more circumspect pace and gave King Alfred a wide berth as he went to the horses' heads, never taking his eyes off the great dog.

Emily strolled up to the front door and it was opened for her by the general himself, a smile of delighted welcome shining upon his countenance.

"My dear Lady Emily, won't you please come in. I cannot tell you how much pleasure you give to an old gentleman this day. Do come in and—Heavens! What have we here? Well, bless my soul!" he exclaimed as he led her into the house. "Aren't you a great fellow! I do not believe I have ever seen his like before!"

King Alfred woofed an acknowledgement of the general's admiration and conferred a slobbering kiss upon the general's hand. Sir Alonzo laughed and dealt a playful cuff upon the dog's broad head.

King Alfred's tail began to wag furiously.

"Oh, he's a beauty! He is of the Newfoundland breed, is he not?"

"Why, yes, he is, Sir Alonzo! How nice it is to find someone who does not fear him and, what is more, knows him for what he is."

They were entering a modest but nicely appointed morning room with windows and a door opening on a small garden.

He drew up a chair for Lady Emily and sat himself down in another. King Alfred came over and laid his massive head in his mistress's lap, fixing his large dark eyes upon the general. Sir Alonzo chuckled and made a sad face at him.

Emily shoved in vain at the great weight and, as she could not budge it, finally commanded: "Enough, King! Be a good fellow and lay down in the corner. You may be sure I'll not forget you when I leave."

The big dog let out a sigh and obediently withdrew to the corner of the room, where he collapsed with a great thump that fairly shook the house. He sighed once again and then went quickly to sleep.

The general shook his head in wonderment. "My, the beast is almost human," he said, and so began a pleasant conversation. What was actually said betwen them for the next half hour was of no great importance, for it was a case of two people chatting to pass the time as they became more and more aware of each other. There were touches of wit and humor exchanged between them, and some cursory discussion of the day's events and how they each spent their time but, during it all, they were measuring each other and confirming the strength of the appeal each had felt for the other from the beginning. In short they were enjoying each other's presence and the time went quickly by.

In conformance to the rules of etiquette, when the very pleasant and cheerful half-hour had elapsed, Emily rose to her feet to take her leave—and the room suddenly exploded!

The door to the garden burst open and two men

rushed into the room. The smaller of the two, with a bare blade in his hand, pointed it at Lady Emily and clapped the larger man on the shoulder, urging him towards her while he turned to face the general. The big man came lumbering towards Emily, his hands outstretched and clutching.

General Beresford leaped forward to interpose himself between Emily and her assailant, but never reached her side as she stood transfixed in horror.

A roaring black fury, great white teeth bared, came charging into the fray, brushing past the general with such force as to send him careening back onto the hearth. Without a moment's hesitation, Sir Alonzo snatched up a poker and started for the villains. But it was almost all over before it had started. Close on to two hundredweight of outraged canine had launched itself at Benson's throat and brought him down, shrieking in terror. Raike stood by, paralyzed, his eyes filled with mindless panic, unable to tear his sight from the savagery his chum was suffering. Then awareness of his own danger came to him and he started to turn back for the door but the general was on him and smashed at his knife with the poker. Raike screamed in agony. It was the very same arm that had suffered a similar fate at their first assault. A second blow caught him squarely on the pate and his scream was cut off as he fell, senseless, to the floor.

Very coolly, the general turned to Lady Emily and remarked: "My dear, I believe His Majesty has had his fun."

Lady Emily let out a quavering breath and said, "Yes," with a tremulous little smile. "King! Heel!"

King Alfred was quite ready to obey the command. The quivering, bloody hulk with lacerated arms shielding its head had been reduced to a proper state of submission and his particular goddess would suffer no further inconveniencing. Obediently, he came to sit by her, his eyes sadly contemplating the ruin he had wrought as though debating if a few more licks might not be warranted.

It had been a matter of seconds, the entire business. The general's man, as he came rushing in, a martial pistol in each hand, came to a stop and gazed in awe upon the scene.

"General, sir, are you hurt?" he asked, full of deep concern.

"No, Higgins, all is in hand. Have a lunch prepared for two." He turned to Lady Emily. "I am willing to forgo the demands of etiquette if you are, my dear. You will stay and join me for lunch, will you not?"

"Dear Sir Alonzo, if you can put up with more than a half-hour of my company, I should be delighted to join you."

"I assure you I can suffer it easily. Can I have something prepared for His Valient Majesty? He deserves the best there is, you will agree."

Emily laughed. "Yes, he does, but I should hate to take his mind off his vigil."

The general surveyed the forms of the two wretches on the floor and smiled. "I should think his work is done and well done but, if it will make you feel easier—Higgins, fetch some stout twine and do the honors to this pair of cullies and, when you inform cook about lunch, have her serve up a nice portion of beefsteak for this brave fellow."

"Very good, sir."

In short order, the would-be assassins were thoroughly trussed up, lunch was served in the dining room, and King Alfred followed Higgins into the garden to do justice to a couple of pounds of fine beef.

Higgins came in to see if everything was in order with the general and his company.

Sir Alonzo looked up and said: "I suppose we should see to their wounds and perhaps give them a bite of something. I intend to be some time at lunch with my lady—their disposition will have to be deferred until we have finished."

"Very good, sir. The animal is standing guard while one of the maids is seeing to the big fellow's wounds. I thought it best to avoid staining the rug any more than was necessary."

The general nodded and dismissed him.

He resumed his conversation with her ladyship. "My lady, any doubts I may have had as to my being in jeopardy are now completely dispelled for these are the very same bravos who set upon me before. I would apologize to you for having subjected you to their attentions, but I should prefer to render you my thanks, my profuse gratitude in fact, for having such a well-trained beast—a most proficient animal indeed. And I would compliment you upon your own fortitude before the enemy. You did not shriek, you did not swoon—I am positively amazed to discover any woman who would not have done either under what were most trying circumstances."

Lady Emily chortled. "Oh, well, you see, Sir Alonzo, as soon as I saw they had no firearms with them, I had not the least concern that King Alfred could come to any harm."

The general laughed heartily in appreciation of her humor and of her modesty.

The meal continued at a leisurely pace and when it was over the general declared: "I believe those brigands have intruded on my hospitality long enough. I shall now take pleasure in delivering them up to Bow Street. Shall you be able to get home without any trouble? I—"

"Oh, do not think you shall go without me, sir! I am coming with you. You do not think I am about to surrender the opportunity of witnessing the expression on Ned's face when we deliver up our prizes. They *are* ours, you know, for it was your poker and my dog that did them in."

Sir Alonzo got to his feet and performed a bow. "My lady, you give my poker too much credit. As it was, it was of little account. I dare say King Alfred could have handled the both of them with perfect ease. Nevertheless, I am proud that you confer any accolade upon my poor efforts," he ended, with a smile of good humor.

Lady Emily, smiling too, arose and they went in to see how the two housebreakers were faring.

The general was all for insisting that Higgins accompany them to assist in guarding the prisoners, but Lady Emily pointed out that it would crowd them all too much, and that anyway King Alfred would not mind in the least devoting all of his attention to them, making any need of Higgins quite superfluous. She pointed out further that if it came to that, considering the lamentable condition that His Majesty had reduced them to, she did not doubt that she and her dog could easily enough deliver them up even without *the general's* help.

Sir Alonzo was quite amused, but he had to agree, and so he instructed Higgins to drive her ladyship's phaeton home and leave word with Lord Carnavon that his daughter was safe with him and that he would be seeing her home in a few hours.

That done, the general's carriage was brought round and their glum charges were transferred into it, along with King Alfred to keep them company. It could hardly come as a surprise to anyone that His Majesty continued to express his disapproval if they even shifted in their seats. It was a mighty unpleasant time that Raike and Benson shared, in what semed to them to be the longest ride of their lives.

Up on the box, Sir Alonzo was quite exhilarated to be seen driving along with such a charming companion by his side; he flourished the ribbons with pride as they passed through the streets of the City.

For those few people who had witnessed my lady driving about earlier in the morning, the sight of her up on a box alongside General Beresford, the well-known national hero, with only a great black, shaggy dog for passenger (the villainous pair were huddled down and could not be easily made out) must have offered such food for gossip as to provide them with a month of dining out. It was probably just as well that they had no means of ascertaining the destination of the conveyance and its colorful occupants, or they'd have been able to dine out upon the story for a year.

Chapter VII

It does not appear in the *Chronicles of the Bow Street Police Office*, and one can only wonder how the eminent chronicler, Mr. Percy Fitzgerald, could have missed it, especially as he took great pride in recording all of the oddities pertaining to that office for the entire period of its existence. Perhaps it was that he himself did not believe what happened that afternoon in early April of 1829 at the Bow Street Police Office. One can hardly blame him, it was so unlikely.

It was in the early afternoon, and Chief Magistrate Denning was busy at his bench, in the process of disposing of a number of cases being brought before him. A noise of confusion at the rear of the chamber made him look up in annoyance. His face fell, then incredulity filled it, and he stood up smartly and stared towards the rear.

Naturally everyone else in the courtroom, seeing the peculiar behavior of the magistrate, stopped what they were doing and turned to look too. Amd what they saw made them gape in wonder, for it was a great black dog that was lumbering into the chamber, herding two torn and bloody men before him, their hands bound and a look of panic in their eyes, and they were followed, no, not by a pair of runners, but by a charming little lady engaged in conversation with no less than General Sir Alonzo Beresford, the hero of Waterloo, himself.

The crowd shrank back and made a generous path for the dog, which King Alfred accepted as his just due continuing his triumphal march towards the high bench until Ned, who had been assisting his father, shouted in the greatest surprise: "Emily!"

With a high-pitched yelp of joy, King Alfred abdicated his dignity on the spot and went charging forward to launch his two hundred pounds at Ned in gladsome greeting. Down went man and dog in one great confused heap and, when the dust had cleared, there was His Highness seated on Ned's chest, slopping at his face with his great wet tongue. Ned was laughing fit to be tied and completely breathless from the great weight he was bearing up. He was altogether helpless as the crowd in the courtroom, infinitely amused and eaten up with curiosity, roared their approval to see the noted runner brought down so neatly.

Lady Emily came running up to kneel alongside, crying: "Is he not a dear, Ned? He has not forgotten you!"

Ned could only gasp: "Indeed, you can see how overwhelmed I am! Now get the beggar off me!"

Emily ordered her dog to her side and Ned got to his feet, still chuckling as he brushed himself off.

By then the general and the magistrate had come up to them, and Mr. Denning, with a quizzical look, declared: "I say, Alonzo, but for your lovely escort, I should hold you in contempt! How dare you interrupt my court when it is in session, with such undignified proceedings?"

The general smiled. "I bring you more custom. These bullies are a bit the worse for wear and may need some patching up before you have them put away. I'd appreciate your taking them off my hands."

The magistrate signaled up a constable and gave him some brief instructions. The officer marched the prisoners off.

Ned, recovered by this time, was full of indignation. He demanded: "What the devil are you doing in this place, Emily? I told you never to come here! It is not fit for a lady to be seen passing the time of day in Bow Street. What will people think?"

"I will tell you all about it—but not here. Where can we go?"

"*You* shall go home, and at once! I'll have one of my men escort you."

"Alonzo, what is all this about?" asked Mr. Denning impatiently.

Sir Alonzo looked about the chamber with an expression of distaste. "Really, Alec, I have not the least objection to relating to you all the details of the affair, but must I do it out here in court like a common criminal?"

Mr. Denning replied: "No, of course not. How bad of me." He looked about and beckoned to a runner close by. "You, Cogshill, fetch Magistrate Roberts in at once, and let him take my place on the bench. I am otherwise engaged." As he turned back to Sir Alonzo, he caught Emily's eye and saw the look of appeal in her face. He glanced at his son's face. It was like granite.

"Ned, take Lady Emily to your office and get her statement while I do the same with Sir Alonzo."

"But, sir—"

"That is an order! Come along, Alonzo. I'll send out for some tea or whatever, and we can have a comfortable coze. Now, just exactly who are those two? . . ." He and the general walked away, leaving Ned and Emily to themselves.

Gritting his teeth, Ned said: "This way, my lady."

She went right by him, her chin in the air, and remarked: "I know the way. I have been here before, remember, and you were behaving just as miserably, if you will recall."

They entered his tiny office. Just as Ned went to close the door, King Alfred shouldered his way in.

The room was little better than a large cupboard and crowded enough with two people. And so, when Ned turned to complain to Emily, only to find her holding her arms out to him, her head tilted back and her dark eyes beseeching, he could have blamed it upon a nudge from the bulky beast when he found her in his arms, and that he was kissing her as though he might never see her again. King Alfred, seeing that all was as it should be, flopped himself down under the desk and went to sleep.

When the intensity of emotion arising from the delightful rites of reunion abated, my lady was ensconced in her lover's arms, pressed close against him on his lap and he, dazed, was reposing in the only chair the little office boasted.

Slowly, very slowly, a consciousness of duty neglected began to return and, with the greatest reluctance, Ned disengaged himself from his lady. With no little difficulty, he contrived to place her in the chair while he took up a position half sitting, half standing against the desk.

"Ned, will you—" Emily began a question.

"Please, my lady, there is something of the utmost importance here. Before you put it out of my mind forever, I pray you will allow me to deal with it. Now, I knew those two queer culls. I was working against them, disguised. They are part of a plot against General Beresford, and I was hoping to use them to bring a villain, Bartholomew by name, into the dock. Of course that is quite out of the window now. What happened? How did Sir Alonzo capture them?"

"Not to take any credit from the dear man, but it was King Alfred"—there was a thump from below—"we have to thank for saving the both of us."

Ned made a sour face. "I should have guessed. It is high time I handed him my red vest. He did as much for you against Bledsoe's blackguards in Biddenham. I do not see what we need of Bow Street, with him about." He smiled as he shook his head. "Sometimes he makes me feel so futile, and he is only a dog."

Emily smiled. "You will not hold it against him?"

He laughed. "No, I think I have learned to have more sense than that. But this changes things. How did it all come about?"

Emily took his hand in hers and, holding it, told him all about the attack. Ned listened intently to all she had to say and then was quite pensive for a time.

He sighed and remarked wryly: "It just shows one that you can never trust a thief. I was to have taken part in the next attack upon the general, but I dare say they thought to do me out of my share. I thought I had done my work so well, too, that it was quite safe to rely upon them. You see, I have been keeping a watch on this Bartholomew the past few days and I never gave thought to—but, oh my God! you might have been murdered!—and the general most certainly, but for King Alfred! And yet if you had not been there with the big fellow—oh, it chills me to think of it! That you should have had to suffer . . . Oh, I would chide *someone* for having permitted you to become imperiled, yet I cannot help but be thankful that you were there with His Majesty. Bless his great heart! The infernal plot might have succeeded but for him!"

He laughed uncertainly and bent down to bestow a kiss upon her—which she, in turn, warmly rebestowed upon him.

"Well, at the least, Sir Alonzo must be more than convinced that our suspicions are confirmed," declared Ned. "Until this point I am sure whatever precautions he was taking were done simply to humor us. But damme! How are we to proceed from this point? Bartholomew is bound to get the wind up when he learns that Raike and Benson have been taken in the act. I do wish we could have avoided that."

"Can you not get either this Raike or this Benson to inform on Bartholomew?"

"Oh aye, there'll not be the least difficulty in *that*," replied Ned offhandedly.

"How can you be so sure?"

Ned gave her a superior glance. "Because it is the topping cheat for them if they do not and Botany Bay if they do. That is hardly any choice at all."

"Topping cheat? Oh, Ned, I do wish you will not use that horrid thieves' cant with me! Whatever do you mean to say?"

Ned laughed. There was a bitter note in his tone as he replied: "I beg your pardon, my lady, but that was Lolly speaking. I do not suppose I shall ever get so far from him as I could wish. Topping cheat is the gallows. They have a choice of squeaking—er—informing and being transported to the penal colony in Australia or keeping mum and hanging."

"Oh. Well then, why do you look so concerned? If that is the case, you have got Bartholomew in the palm of your hand and can take him in charge as soon as you have got what you require from these villains."

"If only it were that easy! First of all I would ask you: if you were a juryman, whom would you believe, Raike who is scum of the lowest sort—we need not consider Benson for he is an imbecile—or Bartholomew who in deportment and appearance is every inch the gentleman? Of course he will deny everything, and with an indignation that must seem genuine, especially as he can call upon some of the best people for a character. Oh, *they* know him for what he is, but they live in his pockets—or else he has got hold of some skeleton hidden in their closets and must do as he bids or face bankruptcy and disgrace. No, if I were Bartholomew, I dare say there'd be no witnesses to any dealings I had had with that pair. My dear, this is not something new or we'd have had the fellow long ago.

"Oh, I cannot believe he is to have it all *his* way!"

"Believe me, he can and will. When I was Lolly, I managed even greater effronteries against my father and O'Shaughnessy—and they had me almost dead to rights!"

"Did you really?" exclaimed my lady, very fascinated. "Tell me about it!"

He chuckled. "Perhaps some other time. Now I am on business, conducting an official investigation."

"I *do* like the way you go about it, dearest, although I should hope that you conduct yourself with a little more reserve with others." And she raised her lips to his.

The investigation came to halt for a few blissful moments.

Ned finally had to put her back down in her seat. "Emily, I pray you will behave yourself. This is serious business and I must think."

"What will you do?"

"It is just possible that Bartholomew, when he learns his cat's-paws have been taken, will make a slip. I do not count upon it, but it is a possibility. He just might, unknowingly, lead us to the party who is behind the plot against the general."

"How can you be so sure that it is not Bartholomew who is the only one involved in it?"

"Because he has no direct motive. Sir Alonzo does not know him. There is nothing to connect them. It must come down to the fact that Bartholomew's profiting from the general's death is strictly a matter of money paid to him to accomplish it; and that would be right in his style. So there has got to be another party who is sporting sufficient rhino to make it worthy of Bartholomew's interest. Now just who that person may be, I have not a clue."

"Well, surely Sir Alonzo must have some idea as to that. I am sure that if someone hated me so much as to wish to encompass my death, I should have a very good idea who that party might be."

"Oh, but the general—slit my wind! But of course— Emily, now see what you have done! You have got me so beside myself I never thought to question him in that regard—and, of course, everyone has assumed that I had! What an incompetent, witless fool you have made of me! I shall have to do it right off. I must go to my father's office at once! I hope he is still there!"

He reached for the door, but Emily grabbed his arm.

"No, Ned! Not yet! Before you go, tell me that you love me!"

He turned around and took her into his arms. "You know I do, my love."

"Say it!"

"I love you, dear, sweet Emily."

They kissed.

She said: "Then, now you will come to call?—and perhaps you will take me to the theater?"

Gently he disengaged himself from her. He shook his head sadly. "No, my dear, nothing has changed. It is not possible."

"Ned, what is the matter with you? Of course it is possible! It is the most possible thing in the world!"

"Emily, I have told you. Not until I can come to you in my own name and with no stain upon it—"

"That is the most ridiculous thing! Surely our love is nothing so puny that it cannot flourish but for a bit of snobbery now and again. It certainly is nothing new to me. If I do not care, how can you care—if you love me?"

"You know I love you and that it is for that very reason that I must put you out of my life so that my questionable heritage can in no way—"

"Oh, stuff and nonsense! I love you, Ned, Lolly, whichever! It is all one to me. I begin to think that you really do not love me at all!"

"Do you think it is not a pain in my heart? Do you think I am not racking my brain every minute to find a way to discover these facts I do desperately desire? Look at what it is doing to me! Even a lowly charley would not have omitted to ask the general, the very first thing, who his enemies are!"

"Well, how long am I to wait?" she demanded angrily. "It is over a week now since you renounced me. What have you discovered?"

"Not a blessed thing, I regret to say. You have got to realize it is not something I am going to accomplish overnight. I have not got the foggiest notion where to begin. I sometimes think I never shall."

Emily was quite hot with him now. "How very encouraging to hear it! Of course you have not and you *knew* you would not! Uncle Alec is worth two of you and he could not! No, Ned, you do not love me at all or you would give up this wild goose chase. It is the most certain thing that did you love me you would never let such asinine nonsense keep you away from me!"

"My darling," pleaded Ned, "I should never be able to hold my head up if you could not be proud of me on every count!"

"Ned Denning, I am not your darling! I am not your love! Sir, I am not your betrothed! My father will see to it that an announcement to that effect is placed in the very next issue of the *Gazette*! And—and, f-furthermore, I never want to see you again!"

She tore open the door and rushed out.

Ned started after her, only to be toppled over backward into his chair as King Alfred erupted from beneath the desk and went charging out after his beloved mistress.

Alec Denning was seated at the desk in his office scanning some notes when the door opened and Ned stepped inside, looking very disturbed.

"Where is the general, sir? I must speak with him," said Ned breathlessly.

Mr. Denning regarded his son with a look of great annoyance.

"We finished our business and he has gone to wait upon Lady Emily to see her home. I should have thought *you* would have seen to *that*!"

"I must speak with him at once!" exclaimed Ned, and was about to rush out.

Mr. Denning cried: "Hold fast, son! I have a bone to pick with you!"

Ned turned and slowly came back into the room.

"Never mind the general! Hmm-mm, and never mind the lady. From the look of you, I'd say she has had quite enough of you. You know, my boy, I may be an old and crusty bachelor, but if I could not give you points on how to handle your love—what the devil have you done now?"

Ned replied quite stiffly: "Sir, truly it is for the best. My lady has agreed to break it off, and that is as it should be."

"You are a cabbagehead if you think she means any part of it! The girl is in love with you! You must have been insufferable to have put her in such a state with you even if she did not mean it."

"I pray, sir, you will let it lie. You are permitting this very personal matter to interfere with my official duties. I have some questions for Sir Alonzo."

"Yes, and I hope they are something to the point! What has come over you? Must I begin now to do your work for you? Do you realize even yet that you never thought to inquire of the general—surely the best source for the information—whom his enemies might be?"

Ned was abashed. "Y-yes, sir, I suddenly realized—that is, my lady brought it up—er . . ."

Mr. Denning shook his head in disgust. "My very best runner—the fellow who, it is my fondest hope, will succeed me—my own son! To omit to do what even the meanest law clerk would laugh to see it had been neglected—damn you, Ned, will you make up at once with Lady Emily so that we all of us can get back to our work and in peace?"

"Your Honor, I pray we will put all of this aside for, even as you have pointed out, I should speak with Sir Alonzo—"

"Oh, shut up and sit down! How can you believe that I would not have remedied your lapse as soon as I had discovered it! Forget Sir Alonzo! I have already examined him on that point. And stop calling me 'Your Honor'!"

Ned knew better than to try to say anything further along that line and drew up a chair.

"Has the general any enemies?" he asked as he sat himself down.

"Yes," said Mr. Denning sourly.

Ned brightened up. "Well, then, if you will give me the list, I shall start to look into it at once."

Mr. Denning tossed a sheet of paper at him.

Ned glanced at it and looked up, horrified. "For pity's sake, doesn't anyone like the man? This is ridiculous!"

"It is more than ridiculous! There are thirty-eight parties listed, and I'll wager it is not a third of the true number. These are only the ones he could recall offhand. He was quite sure there must be many more."

"But Sir Alonzo is a most charming fellow—inclined to be a bit irascible at times, but that is to be expected in a gentleman of his advanced years," said Ned with a chuckle, looking directly into the magistrate's face. Mr. Denning did not deign to retort, but conferred a black look upon him.

Ned went on. "How could he possibly have accumulated such a list? Surely he must be including many with whom he may have had only a mild disagreement."

Mr. Denning shook his head. "No, Alec is not a petty man. The list is credible. You forget, lad, he has been an officer of great power for many years and power breeds enemies as well as friends. I can assure you in such case the former are a deal truer than are the latter. Just think of all the men who may have had reason to hate him; men sentenced to the lash under the articles of war, officers cashiered for cause, relatives of these wretches sworn to revenge—all regarding him as their oppressor, perhaps because he was active in their disgrace or because it was his signature on the document that spelled out their fate. For very similar reasons I could prepare a list like that, but ten times as long."

Ned bit his lip and nodded. "I daresay I am building one myself, of fairly respectable length, too."

"Right. And that is not to number those enemies that any man in the normal way of things is bound to make in his lifetime. No, the list is quite reasonable, blast it! And so you will admit it is worthless as it stands."

Ned agreed. "It is worse than worthless, sir. Bow Street boasts of only eight principal officers including myself. If we all of us were to devote ourselves to the investigation of just those eight and thirty parties and each of us could do one a day, it would take all of five days to do them all. But it is out of the question that we should all be occupied with but this one case, and who knows how far afield we might be called upon to go in tracking down these names? It is more than likely that months would elapse before we had ever done with the list. And, should it turn out the man we seek is not on that list, it would all have been wasted, especially if Bartholomew had succeeded with the general by that time. He would not have been sitting about idly while we were at chasing our tails."

Mr. Denning smiled. "I am encouraged to see that your intellect has begun to sort itself out at last. Good, for we shall have need of all of our wits. I regret to say that mine are not what they are used to being. I can see no clear way to proceed at the moment."

"As I see it, we are left with but one card—but it is a good card, provided we play it properly."

"And that is?"

"Bartholomew himself. For all anyone knows, he is the only person to have the knowledge we seek, and it goes without saying that he will be less than happy to assist us. Furthermore, when he learns that we have got Benson and Raike, I suspect strongly that he will close down much of his business so that his skirts will be clean, in the event we are foolish enough to come after him on the basis of what our pair of beauties have to tell us. And, too, he cannot make another move against Sir Alonzo until he has collected another crew for the task. Now, that he will do in his own good time. He is too cocky to leave the business lay. So there is still time for us to take an action. I propose that, before he does come to it again, I insinuate myself into his confidence and see what I can learn, close at hand."

"No! That you will not do! You have proposed this very same idea time and time again in the past and I still say no! While I would give a great deal to see Bartholomew hang, for some inane reason I have a reluctance to make of your life the stake."

"But this is different, sir! It is worth a bit of risk. We are too close not to attempt it. Our success will not only spell Bartholomew's doom, but we shall have gotten the means of reducing the threat that hangs over the general's head as well. Once having gotten to Bartholomew, one way or another, I'll discover who that third party is. I say all of that is worth the risk!"

"I do not understand you, son! Bartholomew is not so easy to gull. I am sure he must be up to every swindle in the book and may have had the writing of it. It would be neck or nothing with you! You *will* heed me in this."

"But, sir, the general's life is at stake!"

"Aye, we are all agreed on that, and we shall do all that we can to protect him, but that is not to say that you have to put *your* life in the balance so gratuitously— especially after he cut you down so badly at Milliken's."

"Oh, if it were not he, it would have been someone else who would have opened up my eyes. In any case, he is not a bad sort underneath it all. From Emily's story, he would have laid down his life for her and never have turned a hair. That is as much as I could have done, and I owe him for the thought if not for the deed. And bearding Bartholomew in his den is the surest and speediest way of bringing this business to a conclusion. In fact we are at point-non-plus to find any other way to go about it."

The magistrate rubbed his chin. He pondered for a moment and then slowly shook his head. "No, it is far too great a risk. Even as you have said, Bartholomew is bound to stop and think for a while. That should give *us* time to think, too. I am sure that we can come up with a safer and surer way to settle this business. I shall continue to have runners watching him round the clock, and we shall see what we shall see. If nothing should turn up, t will be time enough then to talk of such rash measures as you are proposing. If anything crops up before then, we shall be on it in a trice. Now, Ned, for pity's sake, will you and Emily settle things between you? At this rate I shall be long dead before I can ever boast of having a grandson, I'll wager!"

Chapter VIII

It was business as usual at the ol' Muck and Mire that night, which is to say that for any ordinary Cit it would have been a most unusual experience to enter the place. The patrons were gathered about little wooden tables, three or four of them at each one, heads together in serious conversation. Every now and again a head would swing back and a heavy earthenware mug would swing up. A few gulping swallows and it would come crashing down again upon the table top, to the accompaniment of much smacking of lips and the back of a hand drawn across the face in lieu of serviette.

The air was murky with tobacco smoke from numerous clay pipes of varying shapes, and from black cigars that looked as evil as they smelt. The atmosphere was close and reeked of more than just the smell of burning tobacco. The stench of unwashed, hard-laboring bodies was augmented by that particular foulness, the effluvium of the mud flats along the banks of the River Thames.

The noise of clattering mugs and crude tableware mixed with the dull roar of conversation, which shone with the sparkle of many oaths and much swearing. Occasionally there were hoarse shouts of laughter as some wit displayed his brilliance of mind. Perhaps he was telling a great tale of how he had given the slip to the River Police, or possibly of his latest sojourn amidst the soiled flowers blooming in some Covent Garden nunnery.

At some tables, the conversation was being conducted in hushed and sober tones, and there was the frequent hiding of the lips with a grimy hand to insure secrecy. Obviously at those tables dire plots and plans were being laid, to the loss and great discomfort of some dockside merchant or chandler. No doubt, some morning in the not too distant future an unfortunate good citizen would wake the echoes of the river with curses on the heads of the delinquent River Police, who were never about when one sorely needed them. Lucky indeed would be the merchant if he was given the chance to buy back the goods that were wrested from his warehouse.

The tavern portal swung open and with a breath of dampness from the foggy night without, a lithe figure slipped inside. There was a bright smile on his face as his eyes swept the great room. He appeared to recognize various faces and nodded to himself in satisfaction.

He did not go forward to any table but took up a position to one side of the tavern entrance way and coolly lit up a cigar. He waited.

For a minute or two nothing unusual occurred. Then, little by little, one table after another fell silent and the patrons turned to eye the newcomer. There were nudgings and there were whisperings, there were heads nodding and little hushed discussions sprang up here and there. Finally all was quiet in the tavern as everyone continued to stare at the young man with an air of expectancy.

Like all of his audience, he was quite mud-stained. There was a wiseacre smile on his lips and his cap was set at a jaunty angle. Slowly his gaze wandered over each table; it would stop at one face and then another. There was a peculiar intensity in his face whenever his gaze lingered. His smile never wavered as he watched and waited.

At last a barrel of a man, an authentic mudlark like the young man, shoved back his chair and got to his feet. There was a scowl upon his swarthy features as he swaggered over to the stranger. He frowned sternly as he came to a stand before the young man, feet apart, hands knotted into fists thrust against his beefy hips.

"Who be yer, cully?" demanded the broad fellow.

The stranger's eyebrows lifted and he laughed aloud, but he did not answer.

The mudlark chieftain scratched his head in puzzlement. "There be a familiar look about yer, too familiar I'm thinkin'. Now, who be yer, cully?—and no sass or Natto Binger 'll slip ye a muzzler that'll keep a tooth-carpenter busy wi' yer fer a month."

The young man reached out and pinched the broad fellow's nose hard enough to bring tears to his eyes. The chieftain let out a howl of pain and outrage, as he jerked back and whipped out a knife.

"Are you quite sure that you can, Natto?" asked the young man in clear, perfectly enunciated syllables.

Binger's eyes opened wide in astonishment as he cried: "Split me guts ef it ain't the Nob hisself!"

He let out a roar of laughter as the room crashed with the sound of chairs being shoved back. Most of the crowd began to shout: " 'T is Lolly! 'T is Lolly come back!"

With a roar of laughter that shook the ramshackle building to its foundations, they came rushing over to shake him by the hand and clap him on the shoulder, bursting with curiosity to see him alive and well. It called for a celebration. Lolly was back and the good old times, too, for there was his nibs, right as rain and as brassy as a Lord!

Natto Binger sheathed his knife and put his arm about Ned, pushing all the admiring crowd back as he led the returned hero up to the bar. There he called for drinks all around to toast Lolly and his luck.

Ned slipped a hand into his pocket and came up with a few pound notes which he tossed carelessly onto the bar: "I'll pay the shot!"

Paper currency was a rarity down by the river. It bespoke untold prosperity to his well-wishers. The crowd gasped.

Natto turned to Ned and exclaimed: "Owoo, Lolly! You been up to yer ol' tricks an' been doin' 'em well, I see! Where'd yer disappear to? It's all on five years an' more sence they kilt yer! 'T was that black-hearted O'Shaughnessy as did ye in, we heard tell."

"Aye, he potted me proper, but I made out it was a deal worse than it was and cut my stick when they thought I was done for. Naturally, they'd never let on that I'd given them the slip, and I did not stop running until I had got me across the Channel. I worked the river about Paris for the most part, keeping my own counsel. I've done well enough. I got to feeling a bit peckish to see the ol' Muck and Mire, so I thought I ought to drop in on you lads and see how you were getting on. Is O'Shaughnessy still about?"

"Oh, aye, but he's no bother to us. Since you was kilt, we've left the land side t' others and stayed close to the river. Bow Street 'll leave us be an' the River Police have never been a worry."

"Do you mean to say you've just mucked about the river and left all that lovely loot in the City undisturbed for some lubber to snabble? Hah!" he sneered, rubbing his hands together. "It is high time I did return. Gentlemen, Lolly is back! And Lolly's on the prigging lay! Who'll join me?"

"Now, now, Lolly, things is changed." Natto looked about and measured the crowd.

Ned looked at him, his lips curling. "Come on! You know me, Natto! Bow Street never put the wind up in me! Aye, they napped me once, but never again. I'm a deal older and a deal wiser now, and they are only a deal older."

100

"Nah, nah! 'T is not they runners, lad! 'T is one runner an' they is another."

"You say two runners? What diff—"

"No, Lolly! You took me all wrong! Look, we kin talk together at another place. Me crib's not far off. What say we split a bottle and talk there? Things is changed an' it's worth a water rat's life to leave the river these days."

There was a roar of disappointment from the onlookers. Five years was a long time on the banks of the Thames, and only the old veterans knew Lolly by sight. The younger thieves had had their appetites for their vocation whetted hone-sharp upon tales of Lolly's great successes. To see their hero alive and in the flesh and listen at his feet was all they could have wished for.

"Ah, gentlemen, I am touched, deeply touched. But do you take heart. I shall be back and then we shall see if we cannot liven up the old town a bit. We shall make the Bow Street Beaks earn their shillings and pence once again, mark my words! Landlord, another round for all of my chums!"

Natto and he began to push their way out of the tavern.

Ned followed Natto up along the river bank. It amused him that Natto, without a thought to the contrary, trudged right along through the tidal mud when, had he chosen, he could have gone by way of dry, firm land some thirty feet inland where it was all cobbles. But Ned understood the man's need to maintain his contact with the river. As young Lolly, he had felt the same need, for it was the mudlark's home and his world. It was where he felt comfortable and where he fitted.

At the moment it was all Ned could do to keep up with his companion. It had been so long since he had last stepped along in the viscous, sucking mire that his leg muscles were beginning to complain.

They passed under Waterloo bridge and began to wade along the river frontage of Somerset House. To Ned's surprise, Natto turned in at the arched watergate

101

of the building and led him up out of the water into the building proper. They passed down a long, dimly lit corridor and finally debouched into a large chamber, against one wall of which was a typical mudlark's hut. It was a shedlike contrivance put together from the flotsam and jetsam of the river.

Natto pointed at it and remarked with pride: "A bit of all right, ain't it?"

"You live *here*?" asked Ned.

"Aye. 'T is a far sight better 'n grubbin' about under a dock or in the muck at my age. An' the best part of it is they pays me!" He burst into laughter.

Ned was surprised and did not hide it, especially as Natto appeared to regard the arrangement with great pride and satisfaction.

"You don't say!" he remarked.

"Aye, I do say! They pays me to watch the place o' nights an' I gets me quarters and enough ter keep me 'n vittles an' grog. Now ain't that kind o' 'em?" Natto leered.

Ned frowned. "What's the lay?"

"'T ain't no lay!" said Natto with indignation. "The lads stay clear o' Somerset. Ye don't think I'd crack me own crib or let anyone else into it! An' it's bloody handy to the river, yer must admit."

"Right enough!" laughed Ned. "I take my hat off to you, Natto. You've got yourself on both sides of the law. I could not have done better myself."

"Step inside."

They ducked into the little hutment. It was quite cozy. Squatting on a couple of crates from an East Indiaman, Natto produced a pair of battered tin cups and a bottle, and they proceeded to business.

"Natto, what was it that got your wind up back in the ol' Muck and Mire?"

"Ah, lad, things is changed. Things is changed and 't is powerful sad, it is. The river is the only place for us lads, includin' yoursel'. Mebbe ef they hadna kilt yer, it'd ha' been the same but, Lolly, wi' out yer, 't is worth a water rat's neck ter be discovered half a furlong from the banks."

"Go on!" exclaimed Ned in scorn. "Do you expect I shall swallow your knife? I will, sooner than swallow that flap-sauce! How can things have changed so much?"

"I'll tell yer how! First of all there be a runner, a nob like yersel', Denning by name an' he is fearsome! They calls him the Bow Street Gent an' I thank me Maker that he don' care fer mud or there'd be no life fer us on the river. He's fly, I tell ye, an' up ter ever' dodge in the City."

"One runner? Why doesn't someone pull his cork?"

"Oh, it's been tried, don't yer think it hasn't! But, fer all he is a gent, he kin handle hisself wi' the best—an' what's more, O'Shaughnessy's always lurkin' about, like 'e were his son 'r somethin'. Oh, there's many a good lad o' the cross as has been took by the pair o' 'em an' I'll not distress ye wi' the tellin' o' what condition they was in atter O'Shaughnessy ha' done wi' 'em."

"Hmmmm, but only two of 'em? They cannot be all over the City every night."

"Ah, but they be only the half o' it. Ye see there's Bartholomew! Ever hear tell o' Bartholomew? He came atter you was took."

Ned was not in the least surprised to hear it, for this was what he had come for, anything that would lead him to Bartholomew from a direction that would not compromise his disguise; hence, he was Lolly for as long as would be necessary.

It was the first time in his career out of Bow Street that he had resorted to the role he had lived as a youth, and he had done so with revulsion. It was done at great risk too, for if Lolly and Edward Denning ever became identified as one and the same in the underworld of London, his life, for all of anyone's efforts to protect him, was forfeit. They could not afford to let him live, with what he knew and all the skills he could use to their disadvantage—and had, to the enhancement of Edward

103

Denning's reputation. One false move, one false word, and he would wind up a black-faced corpse floating on the waters of the Thames, picked up by the River Police to puzzle over and then disposed of in a potter's field. And so might he disappear from the face of the earth. No one would know, for he was on his own. Not O'Shaughnessy, not his father, not anyone, knew what he was up to. He had gone ahead and taken the step he thought was necessary in the face of the magistrate's expressed disapproval. As for O'Shaughnessy, the big man would have dogged his trail. Shamus was one man who could never move about the river unmarked by its denizens. After all, he was the archenemy of every water rat, the beak who had done Lolly in.

By becoming Lolly once more, Ned felt that his credentials would be nothing short of impeccable and would serve to give him an edge in his dealings with Bartholomew. The master criminal had reached his present eminence since Lolly's demise, but Ned did not doubt that Lolly's reputation had lived long enough after to have made some impression on Bartholomew. Exactly what, he would soon find out.

"Aye, I have heard a word or two about the bloke. But what has he to say to what a mudlark does?" asked Ned.

"He has got him a crowd o' ugly customers an' they kin do a cully to a turn. Bartholomew has made it plain fer all to unnerstan': the big lays in the City are his'n. Between his business an' Bow Street's there's no livin' fer us in the City even ef you was to lead us, Lolly. An' pickin's on the river is perishin' small. Things is changed an' fer the worse," he mourned.

Ned said: "Perhaps I can do something about that. I think a chat with Bartholomew might help to clear the air somewhat, don't you?"

Natto shook his head vigorously. "Nah, nah, the likes o' you'll never get ter see the likes o' him, Lolly. An' if yer try, what'll be the end o' it? O'Shaughnessy's work 'll be made good on yer. But that ain't the worst of it. Ye've heard, no doubt o' the new police they be talkin' of?"

Ned frowned. "No, I can't say that I have. I've been away, you know."

"It'll be the end o' all o' us, I tell yer! They's going ter be thousan's of 'em all dressed up in regimentals an' they'll be poppin' up all over the place, day 'n' night, too! 'T is bad enough wi' runners 'n' constables 'n' the River Police now. What 'll it be like when they come? They'll be aclappin' their mauleys 'pon yer shoulder ef ye but dare look cross-eyed, I tell yer."

Ned laughed. "Ah, Natto, you must be getting old! You should know what charleys are! One or a thousand, say boo to them and they'll run like rabbits."

"Well, I don' think so an' Bartholomew don' think so neither. He's got the idea they'll be somethin' fearsome 'n he's got the merchants up in arms about 'em." He laughed. "He's smart, he is. He's spread the word that they'd lose their own watchman 'n' charleys, an' their goods 'n' all 'll be at the mercy of a pack o' strangers who couldna care less what happens to 'em as they'll be gettin' their pay from the government an' not from the merchants."

"Aye, he's smart, right enough! Yes, Natto, he's a cove after my own heart. I most certainly shall speak with him. I'll be going to see him in the morning. I'd appreciate your letting me doss down with you this night."

Natto rubbed a heavy hand over his stubbly chin. "Ah now, Lolly, it'd do me heart good to have yer, but times is changed an' times is hard. . ." As he looked at Ned, he winked.

"Of course," said Ned with a laugh. As though by magic a one-pound note appeared in his hand. He gave it to the wide-eyed Natto.

"Crikey!" exclaimed the latter. "A whole cooter?"

"Keep it all—for old times sake. Now I could eat a bite before I grab my forty winks. How about you?"

"Aye, an' there be a tidy bark just down from Copenhagen. It'll be unloadin' in the morning an' the watch is a bunch of us."

"Excellent. Nothing like fresh eggs and Danish ham,"

said Ned as they got up and moved out of the little hut. "And golden butter! Perhaps we ought to pick up a hot loaf of bread on our way. My mouth waters at the prospect."

The morning was close on to eleven o'clock when Ned, in the guise of Lolly, came strolling into Soho Square from out of Greek Street. He was well acquainted with the area, and espied Bartholomew's house off in one corner of the square at once. It was instantly distinguishable from all the other residences by the great fanlight over the large front portal and the two large windows facing upon the square from the first and second floors.

The walk from Somerset House was something less than two miles. He had started out exactly early enough to reach the square just at this hour. His estimate of Bartholomew was such that he calculated to catch up with his man sometime between his arising and his toilet.

He went up to the door and knocked.

It was opened promptly by a mean-looking fellow in livery. There was a bulge under his coat at about the level of his waistband which bespoke a cosh.

The fellow wrinkled his nose in a superior manner and exclaimed: "Phew! Be off with yer! This ain't no stinkin' sewer!" He made to slam shut the door.

Ned deftly inserted his boot and blocked it open as he said: "Now, now, my beauty, a little more respect for a mudlark there, or I'll feed you to my friends, the fishes. I've come to speak with your master, Bartholomew. You may announce me."

The man frowned in a mixture of indignation and puzzlement.

"Now looky here, you river rat—who be you, anyway? You talks like the guv'nor hisself, but you're from the river and no mistake, by the stink an' by the look of yer. That'll buy you naught but a basting you'll not forget in a hurry. Yer new to Lunnon or ye'd know this is the last place for the likes o' you ef yer vally yer health." His hand was sneaking down towards his waist as he spoke.

106

Lolly impudently placed his index finger on the fellow's misshapen nose. Stealthily and quickly his other hand went to the fellow's waistband and gave it a sharp yank. The man knocked away the insolent finger on his nose and stepped forward, raising his fist to smash this upstart down. But he stopped in amazement as his pantaloons, the buttons of his small-falls all popped, slipped down about his knees. Without thinking he stooped to retrieve them. Ned's knee came up sharply to collide with the fellow's face as it came down. With a bellow of pain the bruiser went over backwards, blinded and helpless from the force of the blow.

Ned calmly stepped inside, bent over and collared the man. He hauled him to his feet and maintained his hold while the fellow blubbered and pulled up his pantaloons. The blubbering turned to blistering oaths as he reached out for his tormentor with one hand while, with the other, he grimly held up his pantaloons.

Ned let him take hold of him and immediately the foolish fellow freed his other hand to make good his grip. As soon as the hand had let go of the useless waistband, Ned stepped quickly back. The fellow as quickly stepped forward, only to fall with a crash, his face kissing the floor.

Ned chuckled and said: "Now, my good man, that you have come to a thorough understanding of the value of keeping your pantaloons on, you will do what I say or the next time you forget yourself, I shall kick each and every one of your teeth in, one by one. Get to your feet and take me to Bartholomew! He'll not thank you for keeping *me* waiting."

Just then two more liveried brutes came rushing into the vestibule.

Ned whipped his arm about his victim's neck and whirled him about so that they were both facing the newcomers, the man's body acting as his shield.

He dug his forefinger sharply into the man's back and said, very clearly: "You are a dead man if your friends come a step closer! My gun is an over-and-under, both chambers loaded and primed. You will be first and then one of the others. I'll take my chances with the survivor." He nudged his shield viciously.

The man promptly screamed for his mates to stand off.

Ned was not invading Bartholomew's establishment blindly. He had some idea of how business was conducted therein, having spent many hours, along with his fellow runners, observing the place. He did not think that Bartholomew would trust his retainers to carry firearms, as their use would have only brought the attention of law officers upon him, and that he surely did not wish.

The two men had stopped dead in their tracks and were staring at him, unvoiced threats mirrored in their eyes.

"Now then, we shall all of us march into Bartholomew's presence and you will explain to him the reason for your inhospitality to me."

As though it must end all discussion, one of the men stated flatly: "The guv'nor is still abed!"

"Do you think he would prefer to be awakened by the sound of firearms as I begin to dispose of you?"

The two men exchanged glances.

"I am losing patience rather rapidly! Tarry but an instant longer and there shall be two corpses for sure in this hallway and neither of them shall be mine."

Without another word, they turned and led him into the house, on up a staircase to the first floor. Ned kept a firm grip on his man, never easing the pressure of his finger in the small of the fellow's back.

They came to a door and hesitated.

"Don't bother to knock. We don't wish to disturb the governor just yet, you know," coolly commanded Ned.

They went inside to a dressing room. A quick glance showed Ned the door to Bartholomew's bedchamber. Ned, with his victim still shielding him, sidled up to it.

The two men backed away from him.

Reaching behind him, Ned eased the door open. Even

as it swung open, he whirled about so that his captive must be between himself and the room's occupant. A shot rang out. Ned felt the shock as the ball tore into his prisoner. He let the man fall as he slammed the door to behind him and bolted it.

The curtains were closed and the room was dimly lit. The man on the bed was trying frantically to reload a small pistol when Ned reached him and tore it from his hands. He tossed it carelessly across the room and remarked: "Two barrels are better than one, old chap. You're not as clever as I thought, Bartholomew."

"Who the devil are you?" demanded Bartholomew. "How in hell did you get in here!"

"All in good time, sir. All in good time. But I would suggest you call out and tell your men you do not wish to be disturbed, because I can break your neck in the instant they come crashing through the door."

The man sneered and leaped out of his bed. "Do you truly think you can?"

He was a superbly muscled specimen and his night shirt in no way disguised his broad shoulders.

He started for Ned.

Ned did not budge. "I am a mudlark, as you must have guessed, Bartholomew, and you know how we must struggle from childhood. I hear you have had your men tangle with a few of us, so you must know how well we fight. I tell you no lie when I lay claim to being the best of them. I know all the blows that can kill a man quickly—but enough! I would talk!"

Bartholomew was baffled by this stranger. He knew the fellow could not have been idly boasting, for that he was there bespoke the fact that somehow he had forced his way past three very capable bodyguards. Beyond that there was his speech. It was enough to make him pause.

"Damn! You speak as well as myself! How can you be a water rat? Ah, but wait—there is one I have heard something about! But he is dead! Bow Street snaffled him!"

He studied Ned. "Who the devil are you, man?"

"The very same cully as was cooked by they runners, sor. Aye, 't was O'Shaughnessy, hisself, as done me in, guv'nor, but Lolly was ever too fly for Bow Street," declared Ned, grinning.

There was a crash against the bedroom door. Lolly took a step towards Bartholomew, his hands at the ready.

Bartholomew shouted: "Leave off there! Everything is all right!"

He turned to Ned with a smile. "Aye, I have heard great stories about you, sir, but do not think I believe them all. I'd very much to try a fall with you. Perhaps some day I shall, but not now. This is a precious moment to me and I think I understand why you have come calling. For one thing, I will stipulate you are no ordinary mudlark and, if even half of what I have heard of you is true, I can expect that I may have trouble from the Thames. Am I far off?"

Ned smiled and said: "No, sir. I should say you are smack-dab on the target."

He went to the window and flung the curtains back, lighting up the room. "Time to rise and talk, my lord. Perhaps we can have breakfast together."

"A spanking idea, old man! Now, if I may proceed with my toilet—"

"If you do not mind, I'd like to join you. I am used to my stench, but I do not suppose you are enjoying it."

"Capital! And so very thoughtful of you to have suggested it," exclaimed Bartholomew with a laugh of relief. "I hated to mention it for fear of offending you, old chap."

Bartholomew's two retainers were flabbergasted to see their master issue forth from his bedroom apparently on the very best of terms with that bloody mudlark. They had no time to spare for any comment, for Bartholomew immediately gave orders for them to remove their fallen comrade and see to his wound. They were also informed that if there were any inquiries made regarding the

110

sound of the shot, they were to say that he had inadvertently let his pistol fall to the floor upon arising and it had gone off and, if the tale was not sufficient to satisfy official curiosity, they were to bring the nosy fellow to him.

He turned to Ned and remarked, casually: "Since there are no bodies lying about, a gold coin or two will close the case."

Chapter IX

Shamus O'Shaughnessy, the oldest and the largest runner attached to the Bow Street Police Office, was feeling very put upon. The surveillance of the Bartholomew house in Soho Square had been going on for some days now and in the wee hours of the morning his watch had ended. One would have thought that the relief of a man on watch would be the easiest and most natural thing for runners of vast experience, but no; Barnstaple had been an hour and a half late.

As if that had not been bad enough, the big burly Irishman had discovered, on reporting back to the office before going off duty, that no senior officers were anywhere to be found. Instead of going on home to the nice soft bed waiting for him, for which he was long overdue, O'Shaughnessy had to stand further duty until someone showed up. By rights it should have been Ned manning the office at that moment, and he spent an hour or two rehearsing some choice phrases for the lad. He had gotten together a very satisfactory selection of them and was well prepared to blowing the lad up proper when in walked His Honor, Mr. Denning, a very troubled look on his face.

"Shamus! Where the devil is Ned?" demanded the

magistrate, as though O'Shaughnessy was somehow to blame.

"Sure, an' I thought he was with you, Yer Honor."

"Well, I'd not be asking *you* if he *were* with me, would I? What is he working on?"

"The Beresford case, I'm sure."

"That is hardly any excuse for him to go gallivanting about through the night. Where is his journal? See where he has gone. Hop to it, man!"

O'Shaughnessy's mood tempered quickly before the magistrate's ire but he did not feel good about it, only more put upon then ever.

He went back to Ned's office, where he searched high and low until there on the desk, right before his eyes, was the notebook. His own stupidity galled him to such an extent that he could not help muttering: "Oh, Shamus, I wish ye were someone else so I could give you the tongue-lashin' you deserve!"

He left the office carrying the small buckram-bound volume and walked down the hall to Mr. Denning's office. He went in and laid the book down in front of the magistrate.

Mr. Denning looked up impatiently. "Hell's fire! I don't *want* it! I just want to know where Ned said he will be!" he cried, all impatience.

Shamus, quite familiar with this sort of mood in his superior, picked up the book and flipped through its pages. When he came to the last entry, he read it, looked up, paused and gulped.

"Well?" snapped Mr. Denning.

"The last entry is two days ago. He don't say."

"Oh, he shall hear about this from me! Don't you think he shall not! The very idea of him going off and never letting me know where he has gone! Well, just don't stand about, O'Shaughnessy! Go out and find him and bring him back to me!"

"Yes, sir!" shouted O'Shaughnessy, and he quickly ducked out of the office.

Two minutes later, the big policeman was back.

"Ah, you've found him and quickly! Well done, Shamus!" exclaimed Mr. Denning.

"Well no, sir, I found Lord Carnavon. He wishes to speak with you."

"Dear me, what a time for visitors! Well, we cannot keep his lordship waiting. Show him in! Show him in!"

Lord Carnavon entered and shook hands with Mr. Denning.

"Alec, I came a-purpose to borrow your best man. Peel would prefer to avoid debate on the floor of the Commons, and feels that Ned would make a good showing before a group of merchants who are nagging him to death over the quality of the police officers he has it in mind to staff the new force with. You do not mind, old chap, do you?"

"Why no, my lord, it is exactly what I would have Ned do, but I am embarrassed to have to admit that I have not the vaguest notion of where he is to be found. Er— we seemed to have misplaced him, you see."

"Misplaced him? Alec, you must be jesting! Your best man and your own son and you do not know where he is to be found? I'd say that was damned careless of you. But, great God in heaven, what am I to say to Peel—that I cannot produce my own future son-in-law? You realize what a pair of fools we will look?"

"Do you think I do not realize it? Such a thing has never happened in this office since I took charge of it. Why, it is unheard of! Shamus, have you not the least idea where he could be?"

O'Shaughnessy wrinkled up his face and scratched his head. "He's not in Soho Square 'cause Barnstaple is there. Mebbe he's with the general."

"Go quickly and fetch him. If he's on to something, you will relieve him," ordered Mr. Denning.

O'Shaughnessy, overwhelmed with fatigue, had half a mind to object, but he thought better of it. As he left the office, he dwelt upon the pleasure it would give him when he caught up with the truant and gave him what for.

The two gentlemen had just begun inquiring as to each other's health when O'Shaughnessy was back in to the office again, now in somewhat of a sweat.

"'T is the general, sir, as would have a word with you."

Lord Carnavon and Mr. Denning exchanged looks.

Mr. Denning nodded and O'Shaughnessy leaned out the door and beckoned. In came General Beresford, all smiling.

"Good morning, Your Honor—oh! and how do you do, my lord?"

All the gentlemen shook hands and Mr. Denning remained standing. There just were not enough chairs to go round.

"Ah, Alec," began the general, "I should like to speak to your son if it is convenient. I have another name for his list, you see, and as he appears to put a great deal of importance on these possibilities, I came over on purpose to tell him. It came to me overnight and, perhaps, it truly is not so important—"

"Alonzo, when did you see him last?" asked Mr. Denning a bit sharply.

"Why, it was just yesterday afternoon. He came over to review the list with me—I say, he has a way with dress! You cannot begin to imagine the costume he had on—"

"You haven't seen him since?"

Just then a third caller came in to join the confab.

Lord Carnavon exclaimed: "Emily! I thought you were still abed!"

"Girl!" cried Mr. Denning. "This office is no place for a lady!"

"Ah, my lady, how very charming!" said the general. "Indeed you are looking quite pretty!"

Shamus threw up his hands in despair and started to ease himself out. The little office was now become so crowded, there was not even room left to breathe.

"O'Shaughnessy, stop where you are! May I inquire where do you think you are going?" rapped out the magistrate.

116

"Ter see if I can find Ned, yer Honor!"

"Where is he?" demanded Emily. "I have something to say to him!"

"You'll take your turn, my lady!" exclaimed Lord Carnavon, half-angry, half-amused. "I was here first!"

"With all due respect, my lord, as it is I am in peril of my life, I should think I might have precedence. What say you, Alex?" interposed the general, his lips twitching.

Mr. Denning collapsed back down into his chair at the desk. He was chuckling as he declared: "Now, isn't that just like a constable! He is never around when you have need of him most. This much I will say: If I should get my hands on the scoundrel first, there'll be little enough left of him to interest any of you."

He frowned and suddenly he was on his feet leaning over his desk to General Beresford.

"Alonzo, you were saying something about his costume. Please describe it."

"If you like. He was wearing very rough clothes. Heavy boots and a short heavy jacket, almost like a seaman's but there was a difference, and there was a devilish look in his eye. He even walked differently. Cock o' the walk is the best way I can describe it."

Mr. Denning's face went pale. He looked at O'Shaughnessy, who nodded a mournful confirmation.

Mr. Denning turned to his visitors. "My lady, gentlemen, something is afoot and Ned is—er—occupied. As soon as I can free him from his duties I will make a point of having him call upon you. My lord, I fear I shall not be able to oblige Mr. Peel. It will be a little time before Ned can be made available to him. Now I must ask you all to leave. Er—not you, Alonzo. I want that name."

Lady Emily's eyes were burning into Mr. Denning's face. "Ned is in trouble, is he not?" she demanded.

"I have the fullest confidence that he can handle it, my lady. You are not to worry."

"But I *shall* worry, Uncle Alec. Oh please, *please* tell me how I can help!"

"You can best help by going home and putting it all

117

out of your mind, my lady. You may rely upon it that we shall look after him. Now please go so that I may make the necessary arrangements in his support. My lord, an excuse that my son is engaged in a matter of the greatest importance surely must satisfy Peel. To pull him out of it without endangering more than even himself at this point would be quite impossible."

Emily gasped and tears came to her eyes. "Oh, papa, I feel he has done this thing because of me. I was too cruel to him!" she cried, throwing herself upon Lord Carnavon's breast.

He put a comforting arm about her shoulders and led her out of the office. His face was clouded.

Mr. Denning invited the general to be seated in the only other chair in the room and then told O'Shaughnessy to remain.

"Something is decidedly wrong, Alex, is it not?" asked the general, looking solemn.

"It is nothing for you to worry about, Alonzo. We have—"

"Oh, dash it all, man! I am not concerned for myself! It's young Denning who seems to be in trouble. I have taken quite a fancy to the lad and should be distressed beyond expression if he should come to harm, especially if it is in my cause. Is there danger of it?"

Mr. Denning sighed. "Yes, there is a distinct danger but Ned can take care of himself, you may rest assured. Now then, about this name that has come to you? . . ."

"Ah, yes. Well, all of what I am about to tell you happened so very long ago, I feel a little foolish to tell you of it."

"How long ago?" asked Mr. Denning.

"It was at Badajos, in the aftermath of the siege." The general hesitated.

"If it has a connection with your career, it is worthy of our attention. Pray proceed."

"You probably have heard of the horror perpetrated by our troops upon the fall of the city, but only we who lived through it know to what depths of disgrace the

118

British Expeditionary Forces on the peninsula stooped. All through history, the lifting of a siege has been a signal to the attackers to let loose savagery, looting and raping upon the helpless populace. It pains me greatly, even after all these years have passed, that our troops who, but hours before, had conducted themselves in the finest traditions of English bravery in the attack, once it was successful, should have become beasts by whom no authority was recognized. For a time no power on earth, I do believe, could have restrained their excesses. Many fine officers were slain by their own men as they futilely attempted to stem the horror. I myself took a ball in the arm from a British musket on that night of horror.

"Wellington was astounded and immediately ordered a body of disciplined troops to the town. Only they, together with liberal applications of rope-ends and the erection of gibbets, brought the bloody holocaust to an end. I shall not distress you with the details of what I witnessed, but the number of our men who fell never to rise again *after* Badajos was taken was positively sickening. It was a black time for the British Army and it will be a long time before I can ever forget it.

"I was a lieutenant-colonel at the time, doing my best to abate the horror any way I could until sheer revulsion at the scenes I witnessed overcame me and I could carry on no longer. I will admit that the ball in my shoulder was reason enough to have discouraged me, but what finally did for me was the discovery that a ranking British officer, a man senior to myself at the time, had joined the rioters! Can you imagine my disgust? Can you imagine my feelings?—a *colonel* in the van of the mob, out to pillage and rape?

"Nor was it even something he had done in the heat of the moment, for he had stripped every sign of rank from his uniform! Needless to say, he donned all his insignia but once again—for his court-martial—after which it was stripped from him for good and all. It was my testimony and his subsequent apprehension in that disgraceful state of dress that convicted him. He was a younger son of a noble family and the business was conducted in the greatest secrecy. As it was, the sacking of Badajos was bad enough. It needed no capstone.

"He swore an oath of vengeance against me and was transported back to England and out of my awareness, for our war with the French was engaging all my attention. Shortly thereafter, His Grace had occasion to mark me and invite me to join his staff.

"I never thought about the episode again until last night. Badajos and anything connected with it is anathema to me. But the business did stir in my memory and, despite its having happened all of eighteen years ago, I thought it best to give you the man's name. It is Henry Conway and it is a name that fills me with loathing."

Mr. Denning made a note. "You have no idea of the whereabouts of this fellow?"

"No. Like so many other of the names I have listed, it is to me a name out of the past, perhaps the most repulsive of the lot; yet for all its tarnish just another bit of recollection from a long service history."

"Thank you, Alonzo. We shall keep it in mind. Now I pray you will excuse me. This has been a trying morning and I have fallen behind."

The general took his leave and Mr. Denning turned to O'Shaughnessy.

"Well, what do you think, Shamus?"

O'Shaughnessy shrugged and said: "It is sure that Lolly is back wi' us."

"With us or against us?" asked the magistrate, peering intently at the runner.

Immediately O'Shaughnessy drew himself up and began to splutter in vehement protest. "Ah now, Yer Honor, ye'll no be thinkin'—"

"No, no, Shamus, never! I just wished to clear the air between us. It is a dangerous game the lad has embarked upon and I do not see the need. What have the mudlarks to do with Bow Street business? Since we brought Lolly out of it, they have kept pretty much out of our way and we have been free to leave them to the mercies of the River Police."

"But he is up ter somethin'! That is fer sure!"

"But what? Why don't you go down to the embankments and see what you can find out? Truly, he should not have left us in the dark," complained Mr. Denning.

"I'll learn nothing there. Atter all, I kilt Lolly an' they know me too well—but how can the lad come back to life an' not raise their suspicions again' 'im?"

"I am sure he will have made up some cock-and-bull story to satisfy them," declared the magistrate sourly. "If anyone knows how big a wheedle mudlarks will swallow, he does. Well, if there is nothing that we can do at the moment, we might ask the River Police to nose about a bit and see if they can learn anything that will tell us what he is about. But blast him!" Mr. Denning's fist came crashing down upon his desk. "He has put us in the damnedest position! If he should have need of us, there is no way for us to know—and we dare not interfere! His new—*old* companions would do him in if they got the slightest hint of who he really was. But why he should have thought it necessary to raise a ghost, I cannot for the life of me surmise. And wouldn't you know it, he would have to do a bunker when everyone and his brother has a need to speak with him—not excluding myself."

He slapped his hand down upon the paper before him. "This Conway fellow, for example. It is something he and I should discuss. I have a presentment that there is something here. For an officer and a gentleman to turn scoundrel is not unheard of; but that he should turn beast? That indeed is rare! It draws my attention to him since, for such a fellow, the foulest of deeds are not beyond his contemplation. But here's a puzzle! If he intended the general harm, one would think he'd not have waited some eighteen years before attempting it. Yes, there is something that does not quite add up here."

"Agh, there's no tellin' about black-hearted villains, Yer Honor."

"Come now, Shamus! Think about it! Here's a man who has been broken purely as a result of the action and the testimony of one particular fellow-officer. He swears vengeance and is not the sort who'd hesitate to stoop to any wickedness. Then do you mean to tell me he sits perfectly still for eighteen years, nursing his bloody thoughts, but doing not a thing? I say no. I say there is something missing. The facts are not all here; it is imperative we discover them. The trouble is that I do not know what I am looking for and, therefore, have not a hope of guessing in what direction to bend our efforts."

"What'll you be wishing me ter do, Yer Honor?" asked O'Shaughnessy.

But Mr. Denning was not heeding him. "Dammit! This is what comes of having to rely on a runner deep in the throes of love. If he is going to act the complete cabbagehead, there's no telling what will happen next! If he failed in the first place to request of the general this list of possible suspects, one can only wonder if he himself knows what he is up to. I shall be positively overjoyed if and when he gets himself married. We shall all be at peace and get back to our work. Well, I shall have to look into these things myself. Shamus, I shall go to the general's and see what more I can find out. Something has been missed. I am sure of it. Perhaps, if I can get the general to talk, one of us will be clever enough to see what it is."

Chapter X

Father and daughter came into the Trenchard mansion
and doffed their wraps with absent-minded expressions
on their faces. Having delivered their things into the
hands of their servants, they remained standing in the
hallway, still wrapped up in their thoughts.

Suddenly, at one and the same time, they both spoke.

"Emily, I would have a word with you!"

"Papa, I would speak with you!"

They both of them smiled at each other and my Lord
Carnavon offered her his arm. Together they prome-
naded into a sitting room and sat down close by each
other.

"Well now, my lady, what is it you would speak of?"

"It is Ned, papa. He worries me."

"Yes, my dear, he worries me, too. As you know, I have
a strong liking for him and find him in no way excep-
tionable as a prospective son-in-law. At least that is how
it was, until now."

"But, papa—"

"Let me finish, Emily dearest. It is only your ultimate
happiness that moves me to speak. You know, my dear,
every week there is some story in the newspaper of how,
in the detection of a crime or in the pursuit of a criminal,
some watchman or some constable is hurt or even some-

times slain, and we hardly take any notice of it. After all, it is what they are being paid to do and, if they have had the misfortune to have been less than skillful, well, there is always some other desperate wretch to take their place. Aye, even when it is a runner from Bow Street, as infrequent as that is, it is hardly anything to become distressed about. So it has been with me and, I think you will admit, so it has been with you.

"Now, it is different. For all of Denning's assurances, Ned is in danger. He is having to endure what every thief-taker, every constable, every runner must encounter not once but many times in his career before, if he is so fortunate, old age comes to him and he is pensioned off out of harm's way. Is this the sort of life you wish to share? Will you ever know a moment's peace when Ned is away from your side, commingling with the lowest of the low in some foul dive?"

"But I love him!" protested Emily. "And what has that to say to anything—this talk of danger! If I were a colonel's wife or that of a sea captain, heaven forbid, I would have all of the worry and rarely ever see my husband into the bargain."

"Oh, surely you can be cleverer than that!" her father responded. "Ned is not the only man in the world for you. There are plenty of gentlemen of birth and breeding, from amongst whom you can choose, who engage themselves in peaceful pursuits. Why, a good many of 'em have no pursuit at all and must always be by your side, but I doubt if you would have it," he commented with a chuckle. "In any case, you may pick and choose as you please. There is not the slightest need for you to hang your heart upon this one reckless fool, admirable fool though he be, and gain for yourself needless worry and heartache. Just think of the vulgar females he must of necessity consort with. *That* certainly must give you pause."

"Oh, I shall be jealous, I do not doubt, and he will suffer for it, but it makes no difference. He is mine!"

"Is he truly? He does not think so. All this twaddle

about his birth that has placed your betrothal into limbo hardly speaks so well of his devotion to *your* feelings."

"He is confused—and I could scratch his eyes out! Why must he be so stubborn over something that is so inconsequential? Papa, there is only one thing for it. You have got to get the police reform bill passed and make him the commanding general!"

"Oh? Now it is up to me, is it? Well, my dear, I fear you quite overestimate my influence. As Peel has got it worked out, the new Metropolitan Police will come under himself, as Home Secretary, but it will be governed and administered by a pair of commissioners, senior men who have already been selected. Ned is far too young and too inexperienced as an administrator to be saddled with such a great and grave responsibility. The details of how the organization shall be structured will be pretty much up to the commissioners, subject to Peel's approval. I think I can see to it that Ned achieves a station of rank and responsibility that is respectable in the new organization, but whether he will be elevated to such rank as will keep him out of harm's way, I cannot say, nor would it befit me to move in that direction. He'd not wish me to, himself. I have no doubt that, as Peel thinks very highly of his capability, he will wish to see that Ned is placed where he can be most effective—and that, my dear, will hold whether or no he is Carnavon's son-in-law."

"Oh, papa, you are no consolation at all! Here is Ned laboring under some dread threat that even Mr. Denning knows nothing of—or is not telling me—and all you can do is talk about the prospects of your future son-in-law, who may never survive long enough to ever become your son-in-law!"

"My dear, there is nothing that *I* can do about it at this moment."

"I shall speak with Uncle Alec. Maybe *he* can do something about it."

"You leave Alec be! He obviously has his hands full at this time. Remember, he could not love Ned more dearly

125

than if he were flesh of his flesh, and the Chief Magistrate is one of the most competent men in the kingdom. You may rely upon it, he will do whatever can be done. Quite possibly, he is the *only* man in the world, right now, who has the knowledge and the wisdom to keep Ned safe. Do not disturb him until Ned is safely back."

"Very well, papa, but when Ned is back, he is going to marry me or, birth or no birth, he will wish he had never been born!"

General Sir Alonzo came forward to greet warmly Alexander Denning, as that gentleman was ushered into his parlor.

"I say, Alec, we have exchanged salutations twice in one day. We are become quite the bosom-beaux, methinks."

Mr. Denning smiled and seated himself, at General Beresford's invitation. "I hope it does not take the edge off it that I am here in my official capacity a-purpose to forward our investigation?"

"No, of course it does not. Speaking for myself, any excuse for you to call will serve—and I should hope that, after this business is resolved, our acquaintance will still continue, perhaps on an even more intimate basis. I have managed to acquire a strange taste for the company of Dennings (almost any Denning will do), and sincerely wish that the both of you will feel free to honor me frequently with visits, official or otherwise."

"Thank you, Alonzo. If we do not visit each other quite often, it shall not be for any fault on my part—but I would to business, and the business I have with you is the Conway chap. There is something peculiar about him."

"You do not have to tell me that! I am sure of it!" exclaimed the general in surprise.

"No, no, you misunderstand me. Of course we are all agreed that for him to have got himself cashiered on such grounds speaks volumes for his lack of probity, and bears witness to his strange appetites, but I refer more particularly to his behavior *since* Badajos."

"What behavior? I am sure that I have neither the interest nor the concern for his subsequent behavior. He can go hang for all of me, and I mean that literally."

"It is the absence of any move towards you that is the puzzle. Of all the list that you have given me, he stands out, by character and circumstance, as the one most likely to do you harm. The thing of it that I cannot swallow is that, if he had intended foulness against you, why has he waited so many years to begin it?"

The general shrugged. "Then dismiss him from consideration. I have every respect for your judgment in these matters. If the shoe does not fit, it does not fit."

Mr. Denning shook his head. "But that is just it. It should fit. It must fit. His motive is as powerful as any on your list, but he sounds to me the one most likely to follow through. Are you sure that the assault which took place on Queen's walk was the first of its kind? Were you never set upon before, or had some close brush with danger of any sort? Please think carefully."

General Beresford shrugged. "Obviously the Frenchies arranged a few entertainments of that sort, but they are hardly pertinent."

"Quite. How long were you away on campaign?"

"For the seven years it took us to march up the peninsula to Waterloo. By then I was fatigued and all purpose had gone from my life. It is odd, is it not, that the end of Napoleon should have signaled the end of me, in a sense?"

"I hope you will not take this as impertinence, for it is quite necessary. His Grace ordered you into retirement?"

"Most certainly not! I elected to retire. The duke had every hope that I would remain by his side, but I could not in all conscience continue."

"Now let me understand something. You were away from England for all of seven years—oh, but surely that cannot be correct! After the Battle of Paris, with Napoleon immured in Elba, you must have returned to England for a breather."

"No, I did not, I assure you. I had no reason to return and thought to stay on with the troops of occuption for us as long as I could. It was not until after Waterloo that I discovered how exhausted I was with it all and that, willy-nilly, I must return to England even if I would not find my peace there—but Alec, what in God's name is all of this? Do you suspect that I am my own worst enemy, that you are trying to trace my movements?" he ended with a laugh.

Mr. Denning smiled patiently. "It does sound as if I did, does it not? I am looking to see if perhaps there was an opportunity before this last attack for the fellow to have tried for you." He shook his head. "But no, I cannot see him traveling back to the continent and seeking you out on battlefield after battlefield. He would have been far too obvious." Mr. Denning thought for a moment and then frowned. "I say, there is still a puzzle here and I am not yet satisfied."

"What is so puzzling?" inquired the general.

"That is just it! If I knew what it was I should no longer be puzzled. I just feel it in my bones that I have yet to get all the facts."

"Find Conway and question him. Perhaps he did make some attempt before, but it completely misfired for one reason or another and so was never noticed."

Mr. Denning stared intently at the general. "Something you said just a moment ago, Alonzo, is nagging at me. What did you mean: you'd not find your peace in England?"

"It is not something I care to talk about, Alec, not to anyone. It is a matter of personal sorrow, you will understand."

"Some tragedy here in England that has affected you?"

"Please, Alec, I have no wish to go into it."

"I think you had better, Alonzo. Perhaps this is the very thing I have been searching for."

General Beresford looked off into the distance for a moment. Then he turned to Mr. Denning and his eyes were moist. "If you insist." He paused again. "There was a conflagration and, when it was over, the family home of the Beresfords was completely destroyed and with it, also, all I held dear in this world."

"You had a family? I never suspected! My dear fellow, my heart goes out to you. I have been a bachelor all my life and I know what it is to be alone—but to have had your love and lost it so—so . . ."

Mr. Denning bit his lip and fell silent. He held his peace and let the awful moment pass.

Finally he said: "Alonzo, my friend, I must press you for more details. It is no perverted taste for the morbid that urges me to the distasteful task. It is a matter of routine procedure. You see, it is more than possible that this tragedy has some bearing on our investigation, but I must know more before I may come to any conclusion. If it should fail to shed any light upon the business in hand, I assure you I shall never broach the subject with your again. But your life *is* in danger. You have had ample proof; and as long as you are alive, we must practice every diligence to insure that you remain so. That is why I must pursue every possible circumstance that may relate to it. Distasteful though this business has become, I must pray you will enlarge upon it for me."

General Beresford sighed and nodded. He began to speak in a dull tone.

"I was not there when it happened. I left my wife and my two children at my modest estate in Surrey, just outside of Clapham, to join Wellington in Portugal. I received the news just as we were preparing to cross the Pyrenees into France—"

"July of '13, I make it."

"Indeed, Alec, you are quite correct. I take it that you must have followed our campaigns with more than ordinary interest."

"What was the news?"

"My wife and children had been lost as a result of a

fire at night that had completely destroyed the residence."

"Hmmmm. You have returned to the scene since?"

"No. Not for all the wealth in the world would I ever go to Clapham. Not then and not now. Even though the blackened ruins must have been done away with years ago, those three stones standing in Clapham churchyard are something I cannot bring myself to view. Someday there will be four stones and none of us Beresfords will have ever seen a one of them."

"Who sent you word?"

"The local squire. I forget his name, if he is still the one."

"We can check into that easily enough."

"Check into it?" exclaimed General Beresford. "For pity's sake, leave my dead to rest in peace!"

"Just a few more questions and I will have done."

"Very well. Please get it over with. I wish to put it out of my mind."

"I understand. Perhaps, instead of putting you to the question, I'll tell you some further facts—well, that is too strong. Let us say: tentative conclusions. To begin with, I put it to you that not all in the house perished that night."

"True enough. One of the servants managed to escape the flames."

"A manservant, am I correct?"

"Why, yes."

"Who was he?"

"The coachman. I do not recall his name. It was so long ago."

"How many servants perished?"

"I have no idea. When I left, there was a governess, cook, the butler, and some maids. I am sure that those caught in the fire were not all the same people. During my time away it was up to my wife to see to the household staff, of course. There were bound to have been changes."

Mr. Denning nodded and his eyes were bleak. "Yes, I

130

have enough of a picture to give me reason to believe that I know what occurred. And I have finally got the piece to my puzzle and it is a horrid piece."

"What do you mean?"

Mr. Denning gave General Beresford a measuring look. Then he shook his head. "No, until my suspicions are confirmed, I have not the right to say another word."

The general frowned. Slowly his eyes widened and sheer horror dawned in them. Very deliberately he said: "I never saw that coachman, never thought to look him up! Do you say that it was Conway? That this was all premeditated, cold-blooded murder to avenge himself upon me?"

"It is too soon to say. I would not jump to any conclusion just yet, Alonzo. But I will admit it is the missing piece that nicely ties everything together."

"Nicely! You can sit there and put such a term to the slaughter of my innocent family?" cried the general, beside himself with grief and rage.

Mr. Denning stood up. "Alonzo, it was a far from appropriate choice of word. But if I choose to regard this dire tragedy as only a puzzle, it is because I must keep my mind clear of the intense grief I feel for you, if I am to be successful in bringing this mad fiend to justice. *You* are in no condition to track this beast down and so *I* must remain so. I beg you will remember that I live with these horrors week in and week out. Only by resorting to artifice, and conceits of one sort or another, can I pursue this awful business with an untrammeled mind. I beg you will not judge me by what I may say, for my feelings are hidden and must remain hidden, at whatever cost to myself."

The general got to his feet and put out his hand in understanding. As they shook, he said: "Of course it is a piece with what I experienced on many a battlefield when the young officers were falling to the right and to the left of me. There was grief within me to see it, but there it was kept, and for the same reason. Time enough to lament after the task is done with. Is there anything else you would like to know, Alec?"

"Not at the moment. May I consult with you again if it is necessary?"

"Please do. Feel free to call upon me at any time and for any reason. You will always be welcome, and I promise I shall not put you through another such painful scene again."

Mr. Denning patted him on the shoulder. "I shall, and do you never hesitate to call upon me, Alonzo. I feel as though we are old and dear friends."

When Mr. Denning got back to the office at Bow Street, he was puzzled to see Barnstaple lounging about there. He went directly to his office, where he consulted the duty roster, scowled, and went to his doorway.

"Hoy there, Barnstaple!" he called.

The runner strode up to him and stood stiffly before him.

"What the devil are *you* doing here? I have you on watch at Soho Square."

"Oh, that! Well, 't is like this, sir, Yer Honor, when I see his nibs march up to the door as cool as you please and—"

"His nibs? What door?" snapped Mr. Denning.

"Ned Denning, your son, sir. He was wearing an outfit that was mud all over and he waltzes up to Bartholomew's door cocky as you please. I seen he'd taken a hand in the game an', as we're spread thin enough, I thought it best to come back in, in case I was needed. No use fer two of us to be workin' the same street as it were, sir."

"Oh, you blasted idiot! We had him and now I'll wager we've lost him again!" shouted Mr. Denning, turning purple with anger. "Oh, you are no good to me! Where's O'Shaughnessy?"

"Down to the River Police. He left word."

"How can it be that whenever I need someone he is never about?" asked Mr. Denning of the heavens. "You, Barnstaple, get back to your post at once, do you hear?

132

Don't you dare take your eyes off that house and, if Ned steps out of it, you are to follow, but softly. I don't suppose you will be able to escape his notice, but try to do your best, especially if he is in company with anyone. I'll send O'Shaughnessy out to you as soon as I can, and you will take your further orders from him. Now, go!"

"Yes, sir!" and Barnstaple left the office at a trot.

In the dining room, where they had spent all afternoon after lunch, at conversation and cards, Ned and Bartholomew appeared to be enjoying each other's company.

"So, Lolly, that was a most enjoyable coze we have had, and I am pleased to see you are a regular Captain Sharp with the cards as well."

Ned laughed and tossed a thick sheaf of bills across the table to Bartholomew. "I know a few things. No offense. Here, take it back! I was cheating you blind."

"No, no!" protested Bartholomew, pushing the bills back at him. "Keep the lucre. I knew you had to be cheating, but I'm damned if I could catch you at it. To witness a topping Greek at work is worth the price.

"I dare say you are a man of many talents. I am still impressed with the way you walked through my bodyguards and, of course, vastly amused. Have you used that trick with the waistband often?"

Ned shrugged. "As circumstances might dictate."

Bartholomew laughed and shook his head in wonder. "I should like to have seen it! But I still do not see how you could have gotten away with it. Wellers, for all his bulk, is a fast man on his feet. I've seen him mill down many a cove, yet he never laid a hand on you? Just l-let you p-pop h-his b-buttons—" Bartholomew could not speak for the laughter that was convulsing him.

"It's an old dipster's trick. Direct your victim's attention away from his pockets whilst you give them yours. By touching his nose and letting him knock my hand away, I diverted his attention from the business of my other hand quite long enough for it to reach out and give

133

one sharp yank. Once his pantaloons dropped, it was all over with him."

"Oh, that is perfectly marvelous!" cried Bartholomew, still choking with laughter. "It begins to appear that all the tales I have heard tell of your ingenuity and prowess were not exaggerated a bit."

"You will admit it was better than a calling card and saved us a deal of debate?"

"That it did! And I thank you for it. Well, I think we have a great deal more to talk about. I have a need for a lieutenant upon whom I can rely—a man with brains and spirit, and in my business that is a rare combination, to find both qualities in the one person. You will stay with us the night?"

"Thank you, but no. I'm dossing down with Natto Binger."

"Ah, yes, Natto. I went to a bit of trouble teaching that beauty that his place was down by the river. Cost me a few men to do it, too. I must suppose that *that* is all gone up in smoke, now that you have rejoined the ranks—no, I daresay that I am holding converse at this moment with the chief water rat himself."

"That remains to be seen, but it is something that is certainly worthy of discussion. After all, if my mudlarks could be gotten to fight together, it just might take more men than you have got to teach them their place again, wouldn't you say?"

"I am way ahead of you, Lolly! It is no more than I expected from you. But it appears to me that, as you are probably the only person *alive* who can unite your mud-bedizened cohorts, the obvious and least costly solution would be to shoot you here and now."

"Yes, that would be the easiest way, provided you had the wherewithal to accomplish it—such as this, for instance," remarked Lolly, sliding a small pistol across the table. It slid right up to Bartholomew's hand.

Bartholomew snatched it up and started violently in his seat. "What the devil!" he exclaimed. "When in heaven's name did you lift this little beauty off me?"

"What difference could that possibly make? I did it and you were disarmed without ever realizing it. The pistol is the proof."

Bartholomew examined it carefully. He shook his head in amazement as he pointed it up in the air, cocked it, peered into the chamber, and then slowly eased the hammer back down onto the percussion cap. He laughed. "Burn me if it isn't still loaded! I dare say you have me covered with something else?"

Ned laughed in reply. "You will never know for sure unless you try me."

"Lolly, I like you! I like your style! I admit I had some thoughts that you would be my guest this night, willy-nilly, but now I'll not say more than that it is my dearest wish you will remain. If you do not care to, you are free to leave."

"It would be my pleasure to stay. I just wished to make doubly certain that it *was* my pleasure."

"Quite. You could not have made it clearer. Now, let us go to dinner. Where would you like to dine?"

"We have a great deal to discuss, methinks, and I have not got my best manners back with me yet. I propose we dine in and talk. We have all of London to discuss and, I dare say, that will call for something more than polite conversation."

"Excellent. I'll show you our London of 1829 some other time."

Late that night, when he retired to the chamber that Bartholomew had had prepared for him, Ned was not too displeased with what he had accomplished thus far. Everything was proceeding swimmingly. In fact, it was all going as well as could have been hoped, far better than he might have expected.

As he checked the bedchamber for movable panels and any other devices that might permit stealthy access to him during his repose, he gave thought to exactly what he had achieved this day.

He had established himself in Bartholomew's confidence as a colleague worthy of respect, one with whom the master criminal was not adverse to associate himself. Further, he had made his mark upon the man's underlings so that they'd not attempt his discomfiture or destruction except upon the express orders of their master. By implying that he himself, as Lolly, had all of the mudlarks at his beck and call, he had established a bargaining counter with Bartholomew and that, of course, was the most desirable thing. Thus far, in their talks, he had exchanged promises with his host to the effect that he would let the mudlarks swelter and squirm upon the river flats, in return for which Bartholomew would share with Lolly the administration and the profits of the Lord of Crime's nefarious enterprises. He complimented himself upon his brilliant stroke of reviving Lolly, complete with reputation, and with credentials of a sort that had not failed to impress Bartholomew. In no other way could he have had the least chance of gaining the man's intimacy.

But Ned was not a fool. He knew that he had built himself a house of cards which the least breath of suspicion must blow down, and snuff him out, as well. That risk was in essence the price he had to pay. Nor was his next step so clear to him. Somewhere in this warren of the demimonde, he had got to uncover Bartholomew's particular plot against the life of General Beresford, especially the identity of the principal who was behind it—and when the next attack might be forthcoming. Of course, if he found out the plotter first, there would be no more attacks to follow.

There was no reason to believe that Bartholomew had the least intention of making him privy to all his dealings. It was more likely that he intended to bring Lolly up gradually, giving him only such a share in his operations as would satisfy the mudlark to keep his filthy cohorts out of the City. That aspect of the affair was of the least interest to Ned, but it was necessary that he simulate an interest to gain his ends with Bartholomew.

Ned, of course, had no intention of waiting so long for events to develop. That must make it over-late to help the general. Somehow he had got to stir things up and bring them to a boiling-over much sooner, possibly in a day or so. He did not have much time, he knew, and for more reasons than that he might be unmasked. There was his father, the magistrate, with all of the Bow Street behind him.

Ned had known from the beginning that His Honor would never have permitted him to resume the character of Lolly, so he had not dared to suggest it. But he could not accept the magistrate's refusal to approve any approach at all to Bartholomew. It was a desperate situation and it called for a desperate remedy.

One advantage of becoming Lolly again was that it was bound to throw Mr. Denning and O'Shaughnessy off his track for a time. Sooner or later they must learn from contacts with the River Police that Lolly had reappeared amongst the mudlarks, and then Bow Street would move to catch up with him. He had no doubt that once they had started they would locate him quickly enough, especially as the Bartholomew house was under constant surveillance. He was sure that they would hope to get him out of it but he was equally sure that they would not just come barging in after him. They would try to extricate him without undoing his masquerade; that could give rise to some very delicate difficulties. The least it would do was to make them pause and watch to see what exactly was going forward with him. On the other hand, should they misjudge the situation and move too soon, there was every possibility that they would ruin everything—not excluding himself, he thought wryly. The trouble was that, for the time being, they could not know when to come to his assistance and he could not get free to give them an estimate of the situation.

Before he began to disrobe for the night, he rearranged some of the furniture in the room to make deadfalls so as to surprise any nocturnal visitors. Then he inspected his own over-and-under, made sure it was properly loaded, and, with it close by his hand, composed himself to sleep.

Chapter XI

The next morning when Mr. Denning came into the office he was in a foul humor. It seemed as if, overnight, his well-ordered world had been turned topsy turvy, and all because of that son of his. What was the use in having adopted a charming son if he was not to see him. It was the second night that the lad had not made an appearance. Any word he had received concerning Ned's disappearance was not of an encouraging nature.

Yesterday, O'Shaughnessy had returned with an irate Superintendent of the River Police, Sir Reginald Malcom, and they had had a hot and stormy session.

Sir Reginald Malcom came raging into Mr. Denning's office, charging that Bow Street had been guilty of gross malfeasance in falsely reporting the death of one Lolly, mudlark extraordinary. For nigh on seven years the River Police had enjoyed a sense of relative peacefulness along the waterfront and now that that prime provocator, Lolly, was returned, the mischief was sure to break out all over their heads again.

It took all of Mr. Denning's cunning to cool his colleague's ire down to the point where he could at least get a word in edgewise. He then exerted himself to show Sir Reginald that he was blowing himself up for no real cause. Lolly was dead, so obviously anyone claiming to be him could be naught but an impostor.

He thought to ask if the superintendent had laid eyes upon the upstart. Sir Reginald had had to admit he had not. Then Mr. Denning, mentally crossing his fingers, inquired just how many members of the River Police had laid eyes upon this new Lolly. Er—none, the answer came, but word had gone out all up and down the river that Lolly was back from the dead. It had to be so, for every water rat was going about as cocky as a lord.

Mr. Denning, giving thanks to Ned for having covered himself to that extent at least, then proceeded to point out that Sir Reginald was getting himself all wrought up over nothing. He had not a shred of evidence that Lolly's resurrection was anything more than a tale to bolster the mudlarks' spirits. Obviously it was all a grossly exaggerated rumor and the peace on the river was in no particular danger of being shattered.

Sir Reginald was not so sure but, as a policeman, he had to admit his evidence was less than reliable and so he withdrew his charge, disarmed but not truly satisfied.

And now this morning with Ned still absent, Mr. Denning wondered what other troubles he was about to encounter. He had gotten to rely on the lad to an extent he had never dreamed possible, both here in the office and, so very much, at home.

He sat at his desk very much confused. He was in no mood to sit in court this day, and had just about made up his mind to call in an assistant magistrate, when O'Shaughnessy made his appearance after having completed his watch on the house on Soho Square.

"What have you learned, Shamus?" asked Mr. Denning.

"Nothing to the good, Your Honor."

"What is it?"

"We know he went in and we know he never came out. The two hours that Barnstaple was away from his post appear to have been peaceful enough, but for one little thing. I questioned the people about in the park an' nothin' out o' the ordinary was heard, wi' the one exception."

"Well, what was that?"

"Durin' Barnstaple's absence, a shot was fired in the Bartholomew place. It was heard by more than one and, near as I kin figure it, it couldna been more than a dozen minutes atter Ned disappeared inside."

Mr. Denning frowned. "I do not like the sound of that at all! Hmmmm!"

"Yer Honor, sir, Raike an' Benson have sang their lungs out, more than enough for us to go in an' nab Bartholomew on charges. Then we kin find Ned."

"Yes, I know. I am sorely tempted, but my mind counsels against it. For one thing, such testimony will not be worth much in court, so we shall have the devil's own time of it getting a conviction, if at all. And then, should Ned be making any progress, we shall have ruined everything. Of course one well-placed shot is enough to kill a man, but there has not been any further sign to indicate a man wounded or killed, has there?"

"Well, there's been no sawbones sent fer and they ain't attempted to send anything out o' the place. I'm dead certain they'll not be settin' around wi' a dead corpus in their way an' all."

Mr. Denning nodded as though to reassure himself. "And anyway, what would it serve if we were to go in? If, heaven forbid, Ned is dead, we'll not be of any aid to him. As for Bartholomew, we can grab him any time we wish, so we might just as well give him more rope. He'll hang, of course, but I should like him to lead us to the Beresford fiend before he does. On the other hand, and this I believe, if Ned is still alive in there, then, prisoner or no, he has got something cooked up and will serve it when it is ready. We should only upset the apple cart if we are premature, and that just *might* get the lad killed."

"No," he continued, "although I am beside myself with anxiety for the lad, the best thing we can do at the moment is to wait and see. But, out of consideration for your feelings and mine, not longer than two days. More than that makes no sense to me."

"It will be a very long two days, sir."

"Aye, that it will, Shamus. Who has the watch in Soho Square for this day?"

"Coggshill, sir."

"Good man. You had better get some rest."

"Aye, that I will, Your Honor."

At about that same time, the subject of Mr. Denning's concern was enjoying a sumptuous breakfast with his host. All was good fellowship between them. The fact that the liveried tough had taken a ball in his shoulder had been completely overlooked. After all, there had been no complications. The ball had gone all the way through so that the services of a surgeon were not required, and he had been patched up and was now resting. That he had been made the gull of the renowned Lolly had done something to relieve his embarrassment before his fellows. It was a known fact that Lolly had gulled the best of Bow Street many a time in the past and the River Police even more often.

It seemed to Ned that Lolly's repute had grown all out of proportion during the years following his demise; it struck him that he had been missing a good bet not to have taken advantage of the disguise before this. It was doing so much to make his task easier.

But, as good as his masquerade appeared to be, he could not trust to it forever and, that morning upon arising, he had resolved to force a conclusion somehow, before the day was ended. In fact the invitation of last evening had been a close call. If they had gone out to dinner, it could easily have proved his undoing. Heaven only knows where they might have ended up! Some fashionable club where he would have been hard put indeed to escape recognition, no doubt. It had been an easy move to parry, but a second time and that might bring a question to Bartholomew's eyes.

"Bartholomew, I must say this is quite a change from

142

my usual haunts," Ned remarked as he put his coffee cup down, "and I am indebted to you for your hospitality—but I would not strain it. I was never used to sitting about, you know. Of course, considering the damp and the filth of my usual habitation, that is not to be wondered at. Nevertheless, a man of my habits requires the exercise of both wit and body if he is to get on—and I expect to get on."

"I see no reason not to accommodate you in that regard. I think it would be mutually profitable if, today, we spent going about to view some of my enterprises, at least those which can stand up to examination in the light of day—er—provided it is the least bit overcast, don't you know." He ended with a leering chuckle.

"That has not the ring of trust and confidence that should exist between partners," objected Ned.

"Be easy, Lolly. We have got to start somewhere, and even an entire day will not be sufficient to cover a part of the ground. As to the *sub rosa* aspects of my operations, all in good time, all in good time."

"You begin to amaze me, Bartholomew. For heaven's sake, why, you must be fabulously wealthy! Can your operations truly be of such a vast magnitude as all that?"

Bartholomew, flattered, laughed and waved his hand. "How do you think I can afford all this?" he asked grandly. "And if you but knew how many m.p.'s and magistrates I encourage to dip into my pockets, then, my friend, you truly would be astounded, for those gentlemen are expensive, very expensive."

"I dare say you have got yourself a handful of runners as well."

Bartholomew frowned. "I will tell you, Lolly, the runners, from Bow Street especially, are a most untrustworthy lot. Oh, I manage to see some of them well-paid, but I am sure it is money down the drain. You see, they do not stay bought. I am never sure, as the money is doled out to them, whether it might not be that, instead of buying a modicum of protection, I am in fact buying myself a deal of trouble. Indeed they are a breed apart and not at all qualified to be proper policemen. Of them all, there are two, at least, that I am so sure of I need not waste a penny upon 'em."

Ned's eyes narrowed. "Oh, they are completely your creatures?"

"If only they were! No, quite the contrary. The one is a giant of a paddy, by name O'Shaughnessy—"

Bartholomew stopped in midsentence and regarded Ned in surprise, for the mudlark was laughing.

"What have I said that amuses you so?" asked Bartholomew, visibly nettled.

"Truly, no one can tell me about Shamus O'Shaughnessy! Before he shot me, we were like father and son— you know, a good father with a very troublesome son. It was always Shamus and Lolly between us. No, Shamus cannot be bought or I'd have done it before you ever appeared in the City."

"Of course, I had heard about that. Well, the man is a monstrous brute and absolutely brainless. All he knows what to do is to hammer my people unmercifully. He is become such a thorn in my side that I would give anything to have him done away with. The thing is the man clings to life a deal more tenaciously than the people I have sent out to do him in. Now no amount of money will tempt my most bloodthirsty assassins to even talk of him. I do not like it one bit and must see him put out of my way. I suppose I shall have to import someone from Paris to do the job. At least they will try, not knowing the man they have to deal with. When we get to discussing problems like that, I am sure you will be able to offer an idea or two."

"Quite. But you mentioned that there were two."

"Ah, yes, the second is even worse an antagonist, by far the more dangerous of the pair. Even *I* do my best to avoid his notice. He is very much like me, you see, and that sort of person I should never dare to trust. He seems to have come from out of nowhere and is, undoubtedly, the shadiest of the lot. He is that rare sort of cove whose lay, if you can believe it, is upon the right side of the law. You do not know him, I am sure, for he came after you had departed, I think."

"Your description of the fellow does not ring a bell with me."

"Well, anyway, he has made a damned good thing of it. But then he does have this one advantage, you see. He is of the gentry and so has entrée where I do not. Oh, he is quite a fly one. He has actually had himself adopted by the chief magistrate of Bow Street himself, and goes by the name, Edward Denning. Can you even imagine it?"

"Indeed!" exclaimed Ned, all incredulity.

"Yes! I surmise that he is a relic of some proud but poor family and has had to demean himself to being a runner if he would eat. But never underestimate the fellow, I warn you! For all he is a nob, he is sharp and can turn up in the unlikeliest places. Why, dammit, if you were not Lolly, he'd be just the sort to be sitting in your chair this very minute!" declared Bartholomew, laughing heartily.

Ned, of course, joined him. "H-how d-do y-you know that I am not himself?" he gasped through his mirth and they both of them exploded into laughter all over again.

When they had recovered themselves, Bartholomew cocked a wise eye at Ned and said: "Chum, do not think for one moment that I accepted you on only your say-so. I sent someone down to ease himself into a conversation with Natto Binger. Anyway, as to your being the Bow Street Gentleman—that is what they call him, you know—of course it is quite out of the question. You are good at acting the gentleman, I give you that, but you are not up to me on that score and, as I know I am not up to Denning . . . After all, he is the genuine article, don't you know."

Ned let out a sigh of deep relief. "Well, I must say that for once in my life, I am very pleased not to have been a bred-in-the-bone gent, for I'll wager you'd have slit my throttle ere this."

"It would have been a wager you'd have won hands down, old friend," replied Bartholomew nastily.

Just then a servant came in with a note for Bartholomew.

The master criminal, disregarding his guest, quickly opened and scanned it. Ned was amused. It was a small detail, this gaffe of not excusing himself to his company, but not a slip that Ned would ever have been guilty of. He'd have excused himself without thinking. It gave him a slight sense of superiority in that his masquerade was more perfect than Bartholomew's.

"Ah-hah!" cried Bartholomew. "Now shall everyone come to see how nicely all of London fits into my hand!" As he said this, his right hand closed itself into a fist. "Aye, and all of England, too! By the time the sun sets this day, you and I, my friend, can set ourselves to plunder this glorious country of ours with a will!"

"I say, Bonaparte is long dead, you know, and William the Conqueror has not been around for some centuries. *I* have no pretensions in that direction, so exactly who is to be your handmaiden in this exorbitant venture?" gibed Ned.

"You jeer, do you? Well, I shall tell you! The Honorable Robert Peel! How do you like *him* for my accomplice?"

Ned's heart sank. Could this contriving blackguard have the Home Secretary in his pocket, too? It was incredible—but, if true, his boast would be made good!

"You have Peel in your pocket?" he asked in unfeigned wonder.

"Oh, don't be a damned fool! The man is incorruptible—but he is doing my work for me. Against all opposition, he is introducing his police reform bill on the floor of the Commons today. It will be roundly defeated and that will be the end of it. They'll go on mucking about and, with my influence, it will only be a matter of time before I have bought Bow Street and the River Police— and what I cannot buy I shall destroy! Little by little the entire constabulary of Britain will be mine. I say, I think

146

I shall have myself appointed Home Secretary in a few years. No problem at all to buy the necessary votes for my membership in Parliament. Oh, then we shall see a day of days when I proceed to reform the police of the nation. Just think of it! My own personal army! I say, how would you like to become the Commanding General of the Metropolitan Police Force, Bartholomew-style?"

Ned got to his feet and bowed low. "Mr. Secretary, I shall follow you to the jaws of hell. I am your man, Honorable Sir."

Bartholomew let out an exultant laugh as he arose and came around to Ned. Clapping him on the shoulder, he cried: "Bono! You are the very lieutenant for me! Well, old man, I shall have to postpone our plans for the day, for I must go down to Westminster and witness Peel's defeat. I would not miss it for anything. Care to come along?"

"I'd love to, my friend, but my mates on the waterfront may be getting restless and, now that I know what is in store for us, I had better see to it that they give us no trouble. It will make things sweeter to have them with us than against us."

"That is good thinking, Lolly. You do that and I'll see you back here for tea—but it will be a deal headier stuff we shall be imbibing, eh?" He laughed, giving Ned a nudge in his ribs.

"Here's to my Lord Bartholomew!" cried Ned holding up an imaginary goblet.

Bartholomew, smiling broadly, quipped: "Well, all right for now, but only to begin with. 'Your Grace' would be something *more* my style!"

Ned waved good-bye to Bartholomew as the latter's carriage drew away from in front of the house on Soho Square. Then he began to stroll south towards the river. He went right past Coggshill as though he was not there and the latter took that to mean he was to remain at his post.

As Ned exited the square, he glanced quickly back at

Coggshill. The runner was nonchalantly leaning against a post, watching some children playing about the little park in the center of the square. Ned was satisfied, then, that he was not being followed and proceeded on his way, but not to the Thames bankside. The Bow Street Police Office lay in the same direction, and that was where he was headed. He'd have plenty of time to report to and consult with the Chief Magistrate so that they could put in order any arrangements that either of them deemed necessary.

It was an easy walk and he came down Bow Street at a saunter. He went right up to the building and entered. Barnstaple was on duty near the entrance. As he passed him, Ned muttered: "See if I have been followed."

Barnstaple strode out onto the street and looked quickly up the way Ned had come. He came back into the building and said: "I seen nothin' suspicious."

Ned nodded and went on into the hearing chamber.

Mr. Denning, appearing to be very irritable, was seated at the high bench, listening to a case. He looked up when Ned entered and shouted: "Where the devil have you been!"—thereby throwing the entire courtroom into great confusion.

"Your Honor, with all due respect, may I suggest we retire to your office?" requested Ned with a wink.

"Court is in recess!" proclaimed His Honor. He scrambled down from his high seat to lead his son back to his office.

"So!" he began. "You have managed to find something out from the look of you—but what in Creation are you working at? It would be so very nice if one's special constable was to inform one upon what matter he is wasting his time, especially when one's special constable is one's own son and has not slept in his own bed *two nights running!*"

"Sir, you will admit time is of the essence in the Beresford matter, and you will further admit that you never would have approved this strategem of mine."

148

"You are quite damnably correct, sir! Nor do I approve of it now, no matter what you may have learned!"

"That, I think, sir, is not even a moot point! Lend me your ear. . . ." Ned went on to detail all he had done and all he had learned. As he proceeded with his account, Mr. Denning's attitude underwent a radical change, and all he did was to nod during Ned's recitation.

Ned ended with a question. "Do you think, sir, that Peel's bill stands any chance?"

"If he succeeds in his maneuver to avoid debate in depth upon the floor, a very good one. But I see what you are driving at. If Peel fails, we shall just have to take our chances that Raike's and Benson's testimony will be sufficient to convict him."

"Exactly. I would suggest that, in any event, another man be sent out to assist us. He can take post in the square with Coggshill, for I do not know exactly what will transpire. We shall have to be prepared for any contingency."

"It shall be done. But I shall be getting word of the bill's fate as soon as anyone and we shall move to take Bartholomew at once if it is defeated," cautioned Mr. Denning.

"That means I must move more quickly with respect to the Beresford business. Unfortunately, I am no nearer an understanding of it. So it is difficult to guess at the best ruse to stir Bartholomew into showing his complete hand. I shall just have to play along, with the hope that something will turn up before you have to resort to that drastic step."

"Very well—but in that connection, we have come up with a name: Henry Conway. . . ." He went on to relay the facts that the general had given him, together with his own suspicions in the matter. "I have requested the local justice at Clapham to supply us with all information concerning the Beresford tragedy, and he has informed me that he will come in to town today to discuss it all with me. In fact, I imagine he will be here within

149

the hour. You will wish to sit down with us, I presume."

"I would like to very much, but I fear I shall have to forgo it. I have no wish to be seen like this. I shall go back to Soho Square."

"Not right away. You owe it to Lady Emily to let her see that you are all right. The poor dear is positively distraught and, of course, having been so myself, I could give her cold comfort."

"Sir, it is better if she does not see me. I shall never be able to prove myself worthy of—"

"Balderdash and rubbage! You go to see my lady, and that is an order!" cried Mr. Denning.

"But really! Like this? I'll not have time to change—and change back!"

"Go as you are! Go in the servant's entrance! Deliver something! Get her attention! For pity's sake, you know how to do these things better than anybody can! Now do so, and then get back to Bartholomew's! I'll send O'Shaughnessy out."

"Yes, sir—er—but not Shamus. Until we have a better idea, he ought to be keeping a watchful eye upon the general. For if, in the end, I fail, that is where the brunt of the attack must fall."

Mr. Denning pered at Ned. "You have a feeling?"

Ned nodded. "Yes, I do but I cannot reason it out for you."

"I know what you mean. I have had a similar feeling often enough and have learned to trust it. Do you have the least idea?"

"Bartholomew is so intent upon his ambitions that, if Peel should succeed, the resultant confusion in his thinking—Bartholomew's—might be all that is needed for me to take an appropriate action. It is that vague."

"It is enough. Go and do what you believe to be necessary. And give my love to Lady Emily."

Chapter XII

Emily was in her own little sitting room having an exhaustive discussion with her companion. The subject was the merit, or rather lack of same, in one Edward Denning. Most of her remarks anent that gentleman emphasized his negative qualities and her companion gave her every sign of agreement, even to the extent of thumping his great plume of a tail upon the floor.

"King, you do not have to agree with everything I say. You did like him once, I am sure. My trouble is he has quite turned my head and, really, I ought to turn it right around again."

There was a knock and Timmie entered. He was holding a note which he handed to her, saying: "They be a rough, evil-lookin' cove in the kitchen wi' cook. He said as I was to give ye this an' he'll await you pleasure, m'lady."

Emily, with her brow slightly furrowed, took the missive and broke the wafer. It was short and, glory be! in Ned's hand.

"My lady—If you would speak with me, the bearer will direct you.—Ned."

"Send the fellow to me," she commanded.

"By hisself?" asked Timmie doubtfully.

"Well, of course! Do you not think King Alfred will protect me?"

Timmie giggled and nodded vigorously. He ran off.

A few moments later she heard *his* footsteps in the hall and gazed at the doorway in great anticipation.

Despite the fact that she must know him anywhere, the man who entered was a Ned she had tried to imagine but could never succeed in picturing. The one glimpse she got of him, before King Alfred reared up to place his great paws upon his shoulders and lick his face, was of a very different sort of individual. There was an indefinable air about him that made of him a stranger to her.

Having satisfied His Majesty that his loyalty to his liege lord remained steadfast, Ned came to stand before her ladyship.

"So this is Lolly," murmured Emily as she gazed upon him.

A half smile twisted his lips, but he said nothing.

"You are so—so different! If we were to pass each other in the street, I think I should hesitate to speak to you. There is something so different about you, and I do not refer to what you are wearing. It is in your face, your expression . . ."

"You do not approve, my lady?" asked Ned lightly.

"How do you do it?"

"I assure you it *is* the clothes. Who would think to look for Edward Denning in a waterman's attire?"

"Clothes make the man, is that what you are saying? No, I tell you it is more than that. It is in your face. There is a raffish hardness in your eyes I have never seen before. Oh, Ned, I do not think I could have ever loved Lolly!"

"That is quite as it should be, for Lolly would never have looked so high as you, my lady."

"How long must you go on in this distasteful fashion?"

"My lady, Lolly and Ned are one and the same and it is not meet that you should care for the one, since he is the fool of the two. It would have been wiser to have

152

realized that the Bow Street Gentleman was, in truth, the masquerade."

"Oh, Ned, do not say such a horrid thing to me! You are only making me distressed when I would be so happy to see you again, hearty and whole. When will it all be over and you can come to me?"

"Never, my lady. My labors must ever yield jeopardy for me and my heritage remain a dim thing, always beyond my reach, not fit even for speculation."

"Ned, you would not say so if you loved me!"

"I do love you, Emily, but I am not fit company for you."

"You do not love me!"

"As you will, my lady," said Ned, his expression gone completely wooden.

"Before you leave, Mr. Denning," retorted Lady Emily, "know that our betrothal is at an end. I shall sit down the moment you are gone and indite a notice to that effect to appear in the *Gazette*!"

"I have assumed that you had already done so, my lady."

"Well, this time your assumption will be quite the truth!" she snapped.

"My lady," he said as he bowed and withdrew.

Lady Emily was as good as her word. With tears streaming down her cheeks, she immediately sat herself down at her writing table and penned an appropriate announcement to the *Gazette*. She rang for Timmie, handed it to him to deliver.

As soon as the lad had gone, she laid her head down upon the table and wept silently.

There was time enough, Ned thought, as he strolled leisurely north along Bow Street. It was just as well that he had stopped by to call upon Emily. Now she could no longer doubt his resolve and must make up her mind to forget him. But, he wondered, how in God's name was *he* to forget her? This last scene between them, unlike the first time he had intimated that he must renounce his

153

claim to her, had been performed in cold blood. There had been none of the passion of anger and disappointment to serve as anodyne for the pain it cost him. All that was behind him, its place taken by a wave of dolorous self-pity. Whatever hurt it must cause to Emily would be transitory, he was sure. Once back with the younger set of her own class, he would slip from her memory and she would forget him. Ah, but he, mongrel that he was, must pursue an existence forever haunted by the knowledge that, sooner or late, his duties must bring him into her presence time and again down through the years. Oh, what torture for him such meetings must be—to see her on the arm of some peer, her husband, she happy, living the sort of life he could never provide. But—it was the only way. There was a price to pay to insure her happiness, and fate had chosen him to be the one to pay it.

He was quite thankful that Bartholomew and the Beresford case were demanding so much of his attention and all of his intellect. It was not leaving him time to think about his own feelings—and he had better stop *feeling* about them right away if he was to survive. He had a most intense premonition that something was about to happen and he had best be ready for it.

He glanced up at a church steeple and noted that the day was growing late. He had thought to get a bite at some bakery shop on his way, but he had no appetite and so he continued on, moving a little more quickly.

As he came into Soho Square, he was pleased to see that Coggshill and Barnstaple were both lounging about the square at different points. As soon as it got dark enough they would melt into the shrubbery of the little park and keep on the alert.

Of course, neither one of them was wearing the vest that had given the Bow Street Runners the sobriquet of "Robin Redbreasts." He laughed to himself. The cartoonists in the periodicals made a deal more of that item than any runner worth his salt. Maintaining anonymity was ever more serviceable and went a far sight further towards preserving a runner's well-being than any badge of office. Except in the most routine of street patrols or arrests did he ever have any occasion to don it. Where O'Shaughnessy was concerned, it could not have made much difference. He had been around for so very long and he was such a giant of a man that, scarlet vest or no, everyone recognized O'Shaughnessy of Bow Street.

Ned strolled across the square and went right up to Bartholomew's door. He knocked and it was opened promptly by Wellers, all agrin with his arm in a sling.

"The master ain't returned yet, Lolly."

"I imagine he will be home shortly. How is the arm, old boy?"

"Aw, 't is naught but a scratch. Oh, that were the devil's own caper, that were! Ye gulled me proper that time. Ah, but if I could get me mauleys on yer, 't would ha' been a different tale I'd be telling."

Ned grinned. "I do not doubt it, for I could never stand up to you in a proper mill."

"Ah, yer a big man to admit it, Lolly."

"Thank you, Wellers," said Ned. He went on in, satisfied that he had made a friend.

He went through to the dining room and sat down, after he had poured himself a glass of Bartholomew's very fine sherry. At his ease, he lit up one of Bartholomew's very fine cigars and, between smoking and sipping, the time passed pleasantly enough.

He was just pressing out his cigar when Bartholomew, his face dark with anger, came bursting in.

"He beat me! Can you believe it? That colorless, upright saint beat me! The fools passed the bill! God, what a waste!" He began to pace the floor in a fury. "Close to ten thousand down the drain and I have not a thing to show for it! The New Metropolitan Police Force is as good as patrolling the streets of London this very minute."

Ned contained his joy with a great effort and devoted himself to the puzzle that Bartholomew's strange mood was confronting him with. He could understand the man's disappointment and his anger, but he could not see any reason for his air of desperation and total defeat.

"I say, Bartholomew, why all this heat? So what if Peel has got his police force? I do not see how that changes things so much."

"Ah, then indeed you are a dimwit, Lolly. Do you think we shall find it easier to go about our business with a policeman on every street every hour of the day and night?"

Ned shrugged. "Well, perhaps it will be less comfortable than it has been, but, speaking for myself, I have yet to see the member of the watch, be he charley or runner or constable, that I could not give the slip to."

"Oh? Then are you going to work all the lays yourself? For that is the only way left to you. Only the most skilled in your crew will be able to get away with anything. The others will be nabbed in the act or else they'll not even dare to try their luck. If that satisfies you, let me assure you it does not satisfy me. I'll not stand by and watch my take dwindle to a tenth of what I should rightfully be collecting. And that is all it will be, one week after Peel's army starts its march down the streets of the City. The numbskull! He has now got all of London in the palm of his hand, and I'll wager the greatest odds he'll never take advantage of it. What a hideous waste!"

"You think it will be as bad as all that, do you? I dare say I shall have to go back to the river," said Ned, his voice full of disappointment.

"Do you think for one moment it will be any different along the banks of the Thames? Look you, the River Police have done a rather neat job of fending you off of the boats on the river. These days it is mostly warehouses watched over by charleys and of course that is not so difficult since Bow Street, with little more than a half dozen runners at its disposal, cannot afford to spend any time upon you. But that is going to change now, I tell you. I have had my ear to the ground and I know. Think what it will be, Lolly, when you have to contend with hundreds, nay, thousands, of these new policemen. Be they the worst sort of constables you can imagine, even a few dozen of 'em along the shore and you'll not be having anything like the success you have had!"

"Well, burn me! What's a cove to do? If that is to be the way of it, I had best hie me back across the pond."

Bartholomew stopped in his pacing and turned to him. "No, I have a need for you. Oh, we shall leave this blasted town all right but not for the continent. They've still not recovered from Napoleon's looting. I never thought it would come to this, but I have thought it wise to at least think about it, so I am not as unprepared for this defeat as you might think." He paused thoughtfully. "I have it in mind to quit England for America! They call it the land of opportunity—I have a mind to make that opportunity mine!" he declared dramatically.

Ned's eyes narrowed. He was beginning to feel relieved. If that was how Bartholomew was thinking, then General Beresford, one could assume, was not all that important to him.

"What do you say, Lolly? How does the sound of America, the land of opportunity, strike you?"

"I suppose they do have rivers and, therefore, it follows that they must have mudlarks as well," he said with a smile.

"Capital! Now look you, speed is of the essence—and secrecy. If my people knew that I was about to do a bunk—well, I do not have to say more, you understand. They must not know!"

"I understand well enough. Rats and a sinking ship and all that."

Bartholomew conferred a look of disgust on him. "This is not the time for niceties—or, if that is humor, we can do without it."

"May I inquire what need is there for haste? America will be there for the longest time, considering we tried to end its career twice and failed miserably each time."

"Oh, bother your witticisms at a time like this! What do you think is going to happen here a month from now? Once these Peelers begin to make their presence known, it will be all up with the likes of us. There will be no more fat pickings and our colleagues will find themselves faced with a Tyburn ticket every time they look around. They are bound to get wise to the unhappy prospects and begin to pull up stakes. They'll scatter like the wind out of England. Most of them, like you, will immediately make for the continent, but those who are at the top of the stairs in this profession will see the continent as I see it: picked over and bare. They'll be looking for greener pastures than that and the wiseacres amongst 'em, who have got more than a feather to fly with, will set sail for the greenest pasture of them all: America!

"Well, I intend to get there long before it dawns upon them that the British sun has set for them. And I know just the spot to choose. It is always best to locate yourself in the capital of a country, but Washington is little more than a cow pasture and a ruined one at that, I should imagine. After all, what can be left of it after we burned it to the ground in '14? New York and Boston are both good prospects but they are too far from the capital. I have plans for the United States, and a few congressmen—even a President or two—in my pocket are a prerequisite. That leaves Philadelphia and Baltimore. The former has too much a Quaker flavor to my taste, so there you have it. Baltimore! Open to the sea, only a day's ride from the capital, a perfect place to set up our shop, I think."

Ned was amazed at the boundless ambition of the man. At the same time he realized that he was faced with a dilemma. He knew that Bartholomew was not the principal in the Beresford matter and, therefore, he could not sit idly by and let Bartholomew leave the country until he had gained from him the whereabouts of the general's enemy. Assuming that it was this Conway chap, he needed a clue as to where he might be found. Bartholomew was, to his knowledge, the only one who could provide him with it. And, too, it went against his soul that such a villain as Bartholomew should escape the King's Justice. For the moment, all he could think to do was to humor the man and hope that something would give itself away.

Ned nodded enthusiastically. "I say, you have got it up there all right! You have really put your mind to it and come up with a prize. Have you ever been to America before?"

Bartholomew shrugged. "No, but what has that to say to anything? People are born to be gulls for the benefit of those who can gull 'em and, if I am to have my choice, I prefer English-speaking gulls to any other kind."

"Hear! Hear!"

"Then you'll come?"

"I am completely at your disposal, my lord. I say! They have no peerage over there, you know. What can you hope to achieve?"

"Oh, that is easy!" said Bartholomew. "The only thing they seem to worship in the states. Namely, wealth!"

They both laughed heartily at that and had themselves a bit of brandy to help savor the humor of it.

Bartholomew got up and began to pace the floor again. "Now, we have got to hurry! I shall look into sailings the first thing and—oh, my God!"

He wheeled upon Ned. "How much money do you have?"

Ned pursed his lips, dove his hand into his pocket, and came up with a few pound notes and some coins.

"Is that all of it?" asked Bartholomew incredulously.

"Aye, that is my entire fortune until a week from now when a particular ship comes into dock from Ostend."

"Oh, that is much too late! I tell you we are in a fix! I have only five hundred to my hand."

"Is that all?" exclaimed Ned, incredulously.

"Don't be an idiot, you ass! Of course, I have more than that but I cannot get at it. It is all out in investments. Where do you think the cents-per-cents get the money they lend out? Who do you think sports the gilt for my pets to live on until I call upon them to do their duty for me? We cannot wait for your boat from Ostend and we cannot wait for my lucre either. We have got to set sail immediately. We'll have to arrange for our funds to follow us. We can do that once we are safely settled in Baltimore—but five hundred pounds is just not enough! And we have so little time!" he wailed.

"It will more than pay our fare across the herring pond, I should think."

"And what shall we have left to go to work with when we get there—even live on, for that matter? We need at least three hundred more!"

Ned shook his head doubtfully. "It would take a handsome lay to raise that much. There are plenty of juicy cribs to crack but we'd need time to plan for any of them."

"And we have no time—wait! I have it! Now why did I not think of him before! Yes, I know where we can get at least a monkey, perhaps even more."

"For the asking?"

"Well, it will not be as easy as all that! He's a rough customer, has apartments to let, I think, and we both of us shall have to deal with the loony. Might even have to snaffle the beggar. Are you game?"

"Where shall we find him?"

"Not far. Clapham. We'll leave now so that we can get there by dark."

The name of the place struck a chord in Ned's memory, and he wondered. He shot his eyebrows up in enthusiasm. "Sounds a rum lay to me, Bartholomew!" he remarked approvingly.

Chapter XIII

In response to his master's ring, Wellers came into the room.

"Yes, master?"

"Wellers, have my phaeton brought round with my best pair in harness."

"Hold fast, Wellers!" commanded Ned. He turned to Bartholomew. "We shall be travelling in the dark. Do you have decent lanterns on the rig?"

"Of course, what could I have been thinking of! Wellers, make it the light coach and see the lamps are filled and trimmed. It is too much vehicle for my bloods, so see to it that Lord Nelson and the Iron Duke are hitched to it." He turned to Ned. "Now there's a pair to go with! Not the flashiest beasts, but nothing can stop 'em."

It was difficult for Ned not to believe that Clapham must still be a link with Conway, and this fortuitous turn of events acted like a tonic upon him. He had had nothing to eat since breakfast and now his stomach began to complain.

Bartholomew blinked at him and gave him an odd stare.

"Damme," laughed Ned. "I quite forgot to eat today, there has been so much doing. If you don't mind, I shall go down to the kitchen and have a bit of bread and cheese."

"Well now, there is plenty of time for that. I will have a cold collation prepared. I might as well join you. I imagine we shall have to forgo tea this day, and our supper will be a late one. Wellers, see to it!"

The butler-cum-bodyguard withdrew.

Bartholomew turned to Ned. "You are a waterman, so you should know. What is scheduled to leave for the states?"

Ned shook his head. "I have not been back in my old haunts long enough to be up with the sailings. In any case, we mudlarks are far more interested in what is coming in."

"Goods are goods, coming in or going out!" retorted Bartholomew flatly.

"Not so, Bartholomew! What is going out is for the most part of domestic manufacture and carries no premium. What is coming in, what with the duties on it, we can sell it for a handsome profit, yet at a great deal less than the merchant chumps." He laughed. "We even sell their own goods back to 'em. In short, it's the smuggling lay without having to cross the channel."

"Hmmmmm, yes, of course. Never thought of that. Excellent! No reason why it should not be the same in America and, Baltimore being a port, all our longshore enterprises shall be yours to oversee to start."

"Yes, indeed, there is nothing like a fresh start to put new life in a man."

Bartholomew laughed. "Very good that. We both of us shall be turning over a new leaf. Won't the Archbishop of Canterbury be thrilled to hear of it!"

The food was served and both men began to dine. In a little while they had eaten their fill and, as the carriage was waiting, they prepared to leave.

"Do you have a weapon?" asked Bartholomew as he drew out his little pistol and checked it.

"I have Weller's knife," replied Ned with a grin, and he slipped it out from beneath his rough jacket.

"I don't suppose he gave it to you," remarked Bartholomew with a smile. "But surely you will want something with a greater reach."

Ned flipped his hand and the knife streaked across the room almost too fast for the eye to follow it. It brought up quivering, stuck deep into the paneling. "Now I should say that that is as far as your toy barker will reach with any accuracy—and my way is something quieter, don't you think?"

Bartholomew shook his head in wonder. "Lolly, you are full of surprises! I should never have taken you for a chiving cove."

Ned arose and went to retrieve his knife. "There's many a cully who made the same mistake, and I am sorry to say few of them lived to regret it."

"What? Oh, yes, yes!" exclaimed Bartholomew as the point of Ned's remark came clear to him. "I am learning not to underestimate you, my friend. Shall we go?"

They left the house and Bartholomew mounted up onto the box, saying: "I'll do the driving myself. Hoist yourself up alongside. My coachman would only be so much more dead weight in the event we should have to make a run for it." He was looking over the square as he chatted.

Ned mounted up beside him and they started up.

Bartholomew went along at a leisurely pace, taking the first turn out of the square. Then he headed north.

"Clapham's to the southwest," remarked Ned.

"Didn't you see what was in the square?"

"What was in the square?"

"A pair of redbreasts! Now, hold on!" he shouted, and he whipped up the horses. Rolling along at a great rate, he tooled the carriage into an alley and they tore through it with very little room to spare on either side of them. Fortunately it was deserted or there must have been a tragedy.

Breaking out on Berwick Street, Bartholomew headed south, twisted and turned a bit and got them onto Charing Cross Road, where he slowed the horses down to a more normal pace.

Ned had had to cling tightly to his seat during the wild maneuvers. His heart sank, for he doubted that either Barnstaple or Coggshill had been prepared to follow all that quickly.

As they continued to amble along, Ned remarked: "I saw no runners."

"Well, I did!" retorted Bartholomew. "Did you expect to see red vests when they are stationed to keep a watch on me? In any event, I know all the runners. It's my business to know them or I'd have had unpleasant business with Bow Street long since," he boasted.

Ned could not resist it. "Then you know Denning, too?"

"Of course I do, but the trouble with that fellow is, you never can be sure it is him you are seeing. He is very skilled at masquerade. I'll wager give him but a moment to look at you, and in less time than it takes to tell, you would be having a twin brother."

"You don't say! He must be something new in the Bow Street line. I dare say he could cause you quite a bit of trouble."

"Well, he has not, and for a very good reason."

"What might that be?"

"It will require more than one runner to take me, of that you may be sure and, if I do not recognize him, I'll recognize his chums—just as I did back at the house. He can never get close to me."

"I am relieved to hear it. Now, what about this Raike and Benson pair? Your people?"

Bartholomew gave him a suspicious look. "What do you know of Raike and Benson?"

Ned grinned. "Ah, then they *are* yours! That is the rumor going up and down the river. They've split on you."

Bartholomew glanced at him in disgust. "It was to be expected. They are a pair of bunglers!"

"Then Bow Street has *got* something on you! Maybe it

is best that you cut your stick. Your luck is not holding, it appears to me."

"Ha!" snorted Bartholomew. "Don't think for one moment that Bow Street can scare *me* off! If I'd have beaten Peel, I would certainly have remained here in London. Whatever Raike and Benson might have confessed to in the lock-up, they'd never have been able to repeat it on the witness stand at Old Bailey—not with their gullets slit, they would not. They can thank their good fortune that I'll not need to bother with 'em."

"What do they have on you?"

"Well, aren't we inquisitive!" exclaimed Bartholomew sourly.

"Hell, man, we've a long ride ahead of us! I'm just making conversation. What do you think—I'll be off to Bow Street first thing with the information? Me, Lolly, who they'd like everyone to believe is long dead and buried? For all *I* know the pair of beaks we left behind in Soho might be on the prowl for me! They just might have picked up a rumor that I am about and liable to kick up a fuss or two. Bow Street people are not the brightest in the world, but it never hurts to overestimate 'em, I always say."

Bartholomew chuckled. "Aye, you make your point and, truly, I see no reason to hide the matter from you. After tonight you'll be as much a part of it as I will. Actually this queer fish we are going to call on in Clapham is the cause of it all. Now it is not exactly a secret that, for a handsome fee, I can arrange to have a fellow's problem's given the final solution. Sometimes it is that the wrong person was made the rightful heir or, perhaps, it is that one's partner in business will not sell out or he will sell out or, as in this case, it is just the luxury of revenge that is wished for. This Conway we are going to meet with was an officer under Wellington and he was cashiered by a chap, Beresford. Happened many years ago and now Beresford's a general and retired and our chap is rusticating in Clapham near an old burned-out estate. Apparently he is one of those romantic imbeciles with a taste for ruins by moonlight or some such twaddle. Well, anyway, Conway claims it was sheer injustice brought on by envy, with regard to Beresford's persecution of him, and he would settle accounts. Naturally, I do not give one little damn what his motives are as long as he can stand buff. Well, it seems he can. He has got the rhino. His family refused to have anything more to do with him and they put him on remittance, hoping, I suppose, that he'd go off to Australia or America and lose himself in the wilderness. But he did not choose to do so. Instead he has been slowly amassing some sizeable amount just so he would have enough to afford making an arrangement for the removal of the general from the face of the earth.

"It was but a few weeks ago that I received a note from the old gent and went down to Clapham to discuss matters with him. I never leave these negotiations to anyone else. For one thing it is not safe and, for another, they would never get the prices I do. I saw Conway and we talked. I quoted a price of four hundred pounds and he did not even blink. I'll wager he'd not have flinched if I'd asked six hundred!

"Now this is where those two incompetents, now reposing in the Bow Street lock-up, come into the business. I gave them the lay and, to make a long story short, they made a complete muff of everything. Can you imagine such ineptness? Oh, I hope they rot in quod forever! Imagine it! Beresford's well past his prime—why, he must be as old as my client, of course. Twice they went to do the bit. The first time he beat 'em off with a measly walking-stick, the cowardly louts, and the second time—well, you will not believe it! You absolutely will not believe what happened the second time! It was a dog, a damned lap dog cornered them and they were taken!" He burst into sardonic laughter.

Ned easily shared his mirth. King Alfred a lap dog? What could be funnier!

"I suppose one cannot be too careful how one goes about selecting one's people," remarked Ned.

"Oh, here now, do not go casting reflections upon my judgment! Raike and Benson are assassins of reputation or I'd not have picked 'em. They have done work for me before and they have done it well. I have not the vaguest idea what came over them. Truly, it was the simplest task."

"Is not four hundred pounds a mighty handsome figure for so simple a piece of work? I should have thought seventy-five, even fifty, more than adequate."

"Now there is where you and I differ, Lolly, and you will have to change your style of thinking and come up to the mark with me if we are to get along. Always calculate what the traffic will bear and then add a fifth more. Even then you will invariably discover that your bid is too low by half. That is what I suspect is the case with Conway."

"What about Conway?"

"Well, I know he has my fee in hand and, I dare say, quite a bit more. We shall relieve him of it—kill him if we must. It isn't necessary as far as I am concerned since his hands are no cleaner than mine—but his fate will depend upon his cooperation."

Ned snickered. "Seems a shame to take a bloke's ducats for a job not done."

Bartholomew sniggered. "True, but the old fool can do the job himself. He's hot enough for it."

They were crossing the Westminster Bridge over to the Surrey side when Ned yawned and stretched, looking about him in a lackadaisical manner. He settled back down in his seat and he was very content. His sharp eyes had caught a glimpse of a gig well back in the distance with Coggshill at the reins. There was a feeling of pride welling up within him at the thought that the likes of a braggart like Bartholomew was so far out in his estimation of a Bow Street Runner's capability of hanging onto his man.

He was extremely encouraged. The game was his. Before many more hours had passed, he was sure that both Conway and Bartholomew would be in his bag.

They came over into Lambeth and went east until they came to Kennington Road. Bartholomew turned south onto it, heading for Clapham Road. The sun was going down behind the towers and chimney pots of London just over the river they had crossed and it would be dark by the time they had reached their destination. Everything was quite in order. Bartholomew's mood bespoke his satisfaction and, needless to say, Ned was quite elated with how things were turning out.

"How many shall we have to contend with?" asked Ned.

"Oh, that will be no problem. Not at all. He lives alone with a manservant and a cook. We shall have no trouble with those two. The servant, whom I have seen, is an old gaffer and I see no reason that the cook would not be of an age with him, as they are man and wife. Charity cases, the both of them, I should imagine; just the sort of thing that would appeal to Conway. If he was not as mad as a hatter on this eye-for-an-eye thing, I'd not be surprised if he were as balmy over something else, money, for instance—which would not please me half so well."

He pulled over to the side of the road. "We had better light the lamps now. We shall be coming into Clapham Road and the light is just about gone. It is a straight piece and we'll have no difficulty finding our way. Nevertheless, this is not a time for a smash-up with another carriage."

Ned jumped down and lit the side lamps. It was too dim to see the gig and, if it were behind them, Coggshill would never have lit up his lamps. Even as he wondered whether Coggshill was still trailing them, the gig came up and was by them, going at a brisk trot. It disappeared into the darkness ahead.

Ned smiled to himself. It was a maneuver to let him know that assistance was at hand and, at the same time, to throw off suspicion if any had arisen. Coggshill would be waiting near to the junction a little ahead and would pick them up again as they came past him.

Bartholomew cursed as Ned mounted up to the box. "Devil burn him! Did you see that idiot, driving by as cool as you please in pitch blackness and never showing a light? Damn good thing we stopped when we did to light up or that blamed fool would have run us down, I am sure! It's a damned good thing we are not in a rush, for I have not the least doubt we should be running into him before this night is over."

He urged up the horses and the coach began to roll.

"I wonder about that chap," said Bartholomew as they moved along. "Noticed him behind us as we crossed over. After all, he might have been one of our chums from Bow Street. But now I am sure he is not. Little as I admire those red-vested runners, I am sure the least of 'em has the sense not to go driving about in the dark without a single light burning."

By that time they were coming out upon Clapham Road. Bartholomew eased into it with caution and then urged the horses into a trot. There were scattered lights in the distance, and the silhouettes of desultory vehicles traveling along before them could be discerned.

"Well, that is better," commented Bartholomew. "He is probably somewhere ahead of us. Since they all of them are lighted up, I venture to say he has come to his senses and decided to do the proper. We shall be there shortly. I think it is just as well there is no moon up tonight."

"Aye," responded Ned, "but I'll be glad when it is over and we are safely tucked in for the night. This has been a mighty busy day."

"I never thought to ask—not that it makes much difference now. Did you settle things with Binger?"

Ned shrugged. "Things would have worked out well enough if there'd been the need. 'T was a sheer waste."

"Yes, it was. Oh, well, let us look upon the bright side—and Mr. Henry Conway's wallet is all the brightness we shall need. Here we are!" he said as he pulled the horses to a stop.

"Exactly so, Bartholomew; this is as far as you go! I

arrest you in His Majesty's name on a charge of conspiring to murder one Sir Alonzo Beresford."

"What the devil!" cried Bartholomew, turning to glare at Ned in the dim glow shed by the side lamps. He was fumbling at his midriff.

"It is no use, my dear fellow," said Ned. "Don't you recognize the pistol I am holding on you? I relieved you of it almost as soon as we had left the house."

"Who the devil are you? You are not Lolly after all!"

"Allow me to introduce myself. I am Edward Denning, special constable out of Bow Street. One false move and you shall receive a ball where it will not do you the least good."

He snatched the reins from out of Bartholomew's nerveless hands and called out: "Coggshill! To me!"

At once a horse was heard to start up and in a moment the unlit gig had drawn up alongside.

Drily, Ned remarked: "You had best light your lamps now, as Bartholomew here has a distinct dislike of drivers who drive about all dark."

Coggshill laughed and jumped down. He lit the lamps on his little vehicle and stood waiting.

"What have you got, Ned?"

"Bartholomew, and on a charge of attempted murder for a start. He's told me enough to hang him high on all the gibbets in the kingdom. There will be no lack of evidence once we start rounding up his people."

"Blast you, Lolly—or Denning! You are a most underhanded blackguard and not fit to be associated with! You certainly are no gentleman!"

Ned laughed. "Listen to the pot calling the kettle black!"

"But, dammit, you *are* Lolly! We had got Binger's word on it—he swore you were Lolly! He knew you from of old! If I hang, you will be swinging beside me! Bow Street will only be too happy to see your ghost laid for good and all. You told me so yourself!"

"As to that, my dear friend, the ghost of Lolly was well laid many years ago. I am Denning, the master of masquerade, and that is something *you* said yourself—that I could make myself to be Lolly's twin brother. Well, O'Shaughnessy knew Lolly as well as anybody and I had his help with the disguise and the mannerisms. I fear it is all up with you, my fine-feathered friend. You have been gulled just as thoroughly as Binger. Do you think I should have come to you if I had not been able to fool Binger? So do not feel too badly as you were not my only pigeon. Coggshill, go round to the other side and help this *gentleman* down. Put out your wrists, Bartholomew! I imagine you've never felt cold iron on them before. I doubt that you will enjoy it."

Deftly he fitted the manacles to Bartholomew's wrists and motioned him to descend. Then he followed him down.

He turned to Coggshill and said: "Jamie, the game is not fully played out. In yonder house dwells a Henry Conway. We want him in connection with the assaults upon General Beresford. He's an old lunatic and will be dangerous if he is armed. He's a cashiered officer, so he will know how to use a weapon. I'll go in and take him while you see to this dogmeat's comfort."

"Ned, I know you ain't taking a share in the reward, so do you let me earn mine. You watch his nibs and I'll go in and collar the old goat."

"Very well. Shout if you need help."

Coggshill sauntered up the short drive to the little cottage and knocked upon the door. Ned could just make out that he was talking with someone quietly. The door was closed and Coggshill came back.

"Your bird has flown the coop, old chum. Manservant says he's gone to the City. Very upset and mumbling and drooling sort of—so the butler says."

"What was he mumbling about? Did the man say?"

"Somethin' 'bout doin' it himself, and he was cursing a blue streak. What do you make of it?"

"How long ago did Conway leave?"

"At dark. Damn strange time to start for London, I'd say."

"How is your horse?"

"My horse? Fine. It was an easy jaunt."

"I am going to take him. You take Bartholomew back with you in the coach. We'll chain him to the box. I have got to move quickly. Conway has gone into town to do the general proper, but perhaps I can catch up with him. Did O'Shaughnessy take up a post with the general?"

"Aye."

"Good. Well, let us get Bartholomew snugged down. Up you go, friend!"

In a matter of minutes they had Bartholomew with both of his hands chained to the handrail on the box. Ned was not satisfied and he took Coggshill's set of manacles and chained the prisoner's feet together. While he worked he remarked that Bartholomew was a slippery customer and nothing was to be left to chance. "Watch him like a hawk until you have got him safe inside the lock-up, and remember, he's to have no visitors until His Honor says he may—or we'll wind up with a corpse instead of a defendant. It would be nothing more than what he would have done for Benson and Raike and he still may try to arrange it. Shoot him like the dog he is at the first sign of trouble. If there's a choice to be made, I'd rather have him dead than free."

Ned then mounted into the gig, turned it about and dashed off for London. He went at smart clip. He hoped that if he pressed his beast he might beat Conway to the general's house. Conway would not be in so great a rush since he had no idea that Bow Street was onto him and coming fast.

Chapter XIV

The gig careened wildly as Ned wheeled it sharply around a corner into the street in which General Beresford resided. He rattled up to the general's house and, before the little vehicle had stopped rolling, he had leaped from it and was running up to the door. As he went he drew forth both his own pistol and the one he had lifted from Bartholomew. With the barrel of one of them he rapped loudly upon the door panel, shouting: "Open in the name of the law! O'Shaughnessy, are you all right in there?" thinking to discourage Conway if there was still time.

The door swung open and he dashed in, only to be stopped in his tracks as two great arms wrapped themselves about him and held him fast. In the sudden relief from tension, he began to laugh heartily as the huge Irishman exclaimed: Ned, lad, whatever has got inter ye?"

O'Shaughnessy released him and Ned put his weapons away.

"How is the general? Is he all right?"

"Right 'n' tight, me lad! We ha' been swappin' great tales together. Now what unholy devilment has gotten inter ye? I heerd ye had gone back ter the river."

"Yes, yes, Shamus, I'll tell you all about it, but take me to the general. The gaffer has got me worried sick!"

"Of course, me boy, of course. We're settin' in the parlor. General says as how I takes me orders only from Mr. Denning an' yersel', I has got ter be at least a colonel, an' generals an' colonels ha' been known to take drinks together." O'Shaughnessy winked and laughed as he led Ned into the parlor.

"Ah, Ned, I was sure it was you! Welcome! Welcome! Where in God's name did you disappear to?"

"Whew!" exclaimed Ned, grasping the general's outstretched hand and pumping it vigorously as though he had to reassure himself that, in truth, the elderly gentleman was quite unharmed. "I have quite a tale to tell but, Shamus, are you quite sure the house is all secure? Conway has decided to take matters into his own hands. I raced to get here before him. It would appear that I have won."

"All the good it will do you, for I take the prize!" cried a harsh voice. A grizzled man in a top hat and a dark suit stepped into the room. A large military pistol in his hand was pointed at them. In his other hand he carried a black iron jimmy.

Ned felt horrible. The very noise that he had made on arriving had only served to cover up the sounds of Conway's forcible entry.

As the three of them stood aghast, staring at the intruder, Conway said venomously: "Well, Beresford, it has taken me all this time to see you, the last of your lot, destroyed. I've done for the nest and now it is the viper's turn. Oh, how I wish I could make you suffer the tortures that you condemned me to, but I can see you have company and they'll slay me if I but give them half a chance. They can have all the chance they wish, but only after I have lodged my ball in your heart."

With that he pointed the pistol at the general and fired point blank. Right on its heels a second shot rang out and caught him in the stomach. It was a fearful wound and the impact of the ball slammed him back against the door jamb. His glaring eyes started to glaze over as he slid to the floor, his hand clutching at his midriff. With a superhuman effort, he shouted in a hoarse whisper: "*Damn! Damn! Da—*" He was dead.

And slumped down at the general's feet was Ned. He had hurled himself into the line of fire, had taken for himself the ball intended for the general.

"Lolly!" cried O'Shaughnessy, his voice cracking with horror and anguish. He tossed his smoking pistol aside and fell to his knees before the inert form and drew what was left of Ned into his arms. "Oh, Lolly, lad," he crooned, "ye're not hurt! Tell me ye're not hurt! Lolly, 't is Shamus, yer ol' frien'! Lolly, give us a smile, lad! His Honor's waitin' to have a bout wi'ye. Say, lad, ye'll not be keepin' His Honor waitin' now, will ye?"

Suddenly he came out of his funk and glanced up at the general, who was staring down at the strange tableau, frozen in shock, his face one great question mark.

In a tone of urgency mixed with annoyance, Shamus shouted: "Don't ye stan' there, sir! Ned's been grievously wounded! Help me get him to a doctor!"

The general came to with a start, and a mask dropped over his face. He was all business.

"Higgins!" he shouted even as his man came running into the room all breathless. "Go at once and fetch Mr. Roberts. We have a grievously wounded man here, so let there be not an instant's delay! Report to me with the doctor! Go!"

General Beresford stooped down alongside of O'Shaughnessy. "Let me have him, Shamus. I dare say I've had more experience with this sort of thing in my lifetime than even you."

He gently lifted Ned's lapel aside and bared the wound as, at the same time, his fingers sought the young man's throat. "Thank God!" he breathed. "There's a pulse. We have got to staunch the flow of blood. The ball is just below his shoulder. It cannot have touched his lung or he would be bleeding from his nose as well.

175

It's a bad wound, but I am relieved to say it should not be mortal. Give me your knife if you have one."

O'Shaughnessy handed him a formidable pig-sticker, a great clasp knife, and the general began to cut away at Ned's shirt.

"Shamus, go up to my bedchamber. One of the cupboards has fresh linen. Bring me all you can carry."

"Yes, sir." The runner left at heavy trot.

"Well, that's a mercy!" muttered the general. "The ball has plugged the hole for the time being. Now where in hell is that damnation surgeon? The ball has got to come out!"

Once he had finished doing what he could do with the wound, he sat down on the floor alongside of Ned and gazed long and hard into the young man's face, his lips working as though he was repressing himself.

In a little while, O'Shaughnessy came treading back into the room, his arms loaded with bed linen. He was very startled to see the general bent over Ned. It looked to him as though the general might be praying.

"General, sir, is he . . . ?"

General Beresford shook his head. "No, it is all right! He lives!—But where is that idiot of a doctor!"

And just at that point Mr. Roberts came bustling into the room.

Without a word, he knelt down at Ned's side, took his pulse, nodded, and then looked closely at the wound. "This one can be saved, sir!" He arose and was about to start over to Conway's remains.

"Roberts, forget that one! He is beyond your help! But this one we must save, do you understand?"

"Yes, sir. You!" he called to O'Shaughnessy. "You shall have to serve as my orderly!"

Sir Alonzo stepped forward. "No, Roberts, I shall serve."

"Oh, I say, sir—" the doctor began to protest.

"Surgeon, that young man took the ball that was intended for me! I shall serve him in any way I can."

"Yes, sir. Er—sir, would you be kind enough—"

"Roberts!" snapped the general. "Forget my rank! Consider that this is the peninsula and that is Wellington under your hand. You are the ranking officer in this house until that young man is out of danger! Now what are your orders! Spit 'em out, man!"

"Yes, sir!" The doctor took a deep breath and began to order the general about as though he were a mere surgeon's assistant and the general served him better than any assistant he ever had attend him in his entire military and medical careers.

By the time that dawn was beginning to thin out the night's darkness, poor Higgins was quite run off his feet.

When he had returned with Mr. Roberts, he was immediately put to the labor of assisting the huge Bow Street runner with the removal of that horrid Mr. Conway's body. And it was no more easy to accomplish than it was pleasant. Although Conway had had in life that "lean and hungry look," unlike Cassius he was, nevertheless, quite corpulent and made a bit of a load. As they lurched off down the hall with their gruesome burden, the general was heard to call out: "Dispose of that carrion where you will, and if the resurrection men should evince an interest in it, they may have it for the taking! In truth, I'll give 'em each a gold piece and consider it a bargain!"

Such an awful thought was too much for Higgins, who froze with horror until O'Shaughnessy frowned and motioned with his head to disregard the general and proceed on out.

Having completed the job of laying Mr. Conway's remains out by the front hedge, he was then ordered to take a vehicle and drive to Mr. Denning's residence and bring the magistrate back with him.

Not being one who drove with any great dash, the trip in the darkness was for him an ordeal. The trip *over* to the Dennings' was bad enough, but the trip *back* was such as to put him into a state of mortal terror. Mr. Denning, after the first few yards of travelling at Higgins's

177

timid pace, snatched the reins out of his hands and proceeded to urge the horse along like some lunatic jehu. Needless to say, the return journey was but half as long as had been the one going out. Higgins was sure that his heart had stopped beating a dozen times if it had stopped once, so recklessly did the magistrate drive the carriage.

Mr. Denning, all impatience, tossed the reins back at Higgins and leaped from the carriage while it was still rolling. He raced up to the front door and was met by O'Shaughnessy.

"Where is he?" he demanded, his face pale and taut.

O'Shaughnessy pointed towards the parlor and Mr. Denning strode down the hall and entered it.

By this time the surgeon had removed the ball, and the patient was lying on a sofa, still unconscious.

Sir Alonzo came to meet Mr. Denning and there was look of fatigue on his countenance.

"My boy! How is my boy?" asked Mr. Denning with great anxiety.

The general gave him a strange look and answered: "Your adopted son is out of danger, Alec."

Mr. Denning went to Ned's form on the couch and looked at him. His bandaged shoulder was revealed where the blanket had slipped down. Tenderly, Mr. Denning replaced it.

Mr. Roberts came up to him and the general introduced him. The surgeon explained that everything that could be done for the young man had been done and that, as far as he could tell, there was no danger beyond the usual risk of infection in a wound of that nature. Nevertheless, there had been a great shock to the system and he could not be responsible if the young man was to be moved at this point. He thought that, depending upon the recuperative powers of the patient, six weeks to a month of absolute rest might be required. He believed that the young man was a fine physical specimen and the odds were mainly in his favor if an infection of the wound were to develop. That possibility, of course, he could not predict one way or another.

Mr. Denning listened to every word he had to say and, at the end, he turned to General Beresford with a strong plea in his eyes.

The general placed a consoling hand upon his shoulder and said: "Alec, of course he must remain here! And look you, there is plenty of room. I pray you will stay here with us for as long as you care to."

"I thank you from the bottom of my heart, Alonzo, for your kindness, but I may not. With Ned down and the New Police forming up, I may not impose upon you, much as I should love to. As the press of my duties will permit, I will come a-calling and it will be a blessing to know that he is being cared for by someone who is concerned for him."

"Alec, never doubt it! I should be a corpse at this moment were it not for his sacrificing himself for me."

"Sacrifice?" asked Mr. Denning astounded. "What are you telling me?"

"I shall tell you all about it—but come into the other room so that we do not disturb him. Roberts believes he will sleep through the night. Is that not so, surgeon?"

"Yes, sir, and I shall call tomorrow, in the morning, to see how he is getting on. What time would be best?"

"We keep a military mess in this house, Roberts. Why do you not join us for breakfast?"

"Very good, sir. It will be my pleasure. Good night, sir. If the patient should appear to be in pain before I come, I have left some laudanum with Mr. O'Shaughnessy and instructed him in its dosage. Good night—or should I say 'good morning,' gentlemen? I shall be with you in a few hours."

He departed.

"Higgins, get to your rest, what little there is left of it," said the general.

"Yes, sir. Thank you, sir." And he went off to bed.

O'Shaughnessy stepped forward. "Your Honor, hadn't I best get back to the office?"

"Yes, of course, Shamus."

"In that case, I'll leave the drops wi' you, sir, if ye don't mind."

Mr. Denning looked at him uncertainly and raised a troubled hand to his forehead. "I—I don't know a thing about this sort of thing."

The general intervened. "That is quite all right, Shamus. Leave it with me. I'll see to it."

"Thank 'ee, sir," and O'Shaughnessy left to return to Bow Street.

Taking Mr. Denning by the arm, Sir Alonzo led him gently out of the drawing room and into the morning room. There he sat him down and brought over a decanter and two glasses.

"It has been a strenuous time for us all, Alec, but I do believe that the worst of it is over," he said. He began to pour. "This will help to restore us and we can talk a bit."

"Yes," said Mr. Denning, beginning to take control of himself. "Yes, Alonzo, I shall need your statement as to what has occurred—for our files, you will understand."

"Indeed, I understand," agreed General Beresford with a smile.

Chapter XV

General Beresford raised his glass for another sip. His mouth was a little dry, what with all the pother of this night and having to detail it in its entirety for Alec Denning.

Mr. Denning appeared to be unhappy about something, disappointed, more like. He stared into his glass and remained that way for a moment or so, wrapped in his thoughts.

"I say, Alec, it was a fearful price to pay," said the general, "but it has been paid and I think we should be relieved it is over and at no greater cost."

"Oh aye, Alonzo. I am in complete accord with you on that score. It is the other business that has me disappointed."

"What other business?"

"This night, that dastard Bartholomew was brought in. You will recall he is the man in the middle, as it were? Well, we had hoped not only to have charged him with *this* crime but quite a few others, any one of which would be quite enough in itself to have earned him a rope about his neck. It is something that we have been trying to do for years, but he has always managed to come up with an alibi we could not break. This time it looked as though we might have finally caught up with him. Obviously Ned thought so, too, for Ned arrested him and he is in our lock-up at this very moment. Ned's charge against him was to have been as a result of his partaking in this conspiracy against your life." Mr. Denning shook his head despondently. "But I fear that once again it will not wash and Bartholomew will walk the streets of London a free man."

"I do not see that at all," protested the general. "Conway's body is witness enough!"

"No, it is not. Conway, alive and confessing, would have been all we could have asked, but now there is nothing left to connect Bartholomew to Conway except for what Ned may have to say to it. If Bartholomew was a low criminal of no standing, Ned's word would be sufficient, but I fear that Bartholomew has connections in high places and only incontrovertible fact, doubly confirmed, will be sufficient in this case. English juries can be swayed, especially if the defense can cast any doubt at all on the validity of the charges. With a creature such as Bartholomew is, the least spark of doubt and he will blow it up into a blazing defense of his innocence."

"Good heavens! You are not going to set the fellow at liberty, I hope?"

"No, as long as we have something to charge him with, I shall hold onto him and see to it that he gets his day in court. But if this is all we have to support our charge, I am not sanguine that he will not have the laugh on us. I shall be on tenterhooks in regard to him until I have had a chance to hear from Ned exactly why he thought it wise to arrest Bartholomew at this time."

"Ah yes! Now I do recall that when Ned came to discuss my list with me, he, too, made that very point."

"Hmmmm. Ned knows the law on evidence, and the nature of juries, as well as I do, so it is possible that he has something more to go on." Mr. Denning's mood seemed to ease. "Well, I dare say that I shall just have to be patient until he is well enough to talk."

Now it was General Beresford who appeared to be disturbed about something. He studied Mr. Denning for a while until finally he remarked, rather offhandedly: "Alec, wouldn't you say that 'Lolly' is a rather unusual name?"

Mr. Denning gave such a start that he spilled some of his drink on himself, and at once made a great business of dabbing at the wet spots.

"It *is* an unusual name, is it not?" insisted the general, his eyes never leaving Mr. Denning's face. His gaze was peculiarly intense.

Mr. Denning, still busy wiping away at himself, looked up blankly and replied: "Eh? What is?"

"The name 'Lolly'."

Mr. Denning's eyes turned sharp in their expression. Now he was staring fixedly at the general. "Where did you hear it?" he demanded.

"When Ned fell, O'Shaughnessy ran to him and called him by that name."

"Damn O'Shaughnessy!" Mr. Denning's eyes were now darting about as though he were looking for some way to escape.

"You will admit it is an odd name to call a grown man, I think."

"Damned odd! And damn O'Shaughnessy!" Apparently there was no escape. With a look of reluctant resignation on his face, Mr. Denning nodded at the general and sighed.

He said: "If you know that much, then you must know all. Look you, Alonzo, the information I am about to give you is in the highest degree confidential. If it is misused, Ned's usefulness as a runner is at an end—perhaps even his life."

Sir Alonzo was quite taken aback. "My dear Alec, you make it sound a secret of state."

"Well, no, not quite, but something akin, since His Majesty's government has seen fit to employ him in some delicate matters. I shall have to tell you the entire story so that you will understand what is involved and never use the name or mention it. Was anyone else in the room when O'Shaughnessy made the slip?"

"Only myself."

"Thank God! Though I can understand why Shamus forgot himself. You see the two of them go back a long ways together. Now, Alonzo, I must ask for your word that you will keep what I tell you in confidence."

"I understand and you have it. I owe Ned my life."

"Yes, of course. Well, then, it all began about ten years ago when the River Police came to Bow Street seeking our assistance. It seemed that the mudlarks, their personal pets, were getting out of hand. Now we were quite busy, having our own fish to fry. I sent them away unhappy. It was not but a month or two later that their problems had become ours, and with a vengeance. The mudlarks were forgoing their usual haunts by the riverside and carrying their depredations right into the heart of the City. The merchants and the shopkeepers were up in arms. Mud from the river told them, as well as anything could, where this new wave of house and shop breaking was stemming from.

"The River Police and Bow Street began to work together and, after nosing about and comparing notes between us, the information that we had garnered from snitchers and narks was to the effect that all the trouble could be traced to a small group or band of water rats headed up by, of all things, a mere lad of fifteen years of age.

"Well, I immediately assigned O'Shaughnessy, my best hand, to the task of rooting them out and putting a stop to this young brigand's career; and we all of us felt a little foolish for having got our wind up so, over a mere child's pranks, and put the matter out of our minds—or tried to!

"Alonzo, I consider myself more than reasonably astute in the detection of crime and quite knowledgeable in the ways of the criminal mind, and so you can imagine the shock it was to me to discover that I and all of Bow Street, and the entire River Police Force into the bargain, were engaged in a duel with a master criminal who was less than half our ages!

"And, what was the worst, he knew it and laughed in our faces time and time again. He had his own little group who worked close with him, but he could call on any other band of mudlarks whenever he had a need of them. We would get a message that a small army of rowdies was acting suspiciously in front of some merchant's warehouse, for instance. We'd send men out to investigate, and after a night's outing they would return exhausted and empty-handed. The rascals, as they would report, were mudlarks but they had not done anything to provide cause for their detention. But it never failed that sometime later in the morning, a goldsmith or a wine vendor would be in my office complaining to the high heavens that his shop had been broken into and his stock horribly depleted—and the usual bits of dried river mud all about.

"On suspicion, I would have Lolly brought in after such raids—and with some of the goods still on him, mind you—but it was to no avail. He had bought some or all of them at that very shop the day before, and the merchants themselves would castigate me for badgering the gentleman, their very good customer. Gentleman? A mudlark!—but he had the speech, he had the manner, he had the audacity and, of course, he always paid for his purchases in gold." Mr. Denning shook his head and chuckled.

"The young devil had even more! He had the intellect to force me to play the game according to his rules. For three years I had to live with this thorn in my side, beaten at every turn, and so I was forced to admire him. Here was a case of a criminal who carried out his crimes at the expense of others, of course, but only for their wealth and never for blood. As he explained it to me in later years, killing never struck him as being a particularly profitable lay. I strongly suspect, nay I *know* it went a lot deeper than that with him. After so many battles with him in my courtroom, I gained a liking for the lad. He stood up to me proudly and confident to the point of cockiness. The thought that if he had had the misfortune to be a son to me, I'd have taken a cane to his backside, crossed my mind more than once. But with it, after a while, came another idea. What if I *had* the training of him? What if it were given to me to set his steps upon a respectable path in life? Could he not become just as effective an agent for good as now he was for evil? Why, if he were to be my son, with his intelligence and his abilities, what a worthy successor he would be for me. It was a seed planted in my mind.

"Well, in the long run, the odds were against the lad. O'Shaughnessy is a bulldog and, for all his dull appearance, he is a top-flight runner. He buckled down to the task and I assisted him in every way. All we needed was one slip on Lolly's part and we would have him nailed. Believe me, that is the biggest part of police work, waiting for the slip.

"One day, it came. A rumor that Goldsmith's Hall was to be burgled."

"Goldsmith's Hall? Why not the crown jewels in the Tower?" asked the general facetiously.

Mr. Denning chuckled. "Undoubtedly they'd have been next. I admit if we had not come to know Lolly we never would have credited the whisper, but it was just his style, so we set to work to keep our eyes on him. We are experts at that and we did our work well. I gave O'Shaughnessy explicit instructions on the course he was to follow once he had nabbed Lolly and he was pleased to follow them—for he, too, had come to bear some affection for the lad.

"To make a long story short, Lolly was caught in the act and it was reported that he had been killed, shot by O'Shaughnessy as he attempted to escape."

Sir Alonzo frowned. "I do not understand," he commented.

"You will shortly. When Lolly was brought before me, I informed him of what we had arranged and gave him a choice. He could take his chance with a jury or become a runner. His good behavior and devotion to duty would be his safe-conduct to a life of respectability. He

186

agreed—with reluctance—it was hardly a choice—and since Lolly was the only name he knew, I gave him mine, Denning—Edward Denning, and let it be rumored about that he was a distant relative, to allay any and all suspicion and speculation. That, my dear Alonzo, was the birth and the baptism of the Bow Street Gentleman, now my son and heir."

"Amazing!" breathed the general.

"There never were any charges recorded against Lolly, and with his death the file was closed. Ned's identification is a secret that very few people know. The older runners, Robert Peel, my Lord Carnavon, his daughter Lady Emily, and now you, Alonzo. Ned's future in the New Metropolitan Police Force is assured with the passage of Peel's bill."

"Alec, for your act of mercy, and for your concern for one Lolly, I owe you more than I can ever repay!" said the general, in a voice throaty with emotion.

"Nonsense! It was Ned who took the ball in his shoulder for you, not I!"

"Nevertheless, had you not turned a blind eye to your duty, I should not now be alive to thank you for it. I know what it must have cost you and I cannot say that I, under similar circumstances, could have put my heart before my duty. Believe me, Alec, willy-nilly, you have got me as friend for as long as we both shall live."

"I say, there is no call for such melodramatics, Alonzo. I assure you I am honored and deeply pleasured by the prospect."

A stirring noise from the other room was heard. Both elderly gentlemen rose as one and scurried into the drawing room to attend upon Ned.

He was wide awake and remarkably clear-headed. When he saw the general, he laughed out loud in relief. "Well, Sir Alonzo, you cannot know how happy I am to see you whole. Obviously, that devil missed his aim."

"Not exactly, lad. It seems you managed to get in his line of fire," replied the general.

Ned's eyes opened wide in recollection. "Ah, I rememberl Awfully clumsy of me, wasn't it?" he said and he grinned. "I'll vouch for it that those horse pistols you military use do pack a mighty wallop. How badly was I hit?"

"Bad enough, Ned. The sawbones has rewarded you with some six weeks of rest in bed."

"Has he now? Well, I think—" and he made to rise, only to sink back in defeat. "Whew! Well, I guess it shall be at least more than one at any rate."

Mr. Denning asked: "Ned, are you up to talking for a bit?"

"Yes, sir."

"Well, Coggshill brought Bartholomew in and we have got him safe under lock and key, but Shamus had to kill Conway, which leaves us exactly where we were before. That is, with no strong case against Bartholomew."

"Not to worry, sir. Bartholomew handed himself to me all dressed up like a Christmas turkey. Raid his house immediately and take all its inhabitants in for interrogation. Search the place thoroughly, even if you have to raze it to the ground. His books of account have got to be somewhere about. They'll give you all the facts and figures of his operations. Even if you do not find them, he told me enough so that I can frame questions for you to ask of him and his underlings that will get you all the evidence you need to hang him seven times seven times."

"Well!" exclaimed Mr. Denning, beaming. "You have certainly been a busy little bee!"

Ned smiled. "Indeed, I have been; and do you know, sir, it was a sore temptation not to throw in with him? He had an excellent lay and I am sure I could have done him out of it."

The magistrate and the general exchanged looks and broke into hearty laughter.

Ned looked surprised. "Oh, I say! It wasn't all that funny!"

"Indeed it was not," said the general, "for if Lolly had replaced Bartholomew, who would there have been left to bring *him* down?"

Ned's eyes widened in surprise. He looked at Mr. Denning.

"It is all right, son. The general knows. It seems Shamus let fall your old name in his anxiety over you, so I had to tell Sir Alonzo all."

There was a pleading look in Ned's eyes as he turned to the general. "Sir, I sincerely hope you will not allow—"

"Don's be a fool, boy!" cried the general in great irritation. "It only makes you dearer to me! Now *this* may truly embarrass you," he continued, as he came close, "but the Frenchies have a way of bestowing a mark of their appreciation upon a fellow that we British have always laughed at. I am laughing now."

With great dignity, General Beresford bent over Ned and kissed him once upon each cheek. Then, to Ned's and Mr. Denning's even greater astonishment, he planted one further salute upon the young man's brow.

Chapter XVI

Later in the day, a weary Mr. Denning, in his office at Bow Street (as a matter of form, you will understand), delivered a halfhearted reprimand to Shamus O'Shaughnessy for having compromised Ned's identity. Shamus accepted the mild wigging as his due and expressed appropriate remorse. He then went on to point out that perhaps they had better take further precautions.

Mr. Denning, whose mind was overfatigued, asked testily: "Precautions? What precautions? I have had to explain all to General Beresford and he has promised to keep his lips sealed in regard to the matter."

"Well, sir, we are bound ter make up another tale wi' regard to Lolly's comin' back from the dead. Ef we don't, there'll be o'er much speculatin' an' then they're bound ter wonder how come he wasna bagged wi' Bartholomew and all the rest of his crew, ye see."

"Oh, that damn fool boy! Of course—but, oh, my brain 's weary and I cannot think! Shamus, I'd never have made any sort of a runner. These hours have just about slain me. What do *you* suggest we say?"

"Well, sir, we can let it out that we had him in our fists and blast! if he didna give us the slip again. We could put t out as it was our opinion he cut his stick for the continent."

Mr. Denning smiled. "Yes, that would fit, for that is what Ned told his muckish cronies recently, that he'd just come from there." His smile turned rueful. "Yes, I dare say we shall have to retract our original story about your having shot him to death that first time. But you know, Shamus, that is not so bad. After all, Ned can now resurrect Lolly any time he has a need to. Lolly served us well enough this time." He nodded and now his smile was one of satisfaction. "Aye, I'd say he served up Bartholomew done to a turn."

"That he did and no mistake! But, sir, we had best keep our lad under the covers for a bit. If it should come out that Ned Denning was engaged in tracking down Bartholomew an' Conway an' all, why there's many as will put two and two together an' discover Lolly makes Ned."

"True. It will not hurt. The Conway business does not have to be brought into it. There are crimes enough of a similar nature, and a choice selection of others, that will send Bartholomew to his Maker, right enough. Well, I shall stop off for just a moment to make it right with Sir Alonzo. I am sure he will have no objection to having the Conway matter dropped from the docket—and then I am off to bed, blessed bed!

General Beresford, surprisingly enough, seemed to be reluctant to agree right off. He gave the matter due consideration for a moment or two. Finally he said: "Alec, I shall agree to the proposition but upon one condition—and I warn you, I shall not yield on it."

Mr. Denning frowned. "Oh I say, Alonzo! If I can meet the condition, of course then I shall grant it, but I beg you will remember that if I cannot meet it, this still is a matter that seriously affects Ned's future. In fact, bringing him into the Conway matter could easily end his future before it ever got started."

"I am well aware of that, Alec. Now this is my condition. Ned is coming along much faster than any of us could have hoped for. Mr. Roberts has declared that rarely has he seen such a fine specimen, and he does not doubt Ned will be up on his feet in a week, just so long as he does not overdo—"

"Excellent! Then I shall have him home again with me—"

"No! For that is my condition. As long as Ned is not fit for duty, he must remain with me. After all, Alec, I am about all of the time and can see to it that he is properly taken care of and that he takes care of *himself* properly. I beg you will allow me his company," pleaded the general.

Mr. Denning chuckled and put out his hand to the general. They shook hands warmly and Mr. Denning went in to see Ned.

Two days passed and Ned's wound was causing him no discomfort. Perhaps it was just luck or perhaps it was due to his splendid constitution, but the infection that was almost a concomitant of such wounds never set in. So he was well able to receive the caller who came that day.

Higgins came in with the gentleman's card for Ned and stood waiting.

"Colonel Charles Rowan?" asked Ned, looking up at Higgins. "Are you sure he is asking for me and not the general?"

"Quite, sir. It was you in particular he has come to see and wished to pay his respects to the general after. He did say it was official business, sir."

General Beresford said: "Show Colonel Rowan in."

Higgins gave a little bow and withdrew.

The general turned to Ned. "Something is in the wind, my boy. I know Rowan. He fought with the Light Brigade at Waterloo. Good man. Did a stint recently with the Irish Constabulary. Not too long ago, that. One of the Orange Peelers, you know. "I'll not be surprised if that is who sent him to call on you, Robert Peel himself."

At that moment, Higgins announced the caller and the colonel came in, walking in a brisk manner. Immediately he went up to the general and there was a cordial exchange of salutations. One could see at a glance that here were a pair of brother officers in the truest sense of the term. They had a deep respect one for the other.

The general then made to leave, but the colonel said that he had nothing to say that was of a confidential nature. He then went on to explain that, as a result of the passage of the police reform bill, he had been appointed commissioner to head up the new force together with another commissioner, one Richard Mayne, an attorney of some note, and the two of them were to be jointly responsible to the Home Secretary, Mr. Peel.

"Mr. Denning," he went on to state, "I wish to thank you personally—and assure you that Mr. Peel and Mr. Mayne add their thanks to mine—I wish to thank you from the bottom of my heart for your magnificent work in bringing Bartholomew down. Aside from the congratulations that you have a right to expect from every good citizen, we commissioners are especially grateful, for it allows the new uniformed police force to get off to a fine start. There are, to be sure, plenty of matters to call for their complete attention, but Bartholomew's absence cannot help but make for a quieter London in which they are to work, I should think."

"Thank you, sir. I could wish you to know that this wound of mine will not be of a permanently debilitating nature and I shall be available for duty in only a matter of weeks. I pray you will hold a post open for me. I should be pleased to accept anything, the lowest rank of patrol constable would not be unacceptable to me. I assure you that I can qualify. For references—"

To Ned's consternation, the colonel broke into a loud roar of laughter.

He explained: "You, a constable in the uniformed force? After what you have just achieved?—and that is to say nothing about your accomplishments in the past! I should say not. Why, Peel would bestow the order of the sack upon me and make of my commission fish wrappings if I were to even think of it. Frankly, Mr. Denning, upon the very eve of the inception of the Metropolitan Police force you have brought to our attention a lack that we had not realized, a capability that we overlooked in our planning."

Ned was looking very disappointed. "Then I shall not be getting posted to the new force?"

"No, that is out of the question. You are needed exactly where you are. All we are beginning to organize is a band of policemen, trained to patrol a beat and offer every assistance in the prevention of crime and the apprehension of lawbreakers. To execute such a feat as the collaring of a master mind on the order of Bartholomew will be quite beyond what we have in mind to organize. It is a poor excuse that not one of us thought of it, and it would now be inexcusable if we were not to secure such capability on the instant. For the reason I have been empowered to offer you the appointment as magistrate of the Bow Street Police Office until such time when, after having got the new force upon its feet, we, with your assistance and your father's, can give thought to how best to incorporate the particular talents of the Bow Street runner into some department of the new force."

Ned was smiling uncertainly. "Of course, under His Honor, the Chief Magistrate."

"That we are perfectly pleased to leave between the two of you to settle. All we ask is your fullest cooperation in our support. There is so much that your father and yourself know that we do not and, like beggars, we will accept with humble gratitude any nugget of expertise you can spare us in the aid of our devoirs, our duties."

"When will the appointment begin?"

"I am prepared to swear you in this instant, Your Honor."

"It will be my honor to bear witness, Colonel Rowan!" declared General Beresford, beaming. "Ned, I am so proud of you I cannot express it."

The oath was duly administered and the three gentlemen relaxed and, with glasses filled with the general's finest vintage, they began to compare notes.

Fortified with good liquor, a hearty lunch, and with the knowledge of having gained a worthy and valuable colleague, Colonel Rowan took his leave early in the afternoon.

That night the Beresford residence was honored to have the inestimable company of the Honorable Robert Peel and the Honorable Alexander Denning, who came to attend dinner to celebrate the invalid's having gained his doctor's permission to sit up as well as his other, more glorious, elevation.

After dinner, over their cigars, Mr. Denning made it quite clear that he would step down from his seat in favor of Mr. Denning, the newly appointed magistrate. Ned immediately threatened to resign on the spot. The argument that ensued waxed hot and heavy until the Home Secretary had had quite enough of the two of them and intervened.

Deploring such unseemly behavior in two of His Majesty's representatives on the Bench, he threatened to sack them both if they did not settle down and agree to share the post. "The Home Office will be quite satisfied just so long as there is a Denning at Bow Street. If there are to be two of them managing the police office, then of course we cannot help but be doubly satisfied."

The next day, the Honorable Edward Denning, with General Beresford to assist him in getting about, entertained the entire force of the runners from Bow Street, his friends and colleagues for these past five years.

The general took the occasion to present to Ned his note of hand for five hundred pounds, the amount he had posted as reward.

Ned accepted it on behalf of the men and, holding it in his hand, he made a little speech to them.

"I strongly recommend that you take your share of this money and put it aside. It is not likely you will be seeing any more of the same very often in our future. We have

196

got to rededicate ourselves and get squared away. There will be a comfortable living to be made as runner, what with an increased stipend together with the usual fees and commissions, but that is bound to be all. In short, gentlemen, the days of runners like Sayers and Townshend are, as of this day, behind us. Any runner who expects to leave an estate in excess of £20,000 had better be a great deal sharper than I am, or else he had better turn in his vest and truncheon right now. If not, I'll wager he finds himself in the dock at Old Bailey and, believe me, it is a wager I shall win.

"Gentlemen, we are working against crime, not with it. Those of you who have been laboring in the mere shadow of the law are warned that it will no longer be tolerated. I am sure the practice of posting a reward will continue; but you will not pick and chose your assignments on that basis or any basis at all, not if there are more serious cases needing our attention.

"Now, it has been for almost three generations that we runners have carried on with our special abilities, and we have done it well enough to gain our country's endorsement. We have never been more than a mere handful to police the realm, yet we have garnered a record of achievement that now will insure the continuance of the Bow Street Police Office and its special duties in the face of today's almost complete reformation of the constabulary. Yes, my friends, for the most part, the charleys will be gone, and the local watches are being disbanded even as I speak. Of the old system only the Bow Street runner will remain. That is because there is no one else who can take our place. But I caution you, we shall not be taken for granted. We shall have to prove our right to continue and we shall be measured against the Peelers. You will be well-advised to comport yourselves as close as you are able to the example that will be set by our new colleagues in their new uniforms. We have had, for many years, a reputation that was unchallenged for honesty, loyalty, and devotion. This has become somewhat tarnished of late, and we have got to see that it is newly refurbished. I tell you this: I am going to be doing my damnedest in that direction and will expect not anything less from you."

Admittedly two or three runners were not so overwhelmed with joy at the prospect of having to forgo their takings from both sides of the law, but the immediate prospect of some eighty pounds apiece of reward money—neither Ned nor O'Shaughnessy would be sharing—helped them, for the moment at least, to swallow any forebodings that they might have had.

Chapter XVII

My Lord Carnavon was sitting down to a late breakfast. The sun was well past the meridian; had it not been his first meal for the day, one might have said it was an early tea he was having, without stretching the word too much.

He had arisen very late because he had gone to bed very late, not for the first time in the past few weeks. Once Peel's reform bill had completed its rough passage, he had hoped that it would have signaled an end to the politicking that had been engaging so many of both his working hours and his supposed hours of slumber. But it had not. Peel had required his continued support—the success of the reform bill only spelled out so much more work for his lordship. There were commissioners to select, and Peel had his candidates all chosen. He required Lord Carnavon's influence to help him defeat opposition candidates who, as commissioners, would have eviscerated the whole idea of the new force. And then there were initial objectives to be defined; and once they had gotten them whipped into shape, why, there were the policies that had to be formulated, or the objectives could never be achieved.

It was not the most interesting labor that my Lord Carnavon would have chosen for himself, for he had not the knowledge nor the concern for the problems of an infant police organization, but Peel was a friend, a powerful friend and, what was even more to the point, Fate might yet decide that his daughter would marry a fellow who was more than a little connected with the business. In that sense it was most properly a Trenchard affair.

And so the round of meetings and discussions had continued on into the late hours of each and every night since the passage of the bill—as if it had not been that way for weeks before, while Peel was trying to make up his mind whether or not the time had ripened sufficiently to test his proposition on the floor of the Chamber.

But this week had finally gone by, and Peel was satisfied. All the maneuvering was done with. Carnavon's presence was now become superfluous. My lord could now resume the normal tenor of his life once again. And so he had indulged himself with an overlong night's rest.

For all that he had slept the sleep of the weary, he had not felt he had slept the sleep of the just. The entire rigmarole of all he had just been through had not been because he was concerned for the public's welfare and safety. As far as he was concerned, he could take care of his own and never had, and never would have, a need for a policeman in uniform. The whole blasted business had been undertaken at the behest of his daughter; it was she who had made of it a Trenchard family affair. The damnable thing of it was that he could not be sure now that his efforts would be of any blasted use to her. There was this eternal bickering going on between them over the lad's nonsensical notions and for the life him, my lord could not say if Ned would or would not ever become his son-in-law. Perhaps now that he had the time to look about him, it might be a good thing if he put his foot down and cut through all this persiflage. But that prospect did not particularly hearten him. He knew from past experience that young Denning could be as stubborn as any lout, and that his daughter was every inch a

Trenchard—and no one, not even a Trenchard, would care to tangle with a Trenchard.

He sighed as he picked up his newspaper and started catching up on the doings of the town.

He had not got through the first item when Lady Emily came sauntering in and sat herself down opposite him. He paid no attention to her other than to nod. It was meant as a greeting, but it appeared more as an acknowledgment of her presence.

"Papa, I am excessively bored. I have been thinking we should give a ball to celebrate my disattachment—if that is a word—so that I may rejoin the ranks of the living."

"Quite, my dear" came my lord's voice from behind the paper.

A frown clouded Lady Emily's pretty face. She stared hard at the paper and said grimly: "It shall be the most glorious affair of the season. I shall invite His Majesty and I shall invite Louis XVIII and the Duke of Wellington and, of course, Napoleon Bonaparte, may his soul rest in peace."

"Quite. Anything you say, my dear" came from behind the paper.

"Papa! You have not heard a word I have said!" cried Emily sharply.

Without putting down the newspaper, his lordship peered around the side of it and complained: "My dear, anything you wish will be perfectly all right with me. Now I pray you will let me get on with my reading. I have so much to catch up on." And he ducked back behind his paper.

Emily sighed. "Very well, I will speak with you after you have finished. In the meantime, to pass the time waiting, I would appreciate your letting me have a share of the paper."

Out popped my lord's head. "My dear child, I have now read this one item some four or five times and I still have not the vaguest notion of what it is about. Why are you at me so?"

"I am bored, papa. Give me a part of the paper if you please."

"Oh, for pity's sake!" He laid the newspaper down upon the table and neatly tore it down the centerfold. He retained the part he was reading and handed the forward section to her.

"Now leave me in peace, I pray!" he exclaimed in exasperation, and resumed his reading.

Emily began to peruse her portion and for a moment there was silence in the breakfast room.

Then, at the same time, both father and daughter dashed their papers upon the table top and in tones of shock and indignation, slapping the paper with their hands for emphasis, they began to demand of each other:

"Emily, your betrothal! Who dared to announce—!"

"Papa, he is a cruel beast! He never told me that—!"

And that was far as their exchange was comprehensible. It immediately developed into an unintelligible exchange of charges and countercharges that neither of them responded to. It is safe to say, however, that my lord was wrathfully indignant with his daughter and that his daughter was wrathfully indignant with her fiancé and both of them had the newspaper to thank for fusing their respective eruptions.

For a moment the Trenchard house was filled with a most unmannerly uproar. It was disturbing enough to rouse King Alfred from a short nap. He came lumbering into the room, looked from daughter to father and back again, shook himself and withdrew.

Emily began to laugh. "Oh, papa, His Majesty has just expressed his disapproval. I humbly apologize for my lack of manners."

His lordship chuckled. "For a moment I was a little beside myself, too, and I humbly apologize; but Emily, this is enough to try any father's soul!" he exclaimed, pointing at the paper.

"Why, what have you found?"

"I have found that I have announced the ending of my

daughter's engagement. I think it is just the slightest bit unusual that I have to have recourse to the *Gazette* to learn what it is that I have been doing. Young lady, how do you dare to publish anything at all in my name, especially something I had not the least intention of agreeing to?"

"For one thing, papa, you were terribly preoccupied with more important concerns. For another, it is *my* betrothal and I shall do what I like with it."

"As to the first, surely it would have waited. And as to the second, I will have you know that I am still head of the family and this being family business of the highest importance, I expect to be consulted before any rash action is to be taken and, although you may do as you please about it, it will only be after we have had a reasoned discussion of the matter."

"There was nothing left to discuss. Ned—"

"Ned does not deserve such treatment," declared his lordship sternly.

"Ned does not? You say Ned does not? If the truth be known, it is *I* who am being treated so badly!"

"Stuff and nonsense! Can you not see what you have done to the fellow? Now the world has every reason to believe that we, too, consider Edward Denning lacking and unfit. I would not have that—and I hardly think it was what you had intended."

In a tone of despondency, Emily said: "But what else was there to do? No, that is not at all what I wished, nor do I think any of our friends will really believe that I am serious. But, papa, that is the thing! It is Ned himself who believes it. It might just as well have been he who placed the announcement in the newspaper. I have told you what he said to me at our last meeting. It has been the same thing over and over ever since that business at the Milliken Club. I have not been able to do a thing with him! Oh! If I did not care for General Beresford so very much, I should positively dislike the gentleman for what he has brought upon us! As for Ned himself"—she slapped the newspaper—"one would have thought, engaged or no, he'd have had the decency of informing me in person of his recent elevation. Surely we can still be friends. But no, not even a note these many days. I must be grateful to the *Gazette* for the news. Well, at least it is a relief to know that the honor was not awarded to him posthumously."

"Oh, so that is what Peel had reference to! I wondered. He made an offhand remark that I should have reason to be proud of my future son-in-law. Son-in-law? It has become a wish close to my heart, for I *am* proud of the shuttlehead, but I am at my wit's end with him. I tell you, Emily, you'll not find him an easy one to live with."

"I am sure that I shall never have the opportunity to discover it."

"Well, what is there left for us to do?"

"Papa, there is nothing left to be done. The announcement of the break between us has done it all. As long as Ned has this thing about who he truly is, there just is no talking with him. And if he has managed to exist a full quarter of a century without uncovering a single clue to his identity. I am sure he will go to the end of his days no better informed than he is at present."

"What were you saying about giving a ball?"

"Oh, I was not serious. But it is boring to have to sit alone, and I think I should go down to Ravenswold for a while, a long while. I have friends there in Badenham and it would help me to forget."

"If I thought it would, I should be pleased to have you go. But I know you will not be able to, and I'll not have you indulging yourself in a bout of blue megrims in remote solitude for the rest of your life."

"Oh, I shall be all right, I assure you."

"I see. Then you are not in love with the fellow and never have been."

"Oh, papa, how can you be so cruel!"

"Because you are my daughter, and we Trenchards do not take our love lightly," said his lordship grimly. "Oh blast! You shall not go to Ravenswold. I shall go to that young man and have a heart-to-heart talk with him. The situation has become positively unbearable, and it is fast becoming ridiculous. That I, Carnavon, must sue upon my hands and knees to a—a—"

Emily laughed. "A magistrate, papa! The Honorable Edward Denning! Oh, why must he be so difficult!"

"Perhaps it would be easier if we did throw a great affair. I could take him aside and—"

"He'd never come! And as he is no longer a runner, even his father could not order his attendance. No, papa, there is nothing to be done. I must forget the Honorable Mr. Denning for all t-time."

Tears were glistening in her eyes as she said it. His lordship cursed, arose from his seat and came over to Emily. He bent down and kissed her, patted her on the shoulder and walked out of the room muttering under his breath.

At the Beresford residence in Mayfair, that very same morning, the *Gazette* was also having a great effect.

The general was perusing the paper, a smile of immense satisfaction upon his countenance as he sipped his morning coffee.

Ned came strolling in and, except that his arm was still in a sling to ease his shoulder, he did not apear to be suffering the least discomfort. He smiled and said: "Good morning, sir."

"Good morning to you, Your Honor. I am pleased to see you looking so well."

"Thank you, sir. Indeed I am feeling well and, except that it might throw Mr. Roberts into a fit, I should discard this encumbrance on my arm. If there is any discomfort, that is the only cause of it, I assure you."

As Ned took his seat and Higgins came over to pour his coffee and set a plate for him, the general nodded and said: "Your father cannot help but be a happy man today for you are quite the feature in the paper this morning. They refer to you as His Honor, the Bow Street Gentleman, and praise you to the skies. I have been studying the sketch of your career that they have included. Very impressive, I must say."

Ned's smile turned sour. "The Bow Street Gentleman. They will never let me forget that is where my lineage begins—the Bow Street Police Office!"

"Oh, come now, Ned, you are making too much of it."

Ned fixed the general with his eyes and asked: "Am I truly, sir? Did you not yourself make a bit much of it?"

The general waved his hand in deprecation. "Oh, that! My boy, I was mistaken, completely uninformed. I assure all that will be rectified at the very next meeting of the membership committee. With your new honors, Your Honor, I shall not have to say a word in your behalf. Ha! This record speaks for itself!"

He was riffling through the pages of the newspaper idly as he spoke when something caught his eye. "I say! What's this?"

Ned had been about to point out that nothing could change the facts, or rather the lack of facts, concerning the circumstances of his birth, but he paused—for the general was regarding him with a look of pain in his eyes.

"I should never have thought it of them—and at such a time!" exclaimed Sir Alonzo shaking his head sadly.

"What is there in the paper to disconcert you so, may I ask?" inquired Ned.

"It says here that Lord Carnavon announces the withdrawal of Lady Emily's troth to you. Oh, that is too bad! I thought her such an adorable girl and I was sure of her devotion to you. Now, why should she have done a thing like that? Oh, I am sure she must regret it already! After all, you have just been appointed magistrate and could not hope for a more respectable position in society."

Ned had a knowing little smirk upon his lips. "So she has come to it at last."

"You knew of this?"

"It was I, sir, who called it off."

"Ah, you have found someone else, I take it," said the general, putting a good face upon it.

206

"No, sir. Emily is all I could ever wish. I want no one but her."

"But you have just said it was you who broke it off!"

"And I did."

"Yet you still love her? That makes no sense at all! Ah, then it can only be that Carnavon himself has brought pressure to bear upon you to disassociate yourself."

"No, sir. My Lord Carnavon would never do such a thing."

"Well then, Ned, I would have some explanation. You may think it impertinent of me and perhaps it is, but you must know how interested I am to see you happy as well as successful and this—this business cannot be adding any joy to your life at the moment, I am sure. Nor do I imagine that my lady is in such high gig with it either."

"No, we none of us are. But it cannot be otherwise. I am not the proper gentleman for my lady. She deserves better than a *Bow Street* gentleman—a mere masquerade. Oh, everyone has been kind—more than kind. My debt of gratitude to my father I can never repay, but that is not to say that I have a right to burden the girl I love with my highly questionable beginnings. Perhaps some day I shall discover who I am; and I pray, oh how I pray! that it will turn out that I come of good family. Ah, then—" He fell back in his seat, suddenly very dejected. "Oh, what is the use of it all, sir! By that time—if there ever will be such a time—my lady will have been long married to someone else—a very proper sort of gentleman. Yes, one who knows his own father!"

A look of resolve appeared on the general's face. "Ned, I thought I might wait a little longer before I told you this. I wished to be sure that you were fully recovered, for I have no doubt that it will come as a shock to you. But I see that the time has come for me to say what I have been waiting, with the greatest of impatience, to tell you." He paused for a moment and then declared in a most solemn manner: "Ned, I, General Sir Alonzo Llewellyn Beresford, am your father."

Ned's eyes opened wide in amazement, and then he

smiled as an understanding of what the general was about came to him. "My heartfelt thanks, Sir Alonzo, but there is no need for this. I see what you are at and I am deeply touched—but it will not wash, sir. I already have one adoptive father whom I respect and to whom I am deeply devoted." He laughed. "I have yet to hear of a cove with two such fathers."

"No, Ned, it is not like that at all. You are my true son, flesh of my flesh, blood of my blood. You are a Beresford and so I shall proudly proclaim it to the world."

"My dear General," said Ned, rising from the table, "except for Mr. Denning, I could not wish for a more distinguished sire. You have my deepest respect and my affection forever. I shall not forget what you tried to do for me."

Sir Alonzo said nothing, but there was a shrewd look in his eye as he watched Ned start to leave the room. When the young man was just on the threshold, General Beresford snapped out: "Quickly now, Llewellyn! How do we do it in the cavalry?"

Ned wheeled about, his hand raised aloft as though wielding a saber, and he shouted: "Charge!" He started to run back in to the room only to stop, transfixed, as he stared foolishly up at his arm raised on high. Slowly his gazed descended and fixed itself upon the general's face.

In a weak little voice, he murmured: "P-papa?"

The general nodded. His cheeks were wet.

"Oh God! Papa!" cried Ned. He came rushing over to the general, to fall upon his knees and bury his head in the general's lap, sobbing uncontrollably.

There was a tremendous effusion of emotion in the room, and it was a very long interval that elapsed before the two men could gain control of themselves and begin to converse with anything like usual repose.

To Ned it was more than overwhelming. The last doubt as to his own identity had been completely erased, as the flood gates to his memory were unlocked and thrown wide open. The torrent of recollections that came

208

back to him added much heartbreak, and revivified the shock that had put his past so completely out of his consciousness for all those many years. He had to talk about it. He could not stop himself if he had wished.

Ned was saying: "Yes, it has all come back to me now. That night—that horrible night! I remember I was awakened by screams. It was mama and Ellen. I leaped out of my bed and rushed to the door. Oh, papa, you must believe that I tried to get to them!"

Sir Alonzo patted his hand reassuringly.

"I reached for the doorknob of my chamber door. It was burning hot. My hand sizzled to the touch of it and I could not get it open. Even at that, I did not realize how badly I had burned it until later. I was desperate to get to them. I went to the window and climbed out into the tree. You remember the tree, papa. I had used it many times before to get out at night on the sly.

"By the time I got down and round to the front door, the place was a mass of flames. There was nothing more to be heard but the roar and crackling of the flames. Then the roof came crashing down in a tremendous blaze of sparks, and I heard people out on the road shouting hoarsely and coming towards me. I—I am not at all clear as to what happened then, but the next thing that *is* clear to me is that I had reached the banks of the river and was laving my seared hand in its waters. Then everything is hazy. It is a maze of shifting scenes and shadowy impressions and faceless people. And then suddenly my life as a mudlark begins, it seems. I dare say it was they who must have found me and—yes, I do recall someone asking me who I was, everything was gone from my mind but my name: Lolly."

He smiled sadly. "Poor, poor Lolly. Oh well, he did not turn out so very badly, as well he might have."

"No, he did quite well, my son. You know, Ned—Llewellyn—oh, damn! What shall we call you? Certainly never Lolly!"

"Father, I have lived with Ned for some five years now and it is what I am used to. I should hate awfully to have to get used to Llewellyn, considering that I never truly answered to it ever before."

General Beresford smiled. "As you wish. Alonzo is quite bad enough, but Llewellyn is something worse, I am sure. But I should be sorely disappointed if you will not agree to be known formally and properly as Llewellyn Alonzo Beresford, as is your right. After all, Alonzo and Llewellyn have alternated down the generations of the Beresfords, and I should hate to see the tradition come to an end."

"Of course, father. Family tradition must be something I shall always cherish. I shall wear the name with the greatest pride."

"Thank you, son. And the Beresfords cannot be anything but proud that the scion of the house should have proved himself in their very best tradition. I was used to wondering in my earlier years if, without his breeding and his heritage, a Beresford could yet rise in the world and make his mark strictly on his own merit. You have proved beyond the shadow of a doubt that he can. The family must be forever indebted to you, lad."

"How is the family? I dare say I shall have to call upon them and soon, to renew the ties."

"Time enough for that at your nuptials. They'll all be sure to attend."

Ned gasped. "Oh, that is a sorry mess! Father, I feel a blasted idiot! How can I face Emily now, after making such an ass of myself—and everyone else for that matter?"

"I see no problem. You love the girl, she loves you. Go to her in pride and you can both of you be happy."

"Yes, in my dreams I thought that that was how it would be. But now that it has truly happened, ridiculous though it sounds—well, you do not know Emily if you think she is going to let me off so easily for all the unhappiness I put her through."

The general chuckled. "Spoken like a true Beresford. We never were of much account before the women we loved. I suppose that explains so many of us having taken up the military as a career. Well, I see that I shall have to take a hand in this campaign, as it is more than obvious that, for the moment at least, you are not at all fit for the duty."

Chapter XVIII

Late in the afternoon of that same day, Mr. Alexander Denning made his appearance at the Trenchard mansion in response to a note from Lord Carnavon asking him to call.

He was immediately conducted into his lordship's large study, where he was greeted in a most solemn manner by Lord Carnavon.

They sat down together and Lord Carnavon began.

"My dear Denning, I regret the necessity of asking you to come to me at this time, knowing how busy you must be, but the necessity is clear if you feel as deeply as I do for our two young people."

"Naturally, my lord, I do, and since your note mentioned that they would be the subjects of our conversation I am only too pleased to attend you in the matter. But further, now that we know that Ned is to take over from me, I am suddenly come to a realization of how old and tired I have become. He is young, agile, and intelligent—brilliant, if I do say so myself. I can leave the police office in his hands without worry or regret. And so I am more than anxious to see him settled down so that he can take up the work with an easy mind."

"Good. Now, you will admit that Ned is being particularly unreasonable in his attitude towards the marriage. I am beginning to become quite wrought up over it, as I am saddled with a young lady for whom the world has become over-small and much too dull, and I would see it changed for her. Is there anything you can suggest?"

"I wish to heaven I could, but Ned refuses to discuss the matter with me. I am not any happier about it than are you. He puts a good face upon it and I dare say his being appointed magistrate is some small recompense for his unhappiness with circumstances, but you must understand that he believes he is proving his love by forswearing Emily. Bachelor though I be, I am not so benighted about matters of the heart not to see that here we have an instance where idiocy is being mistaken for devotion—a not uncommon complaint with young people in love, I am sure you will agree."

"I do, I do. But where does that get us?"

"Nowhere, my lord, I am sad to say. But there just is no speaking to him, and if he is to go through life heartbroken and dejected, it is a sorry upholder of the law that he will make. I am truly concerned for him. . . ."

While the two senior gentlemen continued to bemoan the sad circumstances of their young people, to bewail the fact that there did not appear to be any reasonable way to resolving the problem, a caller was announced to Lady Emily. It was General Beresford, attended by another gentleman.

The footman who delivered the message was deeply puzzled by it, but since there was reposing in his pocket a gold coin to insure that that was all he would announce, he did exactly as he had been requested.

Lady Emily directed that they be shown into the drawing room and ordered tea to be prepared. She then looked to see that she was presentable and went down to her company.

As she entered the luxuriously appointed chamber, she discovered the general standing by the window, and alone.

"Sir Alonzo, dear friend, how delighted I am to see you!"

"And I you, my lady."

"But I understood that you came with another party. I would not have him cool his heels without on my account."

"Ah, yes, but he can wait. Before you see him, I would speak with you concerning the young man. You see he is a young gentleman whom I hold in the deepest affection and—well, to be blunt about it—and I do hope you will forgive me—now that your engagement to young Denning is at an end, I should take it as a particular favor if you would allow me to introduce this lad to you."

"Well, really, General, I—" Emily began to protest.

"Oh, surely you can have no objection to meeting with my son, can you? If only as a favor to me? He knows you and has expressed a desire to become better acquainted. I told him that, as I knew you well, there would not be the least problem. Oh, surely, my lady, you are not going to make me lose credit in my son's eyes."

"Your son, General? Why I never thought—you never mentioned—"

"My lady, you do not know the deep pleasure you will give to me if only you will consent to see him. I shall fetch him," said Sir Alonzo, and he hurried out before she could say another word.

Lady Emily was suddenly quite upset. Having had to submit that horrid announcement to the *Gazette* had been ordeal enough. Now she had got to face the excruciating agony of having to entertain what could be no less than a prospective suitor; truly *that* she was not in any mood to welcome.

She was just coming to terms with herself, deciding that she must be resigned to the necessity in view of the affection that she bore Sir Alonzo, when in walked Ned.

He smiled and said: "My lady."

But she saw the sling about his shoulder and the empty sleeve of his coat and that was all she saw.

"Oh, Ned, you have been hurt!" she cried, and rushed

to him full of fear and trembling. "Is it bad? Are you in pain?"

He enfolded her gently in his good arm and kissed her roundly on the lips. A little breathlessly, he declared: "At this moment, I never felt better in all of my life! No, it is nothing at all. Why, it is practically all healed."

She kissed him as warmly. "When did it happen?"

Carelessly he said: "Oh, a week or so back. We had a little set-to with the general's would-be assassin, is all."

She pushed herself away from him. "A week ago and you never told me? Oh, you are a horrid thing! Why, you could have been killed and I'd never have known!"

He chuckled and replied in dandified accents: "Oh, never fear, m'lady. Once had I been slain I should have made it my first duty to have informed you, don't you know?"

She gurgled: "Oh, you are in good spirits again! When shall we be wed?"

He frowned. "Well now, we dare not proceed so fast, my lady. You see the engagement has been called off—"

"Oh, pooh! Everyone that matters knows it was sheer nonsense—oh dear! Not everybody. There is dear General Beresford, who has taken it quite seriously. He has even gone to the trouble of having brought his son to meet me today—Oh, great heavens!"

"Whatever is the trouble, my love?"

"Oh, Ned, the general has gone just this minute to fetch his son to meet me and will be back in an instant with the fellow. Ned, what shall I do? I have not the least wish to meet him. I'd much rather spend this time discussing our wedding with you."

"Surely you have no wish to offend the general. I think you ought to meet with his son."

"Well, I do not wish to offend Sir Alonzo, but surely he will understand that as we are to be married—"

"Tut! tut! My lady, again you rush your fences! We can hardly speak of wedlock when we are in fact not engaged. Truly, Emily, you must be aware how very improper that would be. Anyway that first announcement

216

was quite in error, so it was never binding, you know."

"Ned, what in the world are you babbling about? I know of no error."

"Well then, it appears that I shall have to instruct you. Are you quite sure you have no wish to meet with General Beresford's son?"

"Quite. Why, do you know him?"

"Yes, I do, and I think you really ought to meet him."

"Ned, not now, please!"

"At once, my lady. Allow me to introduce him to you. I present to you Llewellyn Alonzo Beresford. How do you do, my lady, I am charmed, I am sure." He paused. Emily was regarding him as if he were insane.

"My lady, that is hardly any way to greet the son of a good friend," he bantered. "Cat got your tongue?"

"What are you saying, Ned?" she cried.

"So you see, my lady, it is just as well that you broke off your engagement with that Denning fellow, for we have got to announce it all over again and this time, my dear, will you not try to get the name of your fiancé down correctly?"

"Are—are you telling me that it was *you* Sir Alonzo went to fetch?"

"Exactly, my sweet."

"What, are you collecting surrogate sires? You and he are joking, of course."

"No, my dear, this is no jest. Sir Alonzo and I are both of us quite satisfied that we are father and son in truth. It is a long story, how it all came about, but there is something else I would do at the moment than to keep up this inane conversation," he declared, with a grin of invitation.

"Oh, Ned darling, how wonderful for you!"

She threw herself onto his breast.

Outside of the drawing room, in the corridor, General Beresford, grinning fit to be tied, was caught by Lord Carnavon and Mr. Denning with his ear glued to the keyhole.

"Beresford! What the devil are you at?" demanded his lordship.

The general, completely unabashed, looked up and put a finger to his lips. He came away from the door and bowed deeply to his lordship, grinning all the time.

"I have the very great pleasure, my lord, of informing you that my son has just asked your daughter for her hand in wedlock and she has accepted him."

"The devil you say!" exclaimed Lord Carnavon. "Why, damme, I never knew that you had a son! Not that I shouldn't be proud to have the son of such a distinguished personage as yourself, General, for in-law, you understand, but my daughter is in love with young Denning—or at least I thought she was! No, there has got to be some explanation here! My Emily is never so fickle!"

"Oh, disabuse yourself of *that* thought, my lord. I can assure you that my lady is not fickle. Most certainly, it is the man she has always loved that she is going to marry." The general was obviously enjoying himself.

"But that is Denning! I would swear to it!" cried his lordship.

"And I, for one, should never contradict you. You see, my lord, it is with the greatest pride that I have to inform you that Ned Denning is my son and heir, Llewellyn Alonzo Beresford. The last time I saw him, he had been a little shaver, and Lolly was ever the best that he could make of his name."

"Well, bless my soul!" exclaimed Mr. Denning as Lord Carnavon could only stand and stare. "Then he escaped from the fire and ran away and they thought he had perished in it and buried something that they assumed was his—"

"Exactly!" confirmed Sir Alonzo.

"My dear Beresford, indeed, I am so happy for you!" exclaimed Mr. Denning. "To have found a son you had given up forever—and to have found him such a first-rate—er-ahem—" It seemed that Mr. Denning was suddenly encountering very great difficulty in expressing himself.

General Beresford came over to Mr. Denning and put his arm about his shoulder. "Alec, I know what you are thinking and it is wrong. Ned is as much yours as mine! You have been a better father to him than I could ever have been. I'll not thank you for it, for something like that is beyond mere thanks. Alec, bound as we are together by our deep affection for the boy, to term us mere friends is to underestimate the feeling that exists between us very badly."

"Oh, I say!" pleaded my Lord Carnavon. "Won't someone please talk with me? Everyone appears to be gaining a son, whereas I am sure I am about to lose a daughter!"

All this by way of explaining how it was that when Alonzo Llewellyn Beresford, the younger, came into the world he was attended by three grandfathers.

Reading Fit For A Queen

QUEEN-SIZE GOTHICS offer the very best in novels of romantic suspense, by the top writers, greater in length and drama, richer in reading pleasure.

☐ A GALLOWS STANDS IN SALEM—
  A. M. Bretonne   00276-X   1.25
☐ AULDEARN HOUSE—Barbara Riefe   03194-8   1.50
☐ THE ABBOT'S HOUSE—Laura Conway   00328-6   1.25
☐ AN ADOPTED FACE—A. S. Carter   00272-7   1.25
☐ ANCIENT EVIL—Candace Arkham   08559-2   1.25
☐ ANGELICA—Jean Anne Bartlett   08579-7   1.75
☐ BLACKTHORN—Arlene Fitzgerald   03203-0   1.50
☐ THE BRIDE OF CAIRNGORE—
  Jean F. Webb   00376-6   1.25
☐ CASSIA GREAT HOUSE—Iona Charles   08557-6   1.50
☐ THE COUNT OF VAN RHEEDEN CASTLE—
  Scott Wright   08474-X   1.25
☐ THE COURT OF THE THORN TREE—
  P. Maxwell   00592-0   .95
☐ DARK SIDE OF PARADISE—
  Jo Anne Creighton   00390-1   1.25

☐ DARK TALISMAN—Anne-Marie Bretonne   00240-9 1.25
☐ A DELICATE DECEIT—Susan Hufford   00398-7 1.25
☐ THE DEVIL'S GATE—Arlene J. Fitzgerald   03178-6 1.50
☐ THE DEVIL'S SONATA—Susan Hufford   00340-5 1.25
☐ DEVIL TAKE ALL—A. Brennan   00612-9 .95
☐ DRAW A DARK CIRCLE—Iona Charles   03191-3 1.50
☐ THE DREAMER, LOST IN TERROR—
   Alison King   00356-1 1.25
☐ FOOLS'S PROOF—A.S. Carter   00261-1 1.25
☐ THE FOUR MARYS—Rinalda Roberts   00366-9 1.25
☐ GRAVE'S COMPANY—S. Nichols   00252-2 1.25
☐ GRENENCOURT—I. Charles   00264-6 1.25
☐ THE HARLAN LEGACY—
   Jo Anne Creighton   03206-5 1.50
☐ THE HEMLOCK TREE—E. Lottman   00235-2 1.25
☐ INN OF EVIL—J.A. Creighton   00224-7 1.25
☐ ISLAND OF SILENCE—
   Carolyn Brimley Norris   00411-8 1.25
☐ ISLAND OF THE SEVEN HILLS—Z. Cass   00277-8 1.25
☐ KEYS OF HELL—L. Osborne   00284-0 1.25
☐ THE KEYS TO QUEENSCOURT—
   Jeanne Hines (Empress)   08508-8 1.75
☐ THE LAZARUS INHERITANCE
   (Large type)—Noel Vreeland Carter   00432-0 1.25
☐ THE LEGEND OF WITCHWYND
   (Large Type)—Jeanne Hines   00420-7 1.25
☐ LET THE CRAGS COMB OUT HER
   DAINTY HAIR—J. Marten   00302-2 1.25
☐ LUCIFER WAS TALL—Elizabeth Gresham   00346-4 1.25
☐ MIDNIGHT SAILING—S. Hufford   00263-8 1.25
☐ THE MIRACLE AT ST. BRUNO'S—
   Philippa Carr (Empress)   08533-9 1.75
☐ OF LOVE INCARNATE—Jane Croworoft   00418-5 1.25

Buy them at your local bookstores or use this handy coupon for ordering:

Popular Library, P.O. Box 5755, Terre Haute, Indiana 47805   B-8

Please send me the books I have checked above. Orders for less than 5 books must include 60¢ for the first book and 25¢ for each additional book to cover mailing and handling. Orders of 5 or more books postage is Free. I enclose $_____ in check or money order.

Name_____

Address_____

City_____ State/Zip_____

Please allow 4 to 5 weeks for delivery. This offer expires 6/78.

All Time Bestsellers

Buy them at your local bookstores or use this handy coupon for ordering:

Popular Library, P.O. Box 5755, Terre Haute, Indiana 47805   B-5

Please send me the books I have checked above. Orders for less than 5 books must include 60c for the first book and 25c for each additional book to cover mailing and handling. Orders of 5 or more books postage is Free. I enclose $_____ in check or money order.

Name_____

Address_____

City_____ State/Zip_____

Please allow 4 to 5 weeks for delivery. This offer expires 6/78.